JAN 2020 ✕

DARKWATER
TRUTH

Center Point
Large Print

Also by Robin Caroll and available from
Center Point Large Print:

Torrents of Destruction
Weaver's Needle
Darkwater Secrets
Stratagem
Darkwater Lies

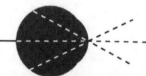

**This Large Print Book carries the
Seal of Approval of N.A.V.H.**

DARKWATER TRUTH

Robin Caroll

CENTER POINT LARGE PRINT
THORNDIKE, MAINE

This Center Point Large Print edition
is published in the year 2020 by arrangement with
RC Productions, Inc.

The text of this Large Print edition is unabridged.
In other aspects, this book may vary
from the original edition.
Printed in the United States of America
on permanent paper.
Set in 16-point Times New Roman type.

ISBN: 978-1-64358-463-8

The Library of Congress has cataloged this record
under Library of Congress Control Number: 2019950806

*In honor of Rebecca Gayle
because your Mémé loves you so much
and I love her and your mommy, Lilo!*

PROLOGUE

1918

"I'm sorry, but I can't keep you." The young woman kissed the baby's head, tears obstructing her view. "I'm only eighteen. I have my whole life ahead of me."

The seven-month-old boy flashed a grin, revealing two bottom teeth just barely visible above the gums. He kicked his little sockless feet, rocking the pram in his enthusiasm.

She handed him a rattle, guilt nearly strangling her, but she had to do what was best for him. Sure, she loved him and wanted to keep him, but she couldn't. She had no means of supporting him and what kind of life could she offer him? Her family didn't have money or social status. If she brought home another mouth to feed, there would be no telling what her father would do.

He gurgled and put the rattle in his mouth. Teething.

She ran a finger along the soft curve of his face. He was such a good baby. Rarely cried, only when he was hungry or needed a diaper change. Smiled all the time.

His eyes grew heavy. It was his bedtime. The August sun had set over New Orleans, leaving

7

only remnant trails of orange blazing in the darkening sky.

Her stomach flipped. She'd take him when he fell asleep. She wanted these last few minutes with him. Lifting him from the pram, she hugged him close. Inhaled the sweet, intoxicating perfume that was universal to babies. His warmth infused her as his little fist wound her hair in his grasp. He cooed and kicked, delighted to be held and snuggled.

She'd been his main source of love and attention. She knew that. He knew that, even at his tender age. It didn't make sense how much she loved him. He'd given her an amount of joy she'd never known possible. She wondered if she'd ever feel this type of love again.

Tears burned her eyes again, and she eased him back into the pram, careful to remove her hair from his grip. He grinned and gurgled up at her, kicking, rocking himself. He blinked again, those eyelids of his so very heavy.

She used a handkerchief to dab her eyes, then her entire face. This was the best thing. Best for her, but definitely best for him. At least this way, he'd stand a chance of being adopted by a family who could provide for him. They wouldn't ever be able to love him as much as she did—never—but they would love him because he was so loveable.

His eyes closed for longer and longer before

they fluttered open. It was time to go. She'd made her decision and she needed to stick to it. She'd told no one—hadn't had time—but knew this was the right thing to do.

The only thing she could do.

Pushing the pram, she made her way down Magazine Street in New Orleans. The gaslights on the street lit her way, but she paid no attention as she strode toward her destination. St. Vincent's Infant Asylum was run by Daughters of Charity order of nuns, and they took in babies without question. It was reported that the nuns were patient and loving to all the infants in their care. That's what she wanted for him: patience and love.

The nuns would adore him. How could they not?

She stopped outside the three-story red brick building. The white wrought iron decorative element seemed too much . . . too ornate.

The baby whimpered in his sleep, as if he knew subconsciously what was about to happen to him.

Her hands shook as she pulled the letter she'd written out of her pocket. She opened the paper, rereading her words once again by the light from the lamp set high on the opening post of the wrought iron fence that surrounded the building.

She'd written about his birth. It was hard to accept that he'd be born out of wedlock, born of original sin. He, himself, was so good. A happy

9

baby. Robust. Cheerful. He brought her such joy.

She continued reading her letter that explained the weeks and months following his birth. How he'd grown to be a delight, despite his rough beginning and his station in life. Her handwriting faltered a little as she explained the recent tragedy that had forced her to place him in the care of the nuns. How she couldn't watch out for him, despite her love for him. She'd written the details of his birth and his family as best as she could. It was her prayer that the nuns would be able to place him in a loving family, perhaps with siblings to grow up with.

That's what she liked to fantasize about—that he would be immediately adopted by a family with a couple of other young children, a big house, lots of laughter, and maybe even a dog. She'd always wanted a dog herself, but they'd never been able to afford one.

He stirred again and she knew she had to move now. If she didn't, things would only get more complicated and harder if he woke.

She pushed the pram up to the stairs. Leaning over, she gave him a final kiss on the tip of his nose. "I love you," she whispered through her tears.

She placed the letter at his feet in the pram and slowly looked up at the entranceway. Dare she knock to make sure he wasn't left outside alone too long? What if someone saw her and asked questions? She didn't want to have to answer questions, certainly not if the police wanted to talk to her.

Was this how Moses's mother felt?

Suddenly the door opened.

She dove into the clump of hedges on the outside of the wrought iron fence.

A nun in full habit stepped onto the concrete porch. "What is this?" She descended the stairs and touched the pram's handle. "Oh, my." She took the letter, read it, then slipped it into her pocket. She gently lifted the sleeping baby and held him against her.

"Come along, little William. You're safe now."

1

ADELAIDE

"Those are definitely human bones."

Adelaide Fountaine tuned out the construction crew's voices. She stared at the bones settled on rubble behind a partially demolished brick wall. The skeleton was on its side, a human skull very visible and very recognizable. Shivers scurried up her spine. It could be worse—they could have found a body instead of skeletal remains.

"We were knocking out the wall, and only made the first swing when the wall crumbled and we saw that." The worker waved his arm around. "Look at that—the real exterior wall is two feet behind this one. Someone put this faux wall up, but they didn't do a very good job."

Addy looked incredulously at the original solid brick wall and then at the fake wall she never noticed in her four years being general manager of this hotel.

"I came and got you immediately, just like we're supposed to do. No one touched anything else as soon as we saw it." The construction foreman nodded as he spoke.

"Yes. You did the right thing." Addy pulled out her phone. The crew had done what they were supposed to do, now she had to do the same. Sometimes, having her dream job wasn't all she'd imagined.

Addy loved the Darkwater Inn, and even though several of the original structures had survived the ravages of time and devastating Louisiana hurricanes, such as Isle Dernière in 1856, Audrey in 1957, Camille in 1969, and Katrina in 2005, it was time for an upgrade. The owner's son, Dimitri, gave her the green light to remodel the Darkwater Inn as she saw fit. After recently spending many months in Europe studying five-star hotels, she was excited about updating the interior while maintaining the architectural integrity of the building. The architect had completed the remodel design just two weeks ago, and construction had begun on Monday—it was only Thursday.

"Hey, Addy." Detective Beauregard Savoie's deep baritone, so familiar and so welcoming, made her smile. Just hearing his voice soothed her frazzled nerves. "How're you this morning?"

The softness of his tone reminded her of his attentiveness on their date last weekend. She let the warmth wash over her as she turned away from the construction crew and their grisly discovery.

"Truth be told, I'm a little freaked. Beau, I need to report something. About the hotel."

"Go ahead." His voice registered that he'd

flipped the switch and moved fully into New Orleans's detective mode.

It'd be nice if officially reporting an incident at the Darkwater Inn were a rare thing. Over the last year, however, that certainly hadn't been the case.

"Remember I told you we're having some renovations done here at the hotel?"

"Yes, I remember."

"The crew was taking down one of the interior walls in the back wing closest to the courtyard and they've . . . well . . ." She cleared her throat. "They've found a human skeleton."

She could hear his quick intake over the connection. "Are you sure the bones are human?" She looked over her shoulder at the bones. "I'm pretty positive. The skull I'm staring at is definitely human." She shuddered and looked away. It might be dry bones and not decomposing flesh, but it still creeped her out. She not only worked here every day, but she called the Darkwater Inn her home as well, living in an apartment upstairs. To think that there'd been a body in the walls for—goodness knew how long . . .

"Clear the area immediately, and get everyone else out of there, too. Assign one of your hotel's security guards to secure the area and don't let anyone in. We'll be there soon."

She nodded, even though he couldn't see her.

"Thanks, Beau." She disconnected the call, squared her shoulders and addressed the construction foreman. "The police are on their way. We need to clear the area."

"Yes, ma'am." He turned to the crew. "Come on, y'all heard the lady. Grab your gear and let's go."

"Is that a hatchet next to the skeleton?" one of the workers asked as he gathered tools.

"More like an axe. Looks like there's dried blood or something on it, too," another worker replied as he wound an extension cord and hung it over his shoulder.

Addy shuddered as she waited for the men. Blood, axes . . . maybe she shouldn't be so surprised. After all, the Darkwater Inn boasted a history almost as old and rich as the Crescent City itself, dating back to the 1840s. To have withstood such a test of time, the old girl had to have her secrets, like the hidden passageways and tunnels of the hotel. But those were mysterious and charming, unlike a skeleton with an axe.

"Can't help but wonder if there are more skeletons," a worker mused.

"If you have everything, we need to clear the area." Addy didn't want to think about there being more than one skeleton in the hotel's walls. One was quite enough, thank you very much. She ushered the men from the construction area, made sure the yellow CAUTION—KEEP OUT tape still securely blocked access to the area, then headed across the lobby to the hotel's security office. Opening the door sent a brush of cool air against her face. Even though it was barely March, they always kept the security office cool because of all the electronic and surveillance equipment.

"Good morning, Addy." Geoff Aubois, chief of security, turned and smiled at her from his leather chair. The large African American man was an intimidating powerhouse, but he was highly sensitive and intuitive as well. Addy trusted him completely.

She rubbed her forehead. "Hey, Geoff. We have a problem."

His wide smile slid off his face and he leaned forward, dark eyes focused. "What?"

Addy quickly brought Geoff up-to-date. "If you'll go make sure no one enters that hall until Beau gets here . . ."

He was already on his feet. "Of course." He turned to Sully Clements, the security officer with the most seniority. "You can reach me by radio if you need me."

Geoff walked Addy out of the security office, and gently touched her shoulder. "Are you okay?"

She nodded. "Sadly, yes. It should affect me more, I know, but after the past year or so . . ."

"I know what you mean."

And he did. He had just returned to work at the Darkwater after having served a year's sentence in prison for killing the man who'd raped his little sister—and Addy—when they were both in college. It left Geoff and Addy with scars from the past but also a deep kinship of understanding.

Geoff turned toward the hall where the renovations were taking place. "Want me to let you know when Beau gets here?"

She nodded. "I'm going to find Dimitri and we'll meet you there as soon as we can."

With a nod, Geoff rushed off toward the locked-off hall. Addy sighed and headed toward the kitchen and Dimitri.

Addy drew in a deep breath as she slipped around wait staff and into the depths of the kitchen. Brunch service was in full swing, one of the biggest meals in New Orleans. Not an early breakfast, since the all-night parties filling the French Quarter and surrounding areas kept people out until the wee hours of the morning. The crowds usually surfaced around ten or so, hitting the hotel's brunch hours. Of course, Dimitri's *pain perdu*, also referred to as French toast, was famous in the District, and many travel food sites had posted raving reviews, so the hotel's restaurant was always crowded at this time.

"Hello, Ms. Fountaine." Yvette, Dimitri's sous chef, smiled at her. Her curly black hair was pulled up under a chef's hat, and her expressive brown eyes sparkled. She set two plates on the steel-plated counter and rang the bell, her ebony skin glistening. "Are you hungry? Can I fix you a plate?"

Addy shook her head. While she adored Dimitri's concoction, knowing there were skeletal remains in the walls of the hotel had stolen her appetite. "Thank you, but no. Is Dimitri around? I need to speak to him."

Yvette's smile widened, indicating the relationship status of Addy and Dimitri wasn't as much of a secret as Addy would like. "He had a meeting this morning. He told me he should be back before the lunch service." She cocked her head to the side. "Can I help you with something?"

Forcing a smile, Addy shook her head again. "Could you tell Dimitri to come see me as soon as he returns, please?"

Yvette nodded. "Yes, ma'am, I sure will." She winked.

Not in the mood to explain why she was casually dating two different men, Addy mumbled a thanks, then headed back to the main lobby to wait for Beau. He'd be discreet, of course, but as general manager, she should be there to meet him.

She didn't have to wait long. Beau and his partner, Marcel, strode through the front door minutes later. Addy stood immobilized by the resolve in Beau as he strode toward her—strong, broad-shouldered, and ready for action. He stopped next to her and looked down at her, concern filling his eyes. At six feet, he towered over her frame by a half foot. His handsome tanned face with its strong jawline and cheekbones caused heat to creep up the back of her neck. She jerked her look to the man beside him, his partner, Marcel, to give herself the moment she clearly needed for a mental shake. The equally tall, powerfully-built African American man's eyes were on fire.

"Where is it?" Marcel wasted no time or energy with small talk.

"This way." Addy turned and led the way to the back wing.

Beau fell into step beside her. "Are you okay?" he asked softly.

She smiled, touched that even though he had a job to do and would do it well, he was still concerned about her. "I'm fine. I mean, this is not how I imagined my week going."

"I can imagine." He let his hand brush against hers as they approached the site.

Geoff gave a quick duck of his head toward them. "Detectives."

"Geoff." Beau nodded back, then pulled out his notebook from his pocket.

"When did you get back on the job?" Marcel shook Geoff's hand.

"Last week."

"What a way to kick off your return, huh?" Marcel shook his head.

"Right."

"So, lead the way." Beau tapped his pen against the notebook.

"Come on." Addy stepped around the tape barricade and made her way down the corridor to the room where the skeleton waited. "The plan is to take out several of these interior walls and make these rooms junior suites. We have so many requests for them." She knew she was rambling, but being in the same space as a skeleton made her jittery. She shut up and gestured to the crumbled bricks around the bones.

Beau intently studied the bones, raking his hand through his light brown cropped hair. "You're right, Addy. These are definitely human remains." He looked over at Marcel. "Call Walt's office and see how he wants to handle this one."

"What can I do?" She hated feeling so helpless.

"Just make sure no one comes back here except the coroner's team." Beau began writing notes.

"You mean the coroner has to come?" Sure, it was technically a dead person, but just bones.

Beau glanced at her and nodded. "His office will make the call as to how to process. Until further notice, no one but authorized personnel are allowed back here, okay?"

"Of course." She stared at the skeleton over

Beau's shoulder. "Any guesses how long it's been here?"

"I couldn't even try." He touched her shoulder. "I'm sure Walt's crew will be able to tell us more when they get here. Why don't you make sure Geoff knows to keep everyone out who doesn't belong here." He turned back to his notes.

Clearly, she didn't belong here either.

DIMITRI

"Come on, Dimitri, you know you've never wanted to run the Darkwater Inn." Malcolm Dessommes twirled his pen through his fingers and stared at Dimitri from across his desk. "It's a great offer."

Dimitri gave a slow nod. "It is, but as I've explained, multiple times now, I'm not interested in selling the hotel."

The pen fell from Malcolm's hand, clattering against the polished mahogany. "But you don't want to run it. Claude did all that and now that he's . . . well, gone, I know you don't want to deal with any of it."

"Gone?" Dimitri snorted. "Father isn't gone by choice. He's in prison." The mighty Claude Pampalon, revealed to be nothing more than a high-stakes stolen arts broker.

"All the more reason to not have to deal with the business of running the Darkwater Inn."

"I don't. Adelaide does." Dimitri couldn't stop the smile from spreading with just saying her name. She was beautiful and kind and caring, and he was blessed to be dating her.

Even if she was also dating Detective Beauregard Savoie. A detail Dimitri chose to ignore for the moment.

"Adelaide is a brilliant general manager and oversees all aspects of running the hotel so I don't have to." She'd been a godsend, that was for sure.

"She can still be general manager, if that's what's making you dig your heels in on this deal. I know you have a sweet spot for her." Malcolm raised his eyebrows and grinned.

Sweet spot? Dimitri was crazy about Adelaide. Had been for the better part of two years, truth be told. It wasn't just her incredible beauty— dark chocolate eyes, fair skin, long dark curls, beautiful smile—it was also her unique combination of spunk, sweetness, strength, and sensitivity that made his heart melt.

He shook his head. "It's not just that. The Darkwater has been in my family since it was built. I remember coming here to visit my grandfather, Henri. So much of my family's history is wrapped up in the hotel. I couldn't sell it if I wanted to." Not that he wanted to offload. He didn't want to run it, but as long as Adelaide would, he was perfectly content to let things stay as they were. This talk of selling and buying was all Malcolm's idea.

Malcolm lifted his pen and began twirling it through his fingers again. "Then how about a partnership? I buy into the company, you can keep controlling interest, and I take over the management, leaving you free to cook to your heart's desire." He set the pen down on his desk. "By me buying in, you'd have capital to conclude the renovations you just started without having to answer to a bank."

Dimitri didn't bother to ask Malcolm how he knew the private details of the Darkwater Inn's renovation project and his recent inquiry to the bank for a line of credit to cover said renovations. Malcolm was one of the youngest and shrewdest, yet brightest businessmen in New Orleans. On most days, he and Dimitri were close acquaintances, if not friends. But today, when he'd asked Dimitri to stop by his office this morning and shown his interest in buying the hotel, Dimitri couldn't help but wonder what Malcolm really wanted.

No better time to find out. "Okay, Mal, what's going on? Why the sudden, and almost desperate desire to own the Darkwater Inn?"

"I need to diversify, and my advisors are on my case to invest in real estate. Namely, hotels because they turn a better profit."

Dimitri nodded. The Darkwater Inn had not just

made a profit over the last decade, but a healthy one—each year better than the one before. It was a good, sound investment, no denying that. "There are other hotels."

Malcolm nodded. "I don't want to get tied up with a hotel chain—those are nothing but a pain in the neck, if you know what I mean. I want something independent. Local. Part of the essence of who New Orleans is." He grinned. "That's the Darkwater Inn."

"Oh, that it is. But why on earth would you think I'd sell it?" Dimitri crossed his arms over his chest and leaned back in the extremely comfortable chair facing the massive desk Malcolm sat behind.

"Because I know you never wanted to run it, and now that Claude's in prison, and Lissette, too . . . well, I thought you might be interested in unloading."

Dimitri straightened. He'd never imagined his half sister would have abducted Adelaide and set up Claude to ensure that she would be the owner, but she had. It was still fresh and raw, and Dimitri had been totally fooled by her. When she first revealed that she was his half sister from Claude's affair with one of his housekeepers, Dimitri had stood up to his father and demanded Claude accept Lissette into the family business, and nobody, nobody, demanded anything of Claude Pampalon.

24

Yet Dimitri had. For his poor little half sister, who not only used voodoo spells on him, if he believed such things were real, but also used her voodoo connections to have Adelaide abducted. He could almost feel the knife wound of betrayal in his back.

"Dimitri?" Malcolm stared at him.

He stood. "I appreciate the offer, Mal, but I'm not interested. The renovations are in budget and Adelaide's overseeing them, as well as everything else. The Darkwater Inn is good."

Malcolm pushed to his feet as well, extending his hand. "Let me know if that changes, won't you? I think we'd make good business partners."

Dimitri shook his hand, but didn't say anything. It was still odd that Malcolm would try such a hard sell to either buy the hotel outright or become business partners. There was more going on, but Dimitri didn't really care. He needed to get back and set up for lunch. "Drop by sometime and we'll grab a bite. I'll make you something off the new menu."

"I'll do that." Malcolm moved from behind his desk and opened his office door. "And you give me a holler if you reconsider either of my offers. They'll stand for a bit." He clapped Dimitri's shoulder.

Dimitri climbed into his car, dropping his sunglasses over his eyes as he slipped behind the wheel. It'd been a very strange meeting all around, but then again, most everything that involved the Darkwater Inn and Claude Pampalon had markings of oddness. Just because the man had gone to prison didn't mean the peculiarity of the Pampalon name had been cleared from the hotel.

Dimitri steered the car toward the hotel. If there were a significant reason Malcolm was interested in the hotel, he'd learn soon enough. Secrets of New Orleans had a way of being uncovered.

Usually when it was least expected.

2

BEAU

"Timothy LaBarre, nice to meet you." The wiry young redhead wearing a jacket with the coroner's office emblem lowered the camera, pulled off his latex glove, and held out his hand.

"Detective Beau Savoie, and this is my partner, Marcel Taton." Beau appreciated a firm handshake and introduction, as well as care taken to preserve evidence. Especially at his crime scene. "Walt out today?" The New Orleans coroner kept threatening to retire, but hadn't yet.

"He's giving a lecture over at the FBI about ritualistic killings by cults."

Beau narrowed his eyes. "Walt's good at that. Is there an uprise in reports of those?" He hadn't gotten any cases lately that could be attributed to a cult, but there were always cults in New Orleans. Usually ones that liked to pretend they were vampires, but there were several who claimed to be religious groups.

Timothy shook his head. "Not yet, but there have been some FBI mumblings about a couple of local groups that they're watching."

Interesting. The FBI usually checked in with

the New Orleans Police Department if they got wind that there was possible movement in a group. Then again, they might have talked to the captain who answered their questions and saw no need to put the precinct on alert.

Marcel glanced Timothy over. "No offense, but we haven't worked with you before. What exactly is your position in Walt's office?"

Timothy grinned. "No offense taken. I realize I look like a teenager." He lifted his camera and took pictures of the wall and skeleton as he spoke. "I'm twenty-four, by the way, and am certified through the American Board of Medicolegal Death Investigators in medicolegal death investigations and have logged upwards of a thousand hours of death investigation experience." He straightened and looked at them.

Beau chuckled under his breath. "Good enough for you, Marcel?"

"Fine." Beau's partner pointed at the bones. "What's your initial impression?"

Timothy squatted in front of the skeleton and rubbed his jaw. "Obviously the skeleton has been here for some time. The clothes have all biodegraded, unless the body was put in the wall naked, which isn't likely because I believe there's a zipper and button there, which indicates he at least had on pants."

"He?" Beau stopped his note taking.

Timothy nodded. "The pelvic bone is narrower

28

and has a more heart-shaped pelvic inlet than a female's open circular one. I'm calling this one a male."

"What else?" Marcel asked.

"Well, without examining and measuring in the lab, it's hard to say, but by what I'm seeing, with the remodeling lines still prominent in the skull, I'd ballpark the lad is around my age— early twenties. There are still strands of short hair attached that haven't disintegrated." Timothy pointed to a gash on the skull. "And that, my friends, is most likely the cause of death." He stood and nodded at the axe propped up against the back wall near the skeleton. "If I were a betting man, I'd guess that's what was used. Initial review is a homicide, gentlemen."

Those familiar tingles tickled the back of Beau's neck. He glanced around the area. "Not much use calling out our crime scene unit."

Timothy shook his head. "I've already called in FACES."

"Faces?" Marcel asked.

"Forensic Anthropology and Computer Enhancement Services . . . FACES. It's a lab that provides forensic anthropology and forensic imaging services to agencies for the state. It's on the campus of LSU Baton Rouge."

Beau nodded. "I've heard of them, but never had to use them before."

"They're pretty awesome." Timothy stowed

his camera in his flip case and reached for his measuring tape and sketch book. "Once they get here, they'll assist with recovery of skeletal remains, then they'll be able to help Walt provide a full report with estimation of age, sex, ancestry, height, time since death, and trauma analysis."

"That's intense." Beau grabbed a pair of latex gloves and slipped them on, then grabbed an end of the tape measure for Timothy.

"Yeah, they can even do facial reconstructions with clay or else digitally-enhanced age progression and postmortem enhancement to help identify the remains." Timothy made notes of the measurements on his crude sketch. "Best part is? Not only are they scary good at what they do, their services are free to all coroners and law enforcement agencies in the state."

Captain Istre would like that. He was always on the detectives about overtime and the budget.

"You've already called them?" Marcel asked.

Timothy nodded as he finished his sketch and stowed the tape measure and sketch book. "Yep. As soon as I got here and realized what we had." He glanced at his watch. "They had a team available to come immediately, so depending upon how long it took them to load up and the traffic on I-10, I'd say they'll be here in less than an hour or so."

"Very prompt." Beau turned back to stare at the skeleton. "So all we know about you, our bony friend, is you're a young man and were killed with an axe to the head."

"And then bricked behind a wall, which would've taken some time." Marcel moved beside Beau. "I'm thinking we should ask Dimitri about renovations done over the years at the hotel."

Beau turned and smiled at his partner. "Good idea. I think you should go talk to him."

Marcel grinned and nudged him. "What? Aren't you the lead detective here? Shouldn't you be the one asking?"

"Go." Beau shoved Marcel toward the exit.

"Are you sure?" Marcel crossed his arms over his chest. "I mean, I might forget to ask him something important or something."

Beau pointed to the hallway. "Go!"

Marcel chuckled on his way out of the area.

"I'm obviously missing something." Timothy smiled at Beau.

"Partner stuff. Not important." He smirked.

"Okay. Whatever you say, man." Timothy pulled a digital thermometer from his case and moved to the skeleton. He took the reading, then made a note. "There are some coins here, too, that must've been in the guy's pockets."

Beau moved closer. "What year are they?"

"Can't tell. They're tail side up. I noticed them when I took the pictures. Once the FACES team gets here and removes the bones, we can grab them as evidence. And the zipper and button." Timothy shoved the thermometer back into the black leather case.

Beau stared at the skeleton again. "I wonder how long he's been in that wall." There was only a couple of feet between the walls where the skeleton rested.

"The coins will help us narrow it down. Zippers have been around since the late 1800s, so we at least have a starting point. Wonder when this hotel was built."

"Mid-1800s." Beau smiled at the young man. "I grew up here."

"Me, too. Well, in DeRidder." Timothy snapped the case closed. "The owner or manager should have records of when renovations were made to the hotel over the years. That'll help pin down some dates."

"Odd that the murder weapon was left there," Beau mused aloud.

"What do you make of that?" Timothy raised an eyebrow.

"Well, it's a statement. Certainly not an accident that it was left, because it took time to wall the body there. If the killer had wanted to get rid of the axe, he had plenty of time."

"Maybe it was an oversight?"

Beau shook his head. "Someone who kills somebody with an axe to the head, then bricks them behind a wall in a hotel isn't going to overlook the murder weapon being left at the scene of the crime. Nope, it's intentional. It's a message."

"For who?"

"I don't know. That's one of the many things I have to figure out." Beau squinted around the room. There had to be easy access. His immediate thought was the murderer had to be on the construction crew so he could hide the body while laying the brick.

Moving closer to the wall the skeleton lay behind, Beau studied the bricks.

"What?" Timothy came to stand behind him, looking over his shoulder.

"I'm no mason, but look at the line of the bricks and mortar here." Beau pointed to the wall where the crew had demolished a large hole. "Now compare that to, say, *this* over here." He moved farther down along the same wall. "What do you notice? Look closely."

Timothy studied the two areas. "The part in front of the skeleton isn't as clean. There is more mortar sticking out."

Beau grinned and nodded. "Indicating someone was in a hurry or didn't care much about craftsmanship." He looked back at the differences. "It's not as uniform either. Definitely not of the same caliber of quality as where the wall started against the adjoining wall." He pointed to just before where the skeleton laid. "Looks like the sloppiness started here and . . ." he walked down to the connecting wall. "Goes all the way to the wall."

"What does that mean?" Timothy asked.

"It means that our murderer might not have been on the construction crew, but knew they were building these walls and what stage they were at. He had a body to hide and knew enough about how to mix the mortar and masonry to finish the wall, even though the work was much more shoddy than the original."

"So it wasn't a worker?"

Beau grinned. "We don't know yet, but my gut tells me no. Even in a hurry, craftsmen take pride in their work."

"But he could've been worried about being caught."

Beau nodded. "True, but he needed to plan enough time to do a sufficient job so that no one would notice. Maybe he had others to help him so it wouldn't take very long."

"Okay," Timothy nodded, "but if not a construction worker, it had to be someone who knew about the renovations and that the tools would be there and the area blocked off."

"Right. That brings in the construction foremen, suppliers, hotel management and staff."

"That's a whole lot of suspects, Detective."

Beau sighed. "Yep, so anything you and the team from FACES can do to help me narrow down my timeline will be a big help."

Timothy grinned like a kid in an ice cream store. "You got it."

Sometimes, it was just that easy. Beau smiled, then stared at the bones and frowned. Other things weren't as easy.

ADDY

"Yvette said you stopped by and needed to see me?" Dimitri strode through her open office door, smile wide.

Her responding smile was automatic. "I did." She stood and met him as he walked in. He put his hand on her shoulder, and she looked up at him. His handsome face was turned toward her expectantly, dark eyes affectionate.

"We've had a bit of an incident."

His smile disappeared as quickly as hers, his look intense. "What now?"

"The renovation crew found a skeleton this morning. The police and coroner are here."

"A skeleton?" He scruffed his hand through thick dark hair.

She nodded and quickly gave him the details, making sure to keep her emotional edge out of her voice. "Geoff's making sure no one goes into the area. Since we already have it cordoned off for the renovations, guests won't be alerted, so that's good."

"What about the skeleton?"

"I don't think they know anything yet."

"Oh, but we do." Marcel crossed into her office. "Sorry, the door was open."

They both turned.

"Then by all means, come in, Detective." Dimitri crossed his arms over his chest and sat on the edge of Addy's desk. "What do you know?"

Marcel grimaced at Dimitri. "It's an open investigation now, so I can't discuss privileged information with you."

The overload of male testosterone in the room could strangle Addy. "What do you need, Marcel?"

"Actually, I'm here to see you, Dimitri."

"And you've found me." Dimitri stretched his legs out in front of him, still leaning against the edge of her desk. "However may I assist you, Detective?"

"Since Addy has brought you up to speed on what we've found, we need some information from you. As acting owner of the Darkwater Inn, of course."

"Of course." Dimitri pushed off the desk and straightened. "What kind of information?"

"We'll need records of all renovations done at the hotel. Dates, locations, basic renovations done . . . that kind of thing."

Dimitri looked at Addy, his eyes wide. "I'm not sure where to find those records. Father kept records, I'm sure, but I wouldn't even know where to begin to look."

"You might have to go ask him, Dimitri." She kept her voice low. As much as she couldn't stand Claude Pampalon, he was Dimitri's father.

"I don't think so."

"Maybe you can call him," Marcel volunteered.

Dimitri glared at Marcel. "Or maybe a visit from the police would encourage him to give up the information more than a visit from the son he feels betrayed him and put him in prison."

Marcel didn't respond, just stared back.

Addy swallowed against the lump in her throat. Dimitri had turned his father in because he was a man of honor. Of integrity. But that didn't mean it didn't hurt for his father to have lashed out at him like he had when he'd been sentenced to eight years in prison.

His father had already given Dimitri power of attorney over the hotel, which he wanted to retract upon his sentencing but couldn't. Their relationship, while always strained, was now all but nonexistent.

That nearly broke Addy's heart. As close as she was to her father . . . well, she couldn't imagine not having Vincent Fountaine as a very strong presence in her life. They might not always see eye to eye, but they loved and respected one another and made the effort to stay close. Every

Thursday evening, she'd join him at his reclusive house for dinner.

Thursday night. Tonight. She'd have something interesting to tell him over the lasagna she was making tonight.

But for now . . . Addy looked around. "I'm sure the records are here somewhere, Marcel. I'll get someone to start searching for them."

He smiled at her. "Thank you, Addy."

She took a breath. "Do you have any idea when the s-skeleton will be removed and that area cleared?" She swallowed a groan and squared her shoulders. What kind of general manager stuttered over a simple word?

"Beau's down there with the coroner investigator right now. I'm sure he wouldn't mind if you asked him." Marcel grinned wider.

Addy could practically feel the tautness rolling off of Dimitri. Guilt assuaged her since it was all her fault. Dating two men at the same time . . . what had she been thinking? Her best friend, Tracey, had told her to date both of them and see which one she had stronger feelings for. She'd been up-front and honest with them about trying to sort out her feelings, but she was to blame for the animosity here.

She turned on Marcel. "I'm sure he wouldn't, but I asked you. Maybe you could go find out for me?"

Marcel stiffened. "You'll be updated as soon as

we can let you know something." He glanced at Dimitri then back at Addy. "Work on getting us those records. We'll need them."

"Of course." Great. Just when she'd begun to feel like Beau's partner didn't hate her on sight, now he did again.

He turned and left the office without another word. She'd talk to Beau about Marcel's attitude later.

"I'm sorry, Dimitri."

"For what? You didn't put a skeleton behind the wall, did you?" He grinned and touched her shoulder.

Even when he was upset, he still went out of his way to comfort her. She couldn't help smiling back. "No, but some people shouldn't tempt me."

He chuckled. "Having a mental image of you taking someone out . . . yeah, that's funny."

She nudged him with her hip. "Hey, you never know."

He pulled her into his arms for a quick hug. "I do know you, Adelaide Fountaine, and I know you would never off someone and put them behind a wall."

She backed up a step, but he still kept a hand on her waist. "Now that I think about it, that is very Poe-ish, isn't it? To brick a body behind a wall."

"Very much so. Maybe that's where the murderer got the idea."

"Do you think so?" She hadn't really considered it, but such an unusual way to hide a body . . . maybe.

"Could be. Either way, there's another murder victim found at the Darkwater Inn. I suppose I should go talk to Beauregard."

A deep baritone spoke up. "No need."

Addy spun, moving away from Dimitri. "Beau. It's not nice to sneak up on people."

The hurt plainly visible on his face as he looked at both of them stole her annoyance.

"I thought I'd give you a status update." Beau nodded at Dimitri.

"Of course. Thank you." She gave herself a mental shake. She had to stop letting her personal feelings interfere with her position. "What's going on?"

Beau gave her that little half-smile of his. "The coroner's office has called in a team to help with extraction of the skeleton. They should be here within an hour. Once they have cleared the bones, we'll gather what evidence there is, then you should be able to continue business as usual."

"I saw a hatchet or axe there when I called you. Is that evidence?"

He nodded. "Everything in close proximity to the victim is evidence. That, in particular, since it looks like a blow to the head might have been the cause of death."

"With the axe?" Her eyes widened. Forget

Edgar Allan Poe, this was taking on a Lizzie Borden feel.

Beau nodded again. "But we don't know anything for sure right now. Timothy, the coroner investigator, said it looked like the damage to the skull could match up with the axe found next to the remains."

"Who kills someone with an axe and leaves the murder weapon next to the body?" Dimitri asked.

Addy shook her head. "Who kills someone with an axe, period?"

"That's what I'll have to find out."

She smiled at Beau. "I don't envy you."

Dimitri's gaze darted from Beau to her, then back to Beau again. "Adelaide will have someone find the hotel's records of when renovations were performed. Is there anything else we can do to help you with your investigation?"

"Not at the moment." Beau spoke to Dimitri, but his gaze burned into Addy. "I've requested a uniformed officer to replace Geoff to ensure the scene isn't contaminated more than it already is. If you wouldn't mind letting us keep Geoff there until our officer arrives, I'd appreciate it."

"Of course." She nodded. If she thought the tension was thick when Marcel was in here, she'd been wrong. Right now, the tension could easily strangle her. Despite what both Beau and Dimitri said, she couldn't continue dating both of them. It was only going to lead to someone getting hurt. Maybe she shouldn't date either man.

She glanced at each of them. Her heart picked up its pace. Both men were handsome in their own right. Both were kind and gentle and amazing men. She liked them both romantically, but also valued each of their friendship.

But she couldn't string them along. She had to make a decision. Sooner rather than later. Before she couldn't even stay friends with them.

1924

"Yes, boys and girls, demons can and do possess people. We must remain vigilant at all times." Mother Mary Margaret walked back and forth in front of the classroom, holding her ruler tightly in her hand.

William squirmed in his seat. He'd heard her talk about this over and over again. It was always the same thing.

"In Luke, chapter four, the Bible tells us about demons and how Jesus drove them out of the men they possessed."

Many in the class sucked in air. Talks of demons and possession scared so many of them.

William didn't want to be scared, but he was. He just couldn't show it. Not to his best friends James, George, and Harold. They were best friends for life and William couldn't look scared in front of them. Even when he was called out. And he would be named in this story, like he had been many times before.

Mother Mary Margaret stopped walking and faced the students, focusing on William. "One of our own here at St. Vincent is here because his mother was a *sinner,* and because she was a sinner, she was where she wasn't supposed to be."

William hung his head. Here it came.

"A man who was possessed by a demon came to the place where she shouldn't have been and killed her."

Other kids looked at him . . . they'd heard the story many times before, too.

"So we must do as we are told and not go where we aren't supposed to." Mother Mary Margaret slapped her ruler against her palm. "And we must study the Bible and pray so that no demon can possess us and use us to do the evil work of the devil."

No one said a word. William wanted to scream. Wanted to cry. He had had a real mom, but satan had taken her from him. He couldn't remember anything about her. Mother Mary Margaret wouldn't tell him anything more about her, but Sister Rosemary had said that a young woman had loved him very much and wanted to take care of him, but couldn't, so she brought him to St. Vincent's.

Had his mother loved him, or was she a sinner like Mother Mary Margaret said? Why did the demon-possessed man kill *his* mother? Why not someone else's?

"You may now go play outside." Mother Mary Margaret dismissed the class.

William hurried outside with his best friends, making sure not to run inside the building or Mother Mary Margaret would make him miss recess and write lines. Even though Harold and George were older than William and James, they all did what William said. He led all the games they played, and made up all the rules.

Sister Rosemary said he was a natural-born leader.

3

BEAU

"Detective Savoie?"

Beau turned to face Timothy, but drew up short before speaking. A striking woman stood beside the coroner's investigator. Beau estimated her to be in her early thirties, with long sandy blond hair, and big soulful brown eyes, but it was her bright and ready smile that snagged his attention.

"This is Dr. Chandler Broussard, the biological anthropologist from FACES."

She shook his hand. "Pleased to meet you, Detective."

"It's Beau." *This* was the anthropologist? Nothing nerdy about this woman. Nothing at all. "So what's the game plan?"

"We'll get in there and remove the skeleton for you. I've spoken to Mr. Kelly, and he's released the bones to FACES for assistance in the case."

Beau grinned and nodded. Good ole Walt.

She began walking toward the taped-off area, Timothy at her side. "I understand there's also physical evidence that hasn't been disturbed that you'll want to retrieve?"

He fell into step alongside her. "A zipper. Button. Coins. All items that haven't dis-integrated, although there's no telling what clothes he was wearing."

She smiled. "You might be surprised. Some-times even though the clothes themselves have biodegraded, there might be a random strand left on a bone fragment. And those zippers and buttons can help determine what clothing was worn, sometimes even pinning down the year."

"Really?"

She nodded and grinned. "Yep. Most people realize different fabrics biodegrade at different rates, but forget about the buttons, zippers, and snaps that don't degrade. Sometimes those items are very specific to a year or fashion which helps date the clothing, even if there's nothing left. Don't rule anything out until we finish our work."

"Fascinating." He knew the basics, yes, but hadn't really considered details.

"I just finished a case where we were able to determine the timeline due to one little snap. That specific snap had been put in blouses in 2008 only, because the company who manufactured them went out of business in 2009. It helped the detectives figure out their timeline and helped solve their case."

"What helped solve a case?" Marcel joined

them from behind. "Hello. I'm Detective Marcel Taton, and you are—?" He held his hand out to Chandler, a smile on his face.

"This is Dr. Chandler Broussard from FACES," Timothy said before she could speak.

She smiled back and shook his hand. "It's a pleasure."

"The pleasure's all mine." Marcel had his charm on full-wattage.

Beau shook his head and started the group walking again. "Dr. Broussard—"

"Chandler, please."

"Chandler," Beau turned to Marcel, "is the biological anthropologist sent to remove the skeletal remains."

"*You're* the anthropologist?" Marcel's eyes opened wide.

Beau swallowed the laugh. "You'll have to forgive my partner, Chandler. He seems to have lost his manners."

She chuckled. "It's okay. I get that a lot. Mainly from law enforcement." She narrowed her eyes as she stared at Marcel. "Hmm. Maybe I should do some sort of study on the mindset of the typical male officer."

"Please don't." Beau laughed. He lifted the tape for the group to step under.

Just inside the corridor, Chandler lifted a large case. "This is my cue to gear up."

"Gear up?" Marcel asked.

"Hazmat suit. I never extract without it." She stepped into the room where the skeleton rested. Two others in the head-to-toe suits were already moving around slowly. "My team."

Beau glanced at them as he pulled out two pairs of latex gloves from his pocket. He passed a pair to Marcel, but looked at Chandler. "Is it okay for us to be here without a suit?" He hadn't considered there would be a danger of exposure to anything, but maybe he should have. Who knew what had been kept behind that wall along with a body?

"I'm sure it's all fine. It's just policy for us." She stepped into the suit. "This really won't take us long. We'll be photographing and documenting as we go. I know you need to retrieve evidence, but we'll share our documents and photographs with you, so we don't need to be stepping over each other trying to get the same shots and such."

"I've already diagrammed, photographed, and documented the scene while we were waiting for you to arrive, Dr. Broussard. I also took one of the few strands of hair for testing," Timothy volunteered.

She smiled at him. "Good job. If you guys could just stay back until we give you the all clear to come in and retrieve evidence, we'll be good to go." She pulled the helmet over her head. "Ready?" Her voice was muffled from behind the plastic.

Marcel gave a thumbs up, and she nodded.

Beau stood beside Marcel and Timothy as Chandler and her team began their work. "Get a couple of evidence bags ready," he told Marcel as his cell phone vibrated. He pulled it from his pocket and read the text message from Vincent Fountaine:

Don't forget to bring the cookies to dinner tonight. And don't be late.

Beau smiled and pocketed the cell. Addy's dad had bet that LSU's star running back would go pro and won the bet. Thus the chocolate chip cookie demand. Addy was on her father about eating healthier, and chocolate chip cookies were Vincent's Achilles' heel.

He watched Chandler work. She was very attractive, no denying that, but she was nothing compared to Addy. He'd known Addy nearly all his life, and been in love with her for most of his adult years. Only this past year had he let his feelings be known, and they were dating.

But it was complicated. She was also dating Dimitri Pampalon.

Addy told them right away that she was dating them both, and while Beau appreciated her honesty, he would rather her not be spending time with the hotel's chef and owner. It wasn't that Dimitri was a bad guy, he actually was nice enough and upstanding, but he was still competition for Addy's attention, affection, and—ultimately—her heart.

That made him very unlikeable to Beau.

"She's a looker, isn't she?" Marcel spoke in a low tone.

"What?" Of course Addy was beautiful. Beau followed Marcel's line of vision. Oh. "Chandler? Yes, she's attractive."

Marcel snorted and shook his head.

"What?"

"You might be all wrapped up in Addy, but that doesn't mean you're unaware, man."

"I said she was attractive."

Marcel laughed and shook his head again. "You've got it bad."

"What?" Heat fanned his face. "You know how I feel about Addy."

"Yeah, but it's gotten worse, if that's even possible."

Beau shifted his weight from one foot to the other. "That's not a bad thing." His feelings for Addy had grown even deeper over their dates. Spending one-on-one time with her romantically only made him realize how much he truly cared for her. He knew she cared about him, too, but in comparison to Dimitri? He just didn't know.

"Okay. You guys can come take some of this evidence now." Chandler motioned them over.

Time to put his personal feelings on the back burner and do his job.

51

ADDY

"So, how's the hotel business going?" Vincent planted a kiss on the top of Addy's head as he sat down at the kitchen table.

"Funny you should ask, Daddy. It's been a busy day." She paused over her plate of steaming lasagna, closing her eyes and sending up a silent prayer.

"Do tell. I did nothing all day but stare at a half-written synopsis for the better part of the day, so please, distract me with anything."

Addy glanced across the table at Beau, who poured Thousand Island dressing over his salad. He glanced up and nodded, so she continued. "Our construction crew doing the remodeling found a skeleton today."

"What?" Her father's eyes widened. As a suspense author, this was right up his alley.

"Even more creepy—it was found behind a fake wall." She shook her head as she pushed lettuce around her salad bowl. "It was like something right out of an Edgar Allan Poe story."

"Really?" Vincent's eyes brightened as he skipped the salad and went right for the lasagna.

She nodded, placing her bowl of salad in front of her father. "And there was an axe found by the skeleton, and an injury on the skull, so that axe is probably the murder weapon. And it might have dried blood on it."

"We don't know that yet," Beau finally spoke. "The lab hasn't determined if that's blood or not. We should have some prelim reports back by tomorrow."

"A skeleton? Any idea how long it's been there?" Vincent absentmindedly took a bite of Addy's salad.

Beau shook his head. "We found coins dated 1917, but the anthropologists will be using the button and zipper found to help narrow it down. We'll get the date the axe was manufactured tomorrow, too."

Vincent took another bite of the salad and rubbed his chin.

Addy recognized his movement—he always did that when his mind was working out a plot twist. "What?"

"That axe . . . just makes me think of the Axeman." Her father moved the bowl aside and pulled his plate of lasagna to him.

"The Axeman?" Addy looked from her father to Beau, who wore a puzzled expression that mirrored what she felt.

"Who's the Axeman?" Beau asked before sneaking a bite.

"Was. He was a serial killer who killed and wounded many people in New Orleans back in 1918 and 1919."

"You're kidding, right? There really wasn't a serial killer called the Axeman." Addy had never heard this before, and she'd been born and raised in New Orleans, only leaving briefly to attend college at Northwestern University a decade ago.

"No, there really was. I remember doing research about him for a possible book." Her father took a sip of tea.

Addy shook her head. "I don't remember you writing a book with any serial killer called the Axeman."

Vincent chuckled. "No, I didn't write it. I got sidetracked with another idea." He rubbed his chin. "Mmm. Maybe I should look at my research again. Especially if this skeleton in your hotel is a victim of the Axeman's."

"There's no evidence of anything like that." Beau grabbed a piece of garlic toast from the warmer.

"Not yet, but there could be, right?" Vincent asked.

Beau shrugged.

"Tell me more about the Axeman, Daddy." How had she never heard about this bit of New Orleans history before?

"Let's see." He rubbed his chin again and his eyes took on that faraway glisten as he spoke. "Back in early summer 1918, the first murder happened. Someone broke into a home by chiseling through a panel of the door. He cut the throat of the couple who lived there with a straight razor, but then bashed their heads with an axe owned by the couple. They both died."

"How gruesome!" Addy shivered.

Her father nodded, but he took another bite of the pasta dish. "The Axeman got the moniker because his main murder weapon was an axe, usually owned by the victims themselves."

Beau swallowed the last of his salad and leaned toward her father. "How many victims were there?"

Vincent let out a breath. "Hmm. I think it was something like a dozen or so, but not all of them died. If memory serves me correct, I think about half of them lived."

"Why did he do it? What was his reasoning?" Addy tore off bits of the garlic toast, but she'd pretty much lost her interest in supper.

"Don't know. He was never caught."

"What?" Beau nearly choked on his bite. He coughed, reached for his glass of tea, and took a big gulp.

Vincent nodded. "He was never caught. No one knows who he was or why he did what he did, but he wrote a letter to the paper that they published."

"You're kidding." Addy couldn't believe she'd never heard so much as a whisper about this before.

"Nope. He wrote a letter to what was then the *New Orleans Times*. In it, he claimed to be a demon from hell."

Beau set his glass on the table very slowly. "A demon?"

"Yep. Strangely, in the letter, he gave an exact date and time he would be in New Orleans. He said he was a fan of jazz music and when he came through the city at that exact time, any house that had jazz music playing would be spared."

"You're kidding," Addy said again. Her dad had to be messing with them.

But Vincent shook his head. "No, I'm dead serious, forgive the pun. He really put that in the letter that was published. And people believed him. There was even a ragtime jazz tune written and published in 1919 called 'Axman's Jazz (Don't Scare Me Papa)'. You can look it up."

"It's crazy that we've never heard this before." Beau shook his head.

"Right?" Addy pushed her plate away. "I can't believe you did research on it and never said anything to me."

Her father chuckled. "It was years ago, Addybear, before you came back from college."

Everyone at the table sobered. Only a year ago she'd been able to share with Beau and her father what Kevin Muller had done to her that caused her to take time off from earning her degree in hotel management. While the sexual assault had derailed her, she was one of the lucky ones—able to overcome the tragedy. Geoff's little sister wasn't so lucky. She hadn't been able to talk to

56

anyone, and the toxicity of what happened to her had caused her to commit suicide. Horrible that one person could cause so much destruction.

Apparently, so had this Axeman. Addy cleared her throat. "That specific night . . . did he kill anyone?"

Vincent smiled and shook his head. "No. Apparently all of New Orleans' dance halls were filled to capacity that night and all available bands played at parties at hundreds of houses in town. It's reported that pianos were banging out jazz tunes all evening. The Axeman kept his word and didn't kill anyone."

"They had no suspects of who he was?" Beau asked her father.

"Oh, they had suspects, of course, but no evidence on any of them. None of the homes were burglarized, so robbery wasn't a motive. Some thought the crimes were racially motivated since the majority of the victims were Italian immigrants. Some wondered if it was business related as several of the victims ran grocery stores attached to their homes where they were attacked. But no one really knows for sure."

"If he wasn't caught, the killings just what, stopped?" Beau asked.

Vincent nodded. "It was baffling to police back then, too. The last victim was around Halloween in 1919. No murder or attack after that was ever attributed to the Axeman."

Addy tossed her napkin on the table. "So why did he stop?"

"That's the mystery, my dear." Vincent took a final bite of the lasagna. "Some say he moved out of town. Some thought perhaps he really was a demon and returned to the bowels of hell." He shrugged and wiped his mouth, then set his napkin on his plate. "So if this skeleton of yours is one of the victims, maybe it's time I think about writing that book."

"It's not my skeleton." Addy stood and took her bowl and plate to the kitchen. "But it's creepy to think it could've been one of the Axeman's victims. I mean, the hotel was around back in 1918 and 1919." She scraped her food into the trash and set the dishes in the soapy water in the sink. "Were any hotels or inns crime scenes for any of the Axeman's victims?" She certainly didn't want to think the Darkwater Inn had that special distinction.

Vincent stood and brought his dishes into the kitchen as well. "No. There were grocery stores below some of the apartments, of course, but I don't think any actual attacks happened in any of them."

She let out a sigh. "Then the skeleton probably isn't a victim of the Axeman." She took her father's empty dishes and slipped them into the sudsy water. "I'm guessing none of the victims were bricked in behind a wall or anything, huh?"

Her father shook his head and finished off his tea before handing her both his glass and hers. "Not that I found, but maybe I missed something in my research."

She shuddered. "You know, it's one thing to read about stuff as fiction, like in Poe's stories. It's really freaky to hear about the Axeman's murders that really happened."

"Truth is always stranger than fiction, sweetheart." Vincent put cling wrap over the dish of lasagna and slipped it into the refrigerator. "But I'd sure like to get a look at the area. How about I drop by the hotel and take you to lunch tomorrow?"

Addy glanced at Beau. "Is that okay? I mean, are y'all finished up?"

He nodded. "Chandler said they were done, so you should be clear."

"Chandler?" She didn't know anyone named Chandler.

Beau's cheeks turned a little pink. "She's the biological anthropologist from FACES."

A strange feeling spread in the pit of Addy's stomach. "She?" Was this . . . jealousy?

Beau nodded, not saying anything, but the pink in his face deepened.

Addy found herself at a loss for anything to say, which was very unusual.

Her father looked between them, then clapped his hands. "So, where are my chocolate chip cookies?"

4

DIMITRI

Dimitri flipped through the file Adelaide's assistant had brought him bright and early this morning. How she'd found the records of the hotel, or where, he hadn't a clue, but he was thankful they'd been located and he didn't have to make a visit to his father.

"Excuse us, Dimitri?"

He turned at his name to find the two detectives and a beautiful blond woman standing in the doorway to his small office in the back of the kitchen. "Yes?"

Beauregard motioned to the woman. "This is Dr. Chandler Broussard, the biological anthropologist working with us on the skeletal remains."

She smiled, her large doe eyes framed by long golden hair in a loose ponytail.

Dimitri wiped his hands on his apron and held out his hand. "Dr. Broussard."

"It's Chandler, please."

The warmth of her hand radiated up his arm and he held her hand just a nanosecond longer than needed. "Nice to meet you, Chandler. How may I help?"

"We took the skeleton back to our lab at LSU yesterday and our forensic artist started reconstructing the skull. We began running preliminary tests, but much of what will help the most will be figuring out the date the body was bricked up." Chandler leaned her hip against the office doorjamb. "I'm hoping maybe you can give us some starting points."

Detective Marcel Taton nodded. "The scene has been cleared, so you can let the construction continue."

Beauregard added, "Addy said she had the hotel's records sent to your office."

Dimitri nodded, then gestured to the chairs in front of his desk. "Please, sit." He sat along with them and tapped the folder. "I hadn't even had time to look yet."

Beauregard pulled out his notebook and pen, while Chandler opened a tablet. Marcel just stared at him. Dimitri resisted the urge to grin. Chandler and the detective were probably very close in age, but their tools . . . well, Beauregard was definitely old school while the beautiful woman looked to be more on the cutting edge of technology. If memory served him correctly, Marcel had almost a photographic memory and never took notes.

He scanned the information of the first page. "The hotel was built in 1842 by Pierre Pampalon, who, apparently, was my great-great-great-great-grandfather." The history of his family was rather well documented in the files, complete with pictures of his ancestors. He would go through the file in detail later for familial connections, but for now he'd focus on renovations to the hotel. "The first recorded remodel was in 1899. It was a full remodel orchestrated by Robert Pampalon to update everything prior to 1900." Black and white photos were included. "Looks like he threw one shebang of a New Year's party." He slid the photo across the small desk.

"The three coins we found around the skeleton were dated 1917, so it would have been a remodel that date or later," Marcel commented.

Chandler handed him back the photo, smiling.

His thoughts rattled for a moment as he placed the picture back in the folder and scanned the pages. 1917. Remodel after 1917. "The next remodel was in 1938 by Louis Pampalon." He scanned over the receipts and notes. "Looks like a new wing was added, but I'm not too sure where exactly."

Beauregard glanced up from his notebook. "The updated floor plans should have been filed at the parish courthouse. I'll have someone check that out."

Dimitri returned to the folder, flipping to the next page. "The hotel was updated again in 1958 and 1959, following hurricane Audrey." He shook his head at the pictures. "I remember hearing about this one in school. So much devastation."

Sighing, Dimitri went to the final page in the file. "My father remodeled in 1970 after hurricane Camille, but it was mostly just to repair and update the structural integrity of the building. We remodeled again in 2006 after hurricane Katrina, but I know the area where the skeleton was found wasn't included."

The detective tapped his notebook. "So, the best options for our skeleton to have been placed would be 1938 or 1958-1959."

Dimitri nodded. "Considering the date of the coins and the construction notes I have, I'd say that's the best bet." He closed the file. "Now what?"

Chandler smiled. "We work on dating the button, zipper, and axe as well as test the bones themselves. We should be able to find some good clues—maybe even solid evidence."

"The coroner investigator said he thought the skeleton was a male," Marcel said.

She nodded. "I concur. The shape of the pelvis pretty much is conclusive. Following my initial inspection of the skeleton, I also concur with his approximate age, early twenties. He was almost six feet—five-eleven, to be exact, and was of slight build. I'd guesstimate him to have weighed about one fifty to one seventy, give or take. Tests on the hair indicate he had short, wavy hair that was dark brown." She set her tablet on the edge of the desk and reached back to adjust her ponytail.

A faint waft of her perfume reached Dimitri. Sweet. Flowery. Almost intoxicating.

Sitting back in the chair, Chandler continued. "My team will be running the skeleton's teeth impressions to try and match up dental records."

"Can those go back to 1917 or further?" Dimitri had no idea when dental records started being kept, and honestly, he truly didn't care, but he found himself wanting to continue to engage in conversation with the young anthropologist.

Chandler flashed her easy smile. "They go back to the mid-1800s. The first documented dental evidence presented in a United States court was in 1849. Helped prove a murder case."

"Interesting." Dimitri locked stares with her. "And interesting you can tell so much about his hair."

"You'd be amazed at the information you can pull from someone's hair. It's a part of you that sticks around."

The detectives stood, Beauregard pocketing his notebook. "Thanks, Dimitri." He paused, glancing at Chandler, then back to Dimitri. "I think that's it for now."

Chandler stood, prompting him to as well. She grabbed her tablet. "That's all I have at the moment." She reached across and shook Dimitri's hand. "I'm sure we'll be working together on more information before the case is over."

"I hope so." Interestingly enough, he truly did.

Dimitri didn't sit after they left. He found himself a bit restless feeling. Maybe a little walk would help bring him back into focus. He suddenly wanted to see Adelaide as well. Slipping his cell phone into his pocket, he passed through the kitchen and into the restaurant.

He had no intention of stopping, but he couldn't help slowing his pace as he wove around the tables. The crisp linens with polished silverware stood out fresh against the dark tables. Small vases with fresh flowers sat on each table beside the ornate salt and pepper shakers. The little details were what made all the difference. An extra dash of cayenne here . . . a pinch of minced crawfish . . . a dab of garlic butter . . . a shot of cooking sherry . . . all little things that made something average stand out. He straightened a vase on one of the tables as he made his way across the lobby.

"Dimitri!"

He turned, the smile already on his face at the sound of Adelaide's voice. She rushed toward him, her father trailing a little slower behind her. "You remember my father, Vincent?"

"I do." He shook her father's hand. "Hello, sir."

"Dimitri." No mistaking the hint of hesitation in his voice, nor in his posture as he turned as if to place an invisible shield extension between Dimitri and his daughter.

Adelaide must have sensed it as well because she took a step closer to him. "Dad wanted to come see where we found the skeleton. You don't mind?"

It's not an exhibit. He bit back the retort and forced a smile. Where had that thought come from? Adelaide always looked out for the best interests of the Darkwater Inn. "Of course not." He couldn't imagine why he'd thought such a thing. It was very unusual. He widened his smile to include her father. "I spoke with Beauregard and Chandler. He says the police have cleared the scene and we can have the construction crew return to work."

She nodded slowly. "They'll be back Monday morning at eight. Luckily, they weren't spooked off of the job."

"That's good news."

"So you met Chandler?"

His muscles tightened involuntarily. "I did. She seems like a nice woman. Smart, apparently, as well."

"I haven't met her yet." The question in her eyes made him look away.

What was wrong with him? He didn't quite feel like himself. "You should. You'll like her."

"You think so?"

He smiled and nodded.

"Ms. Fountaine, Mr. Pampalon . . . just the two people I wanted to speak with." An older, curly-haired woman rushed toward them. "And . . . you are . . . you can't be . . . it is . . . you're R.C. Steele, aren't you?" She squirmed her way into the group. "Are you here about the body?"

She looked familiar, but Dimitri couldn't place her. "What? Who are you?"

Adelaide's face tightened. "Surely you remember Allison Williams, Dimitri? She's the reporter from WDSU."

"Ah, yes." The one who seemed to always know about incidents at the hotel before everyone else.

"You're Mr. Steele, aren't you? I recognize you from your old book jackets. They don't put your picture on the new ones, I'm guessing because of that stalker issue you had some years back, right? Anyway, I've been a fan for a really long time." If she tried to stop talking, Dimitri was pretty sure she would trip over her loose tongue. "So, are you here about the body they found? Ooh, are you doing a book here?"

Adelaide effectively spun her father away from the nosy reporter. "Dimitri, would you mind escorting our guest where he needs to be, please? I'll speak with Ms. Williams." She took the reporter by the arm and led her across the lobby.

"That woman's a menace to herself and others," Vincent mumbled under his breath.

Dimitri chuckled. "No argument here. Come on, let's get out of here before she breaks loose from Adelaide's grip." He turned toward the area that had been blocked off with yellow caution tape.

Vincent glanced over his shoulder, then followed Dimitri. "Don't sell Addy short. She can handle the likes of that woman just fine."

"Oh, I know she can. She has. Multiple times." Dimitri lifted the tape for Adelaide's father. "I have full confidence she can handle whatever or whomever pops up."

"I do as well."

Dimitri didn't know her father well enough to read him. He'd always felt like Vincent Fountaine didn't approve of him for some reason. Sure, most people had run-ins with Claude and that tainted their image of his son, but surely Adelaide had told her father that Dimitri wasn't like Claude.

Or maybe she had sung his praises too much and Vincent didn't like that. After all, weren't most men overprotective of men interested in their daughter? Dimitri couldn't blame Vincent for that. Adelaide was quite a special lady.

"Here we go." Dimitri stopped short of where the skeletal remains had been removed. "That's where they found it."

The entire area had a fine layer of dust over everything. Shoe prints and equipment marks were trailed all over the floor. The protective plastic sheet over the large window prevented the sun from coming in and cast eerie shadows over the room.

Vincent made an undistinguishable sound as he moved toward the wall. He ran his hand over the bricks until he reached the part where the construction crew had knocked out the part. He stepped right beside where the skeleton had laid. He turned to face Dimitri. "Beau told us there was an axe found here, too. Do you know where it was?"

Dimitri nodded. "Leaning against the back wall. Right in front of where you're standing. You should be able to see the mark on the floor." That's what Beau told him. That's right. Adelaide's father was like a surrogate father to Beauregard ever since Beauregard's father had died in the line of duty before he was even a teenager. Naturally, Vincent would hope that his daughter would fall for a man he'd known practically his whole life. Maybe that's what Dimitri was feeling subconsciously from Vincent.

Adelaide's father continued his inspection of the area.

"We reviewed the hotel records today and determined that the most likely time for the body to have been put here would have been either during the renovations of 1938 or 1958." Dimitri didn't know why he blurted that out—perhaps some deep-seated need to impress Vincent in order to level the playing field between Beauregard and himself?

"Fifty-eight, huh? Audrey?"

"Yes, sir. My grandfather, Louis Pampalon, did a renovation and remodel after the hurricane."

"And in thirty-eight? A hurricane?"

"Not that I'm aware of, sir. Just the hotel records reflect that a major renovation and new wing was added at that time."

"Here?"

"I don't know. Beauregard said he'd have someone check at the parish courthouse to see where the wing was added."

Vincent grunted and returned to surveying the area. "Beau said they found coins dated 1917 here, most likely from the victim's pocket."

Dimitri nodded. "So I'm told. Chandler said she'll be looking into dating the button and zipper they found and will weigh that with what they learn from their tests on the bones."

Adelaide's father stopped milling around the space and locked his gaze on Dimitri's face. "Chandler? That's that anthropologist, right?"

Dimitri nodded, a strange lump filling the back of his throat.

"I heard she's a pretty gal."

Dimitri nodded again, not trusting himself to speak.

Vincent stared for another moment before letting out another one of his undistinguishable sounds.

Should he expound? Explain? Dimitri didn't know what he should or shouldn't do or say. He didn't know what Vincent thought. Sure, he'd noticed Adelaide's expression change when she mentioned Chandler, but . . . wait, how did Vincent know Chandler was pretty? Did Beauregard say something? Was Adelaide jealous because Chandler was hanging out with the detective?

No, he wouldn't allow himself to wallow in such high school boyish thoughts. He'd turned the entire situation over to God and would accept the way things played out. While he felt like he and Adelaide belonged together, he wouldn't stoop to playing the doubt and guessing game. It did no one good if he did.

His cell phone rang. Dimitri checked the display. He turned his back toward Vincent as he answered. "Hello, Zoey."

"Hi, Dimitri. Did I catch you at a bad time?" Zoey's voice held a huskiness to it, but also a smoothness. Kind of like a well-aged whiskey.

Dimitri glanced over his shoulder—Vincent had gone back to his inspection of the area. "No, it's fine. What's up?" He and Zoey had a special friendship. While she'd once been a frequent—ahem—visitor at the Darkwater Inn's bar to meet

71

men for money, she'd been a desperate single mother in need of a means to support her son. Dimitri had reached out to various friends and was able to get her a job in one of the warehouse district's art galleries. She'd been grateful, but his friend had been even more grateful, telling Dimitri that Zoey had a natural eye for art and was a great asset to her gallery.

"I wanted to ask if I could use the Darkwater to host a special show for a local artist. This artist is pretty amazing, Dimitri."

"I don't know. There's a lot going on right now." He watched Vincent count off steps from the wall.

"Please. Just a dozen or so paintings, and it'd be a small group of no more than fifty, seventy-five tops."

"You'd really need to talk to Adelaide about that, Zoey."

"I was thinking we could have it in the restaurant. You could make some of your famous and scrumptious hors d'oeuvres for the evening. Please, Dimitri." Her husky voice dropped a decibel.

"So you want me to cater this shindig as well, huh? I'm betting pro bono, too?" But he smiled as he spoke, already mentally flipping through the recipe book in his mind.

"Please. I'll really owe you big time, Dimitri."

He made a point to sigh very loudly. "When?"

"Next Friday?"

"A week from today? Are you crazy?" He would have to make arrangements to close the restaurant to the general public, special order items he wanted to serve, arrange for staffing to serve . . . so much.

"I know it's a lot, I do, but this artist's father is a religious nut and really formidable and we finally got his blessing for a show so we want to set it before he changes his mind."

This could be a disaster, or it could be a wonderful event. It'd been a while since he'd worked outside his comfort zone. Dimitri watched Vincent intently typing on his cell phone. Maybe this was just what he needed— something fun to keep his mind off everything else. He'd handed the reins of the Darkwater Inn over to Adelaide. He trusted her, so he should let her handle this.

"Dimitri? Please? I wouldn't ask if it weren't really important to me." Zoey's voice cracked again. "This artist is important to me."

"Then how can I say no? I can't wait to meet this young man."

"Yes? You'll do it?"

"Of course, but you knew that when you asked, didn't you?" The smile crept back on his face.

"Thank you, Dimitri! Oh, I owe you so big. I promise, I won't forget this."

He chuckled. "What time on Friday?"

"Seven to eleven. I've got to run. I need to make calls. Invite people. Oh, thank you so much, Dimitri. You're gonna be blown away by this guy's talent. He's amazing. And all his work has a religious bent, so I know you're gonna love it."

"I definitely can't wait to meet him. What all do you need me to do to set up?"

"Nothing. Just work your magic with the food and I'll do the rest. I'll come by Friday morning and set up the easels with the artwork and everything. I'll even move the tables around myself if I have to."

He laughed again and shook his head. "I have staff who will do that."

"Okay. Seriously, Dimitri, this means a lot. Thank you."

"See you Friday." He disconnected the call and slipped the phone back into his pocket. He'd need to start planning right away—tonight.

Vincent stepped alongside him. "You grew up in the hotel, like your father and his father before him, right?"

"Um, yes, sir."

"Let me ask you something . . . have you ever heard of the Axeman?"

5

BEAU

"Report is back on the axe." Marcel met Beau at their desks as soon as he returned from his lunch break. Although, taking Columbo to the vet could hardly be considered a break of any sort. His cat was obese, the vet lectured every single time Beau took him in. Also, Columbo hated the vet. The normally docile feline became a ball of claws and teeth every time Beau pulled out the cat carrier. Today's adventure had left him with two long scratches on his left forearm.

Beau took a seat behind his desk. "Don't keep me in suspense."

Marcel parked himself on the edge of Beau's desk, opened a file, and read aloud. "The axe is a 1935 Sager double bit axe, manufactured in 1935, and is a swamping pattern. Its wooden handle is thirty-six inches long, and the head is right at twelve inches long, and it weighs almost four pounds."

"Sturdy."

Marcel nodded. "Yup. Company was founded back in the late 1800s, so they had time to really perfect their designs. They created the chemical treatment method to reduce oxidation and prolong the finish of the metal."

"Sweet. So was it blood on the axe?"

Again Marcel nodded. "Yup again, and before you ask—yes, it was human. Nolan said they are trying to pull enough to get a DNA sample. Right now, he said that the blood is B negative, one of the rarer blood types. Nolan said only about one person out of sixty-seven in the United States has that blood type."

"Rarer is better in this case, in the event we can't get DNA." At least Nolan was assigned the case. While everyone in the CSU was good at their job, Beau had always appreciated Nolan's dedication and his particular attention to detail.

"Yep. Nolan said Robert's doing some new type of testing to see if he can pull off any finger or palm prints."

"That would be nice."

Marcel shut the folder and tossed it onto Beau's desk before moving to sit behind his own desk. "Nolan said they're still looking into the button that we recovered, but initial finding is that it's from men's dress slacks from mid-to-late 1930s. According to what they've been able to find out thus far, the button used wasn't on jeans or work pants, but were found on slacks that catered mainly to upper class."

"And the zipper?"

"It was also used in dress slacks during the same time period."

Beau flipped to a new page in his notebook and began writing. "So what we know about our victim is he was male, early twenties, stood five foot eleven, weighed around a hundred and fifty to a hundred and seventy, had a slight build. He had short, wavy, brown hair. Based upon his clothing, he was probably upper class, which would match with him being a guest of the Darkwater Inn."

"So you think he's a guest, not a construction worker?" Marcel crossed his arms over his chest and leaned back in his chair.

"Not if he was wearing slacks for upper class, I wouldn't think."

"Good point." Marcel sat forward, resting his elbows on his desk. "What else?"

"He might have B negative blood type, and he was murdered, possibly with a Sager axe." Beau tapped his pen against the notebook. "Anything else?"

Marcel shook his head. "Not yet. So, what do we know about the killer?"

"Even less." Beau flipped to the next page in his notebook. "He knew about the construction details going on at the Darkwater Inn, or at least he had to know the schedule. I can't see anybody sneaking in a ton of bricks and mortar without reason."

"Member of the construction crew?"

"Maybe. Or he could've been an employee of the hotel."

Marcel nodded. "Maybe his fingerprints or palm prints will be found on the axe."

"If the axe is confirmed to be the murder weapon."

"Nolan said Timothy sent all the dimensions and such to Dr. Broussard. We should hear back today if it matches up. Nolan said if Dr. Broussard needed the actual axe to confirm, he'd send it to her lab." Marcel grinned. "So you know she had to make some sort of great impression on Nolan for him to volunteer to loan out any pieces of evidence."

"Wow." Nolan wasn't even keen on Beau and Marcel handling anything if it could be avoided.

"Seems she's pretty adept at making good impressions. She's quite the looker."

Beau nodded. "She's an attractive lady."

"And smart."

"Obviously."

"And single."

Beau looked up from his notebook to his partner. "Excuse me?"

Marcel chuckled. "She's single. Not married. Doesn't have a boyfriend, either."

"You quizzed the anthropologist working our case?"

"It came up in our conversation."

Beau let out a snort. "I just bet it did."

"Hey, I'm hurt." Marcel put his hand over his heart and tried to put on a wounded look, but his big grin diffused the sincerity of his gesture.

"Please tell me you didn't ask her out." Beau shook his head. His partner was known as quite the ladies' man. He supposed Marcel was handsome enough—he'd been told many times over that he resembled the actor Taye Diggs, and he took excellent care of himself. He could easily bench press more than any of the other detectives in their precinct, including Beau, but Beau would never admit to that.

"Nah. I don't think I'm her type."

Beau laughed. "I thought you believed all women found you irresistible."

"Most do." Marcel shrugged. "But this one? Well, she seemed pretty interested in Dimitri."

That grabbed Beau's full attention. "What makes you say that?"

"Just the way she looked at him when we were in his office yesterday. I can tell these things."

"Any woman who doesn't swoon at your feet must be attracted to someone else, is that it?" Beau grinned.

"Well . . . not every woman, but most of them."

"Savoie! Taton!"

Both men jumped at the sound of the captain's bellow across the precinct. "My office. Both of you. Now."

Beau grabbed his notebook and rushed toward Captain Istre's office, Marcel matching his steps. "What did you do now?" he mumbled under his breath.

Marcel shook his head. "Me? I haven't done anything."

They stopped at the threshold to the captain's office.

"Come in and sit down. Shut the door." The captain had already plopped back down in a chair that creaked under his weight.

Marcel shut the door, then they both sat on the edge of the chairs, facing the captain.

"This case you two caught . . . the skeleton at the Darkwater Inn. Where are we on it?"

"Not much of anywhere yet." Beau quickly filled the captain in on the facts of the case.

"Doesn't sound like you have any leads on the victim or the crime."

"No, sir. We're waiting on reports from the evidence as well from CSU and the FACES unit," Marcel volunteered.

The captain let out a loud and gruff harrumph. "Are we giving out guided tours of crime scenes now, detectives?" Annoyance accentuated the worn lines of the captain's stern face.

"Um, no, sir." Beau couldn't imagine where this was going, but he was pretty certain the captain was about to let them know clearly what he meant.

"Then perhaps you could explain to me why not only a suspense writer was at the crime scene but also a local news reporter who ran the story on the noon newscast?"

Oh, no. Beau's stomach twisted.

"By your expression, Savoie, I'm guessing you know what I'm talking about."

For years, he'd been Vincent Fountaine's law enforcement source for his novels. Nothing specific, of course, but to verify procedures and policies and the such. Still, following a stalker incident several years ago, Vincent became very secretive about his life to the point where not many people knew that the famous bestseller R.C. Steele was really Vincent Fountaine. "Um, sir?"

"The noon newscast was filled with shots of the Darkwater Inn, reporting that a skeleton had been found within its walls and it was noteworthy enough to bring out one of the most popular suspense authors of today, who just so happens to be, in real life, the father of the general manager of the hotel. Would you care to explain why you didn't think this was important to reveal to me?"

"Well, sir . . . um . . ." He didn't quite know what to say. Vincent had become paranoid regarding his identity after too many stalking incidents. To be identified—on the news—would completely affect his life. Not to mention that the story shouldn't have been on the news at all.

"It's water under the bridge now, since Allison Williams reported it on the news. I'm sure there will be major repercussions regarding this case."

This was even worse than Beau could have imagined. Vincent's identity revealed on the local network would be picked up, no doubt. And that he was at the scene . . .

"Any idea how the news even got wind of this?" The anger in the captain's voice had dissipated a little.

Marcel shook his head. "I don't know, sir. We've suspected for a while that there was a leak in the department somewhere since the same reporter, Allison Williams, seems to be able to report on things almost immediately."

The captain pointed at them. "Find the leak and plug it. And do whatever damage control you can revolving her report. We've already got a call from several of the station's affiliates wanting comments. This isn't just going to die away."

Beau and Marcel both stood. "Yes, sir," they said in unison before rushing from the office.

"If I find out who keeps feeding that woman information . . ." Marcel slapped his fist against his palm.

"It's made our job harder on several cases now." Beau shook his head. "Vincent is going to be furious. Addy, too." He hated to think how angry both would be. He was mad enough over the report, and he hadn't even seen it.

"As they should be. Man, that Allison Williams . . . it's past time somebody put a plug in her outlet."

Beau nodded. "Why don't you put your charm to use on the ladies in the records room, dispatching, wherever, and see if you can get a lead on Allison Williams's source? Somebody around here has to know something."

"On it." Marcel turned and headed down the other hallway of the precinct while Beau returned to his desk. His phone buzzed before he could even sit down. He snatched it up. "Detective Savoie."

"You have a visitor up here in reception. A Dr. Broussard. She says she has some information for you on a case you're working."

"Yes. Send her back, please." He hung up the phone and waited until Chandler rounded the corner. The uniformed officer pointed the way to his desk before turning back toward the reception area.

Beau met her midway across the open precinct detectives' den, as he referred to it. "Chandler, you didn't have to come all the way down here." He shook her hand, then led her to his desk, pulling out the chair beside it for her.

"It wasn't any problem." She sat. "I had to drop off some reports at the coroner's office anyway, and I thought you might be interested in hearing the news firsthand, in case you had any questions."

Beau sat in his chair and pulled out his notebook and pen. "What's that?"

"The axe was definitely the murder weapon. The skull has a three-and-one-third-centimeters-deep gash on the left side of the skull just above the ear. The sheer force of a blow with enough force to cut that deep into the skull would kill anybody. The length of the gash on the skull matches with the axe perfectly." She crossed her legs and tapped her short, unpainted fingernails on her knee. "Due to this information, and the fact that the axe was left by the body, I'm going to work off the assumption that the blood found on the axe belongs to the victim. I'm hoping your CSU results can pull a DNA profile, which if matched, we can confirm with blood typing and dental records."

"Have you had any luck with those?"

Chandler smiled and shook her head. "Those take a little more time. We've made the impressions and are running searches. If you have any type of time frame you think the murder could have been committed, it would be helpful for me as I search for missing persons."

"You think the victim was a missing person?"

She grinned again. "I think the murderer went to a lot of trouble to hide the body, so I'm going to assume someone had to miss him. If we get lucky, someone filed a report and that will give us some information to start our searching."

Beau flipped to the victim page he'd made in his notebook and read what he'd written, explaining about his upper-class theory because of the button and zipper.

She nodded. "If he was upper class, that might actually help us even more. When the wealthy go missing, they're usually reported as missing."

"Yeah." He jotted down the notes about the blow to the head.

"Especially if they go missing while on vacation or something. If they were a guest of the hotel."

He hadn't considered that right off the bat, although it did make sense. He made a note in the margin of his notes. "I'll check out any reports that were filed on missing persons from the Darkwater Inn." It was as good of a lead as anything else they had at the moment.

"So, detective, what's your gut telling you about the time of the murder?" She smiled. "I've worked with enough law enforcement that I don't ever discount a cop's gut instinct. They usually tend to be pretty accurate."

He glanced at his notes and shrugged. "I don't like to guess." He dealt in facts . . . in absolutes. He didn't like guessing and certainly didn't like discussing guesses outside of his partner.

But Chandler smiled so widely, she disarmed

his resistance. "I'm not asking you to commit to an answer, just what you think, based on your training and experience."

It was hard to deny the woman when she turned her charm on. Too bad Marcel had written her off—the two of them would be a formidable pair.

Beau let out a sigh. "Well, looking at just the evidence I have right now, if I were pressed, I'd say my best guess would be the murder and stashing of the body had to be during the 1938 remodel."

"That's exactly what I think, too, based upon what we know and my experience." She sucked her bottom lip, making a slurping type of noise before letting it go with a pop. "Upper class . . . are you thinking he was a guest of the hotel?"

"That's kind of the way I'm leaning."

She nodded. "Makes perfect sense. I wonder if the hotel has guest ledgers from that time."

"Maybe." He hadn't really considered that. "I could ask Addy."

"Or I could ask Dimitri." Her face brightened a little bit. Just enough that someone trained in microexpressions would notice. "I mean, if they kept a ledger and one of their guests went missing, maybe there would be some documentation, right?"

Marcel's insight wrapped around Beau's mind. Maybe his partner *did* know more about the female gender than most. "Maybe."

"I mean, it wouldn't hurt to ask Dimitri to look, right? Especially if we could find a name that matched a missing persons report you might find, right?"

"There's no harm in asking."

She nodded. "I think I will." Chandler glanced at the floor, the apples of her cheeks turning a little pink. "So, um, would you happen to know if Dimitri is involved with anyone or anything? I didn't see a wedding ring but . . ."

"No, he's not married." This was awkward. On one hand, it was great that a beautiful woman was interested in Dimitri. On the other hand, it put Beau in a tight place to explain Dimitri's interest in the woman Beau was also dating.

"Is he seeing someone specific, do you know?"

"I know he's dating, but not in a monogamous type of relationship." That was the truth. The monogamous part might be only because Addy had feelings for both Beau and Dimitri, but it was a fact.

Chandler smiled. "Good. I mean, oh. I just wondered is all. He's very handsome and charming and he does own a hotel."

Beau chuckled. "He does at that." He shouldn't have the giddy feeling at the thought of Dimitri and Chandler becoming involved.

But he did.

She stood. "Well, I think I'll go ask. If I find out anything, I'll call you, okay?"

"I'd appreciate that." He stood and shook her hand. "It'd help me on the case tremendously."

"Sure. I'll be in touch." She walked with a bounce toward the reception area.

As Beau returned to his seat, a heaviness settled in the pit of his stomach. He'd been truthful enough with Chandler, but he didn't want Dimitri taken out of contending for Addy's heart. If Dimitri and Chandler connected, would Beau get Addy out of default? He didn't want that.

He wanted Addy to be his, more than he wanted to draw his next breath, but he wanted her to want him. Wanted her to choose him.

Wanted her to love him.

That meant she had to choose between Dimitri and Beau. She had to make the choice, not have it made for her. Otherwise, he'd always wonder. That was no way to have a relationship. Not one that would last, anyway.

In that moment Beau knew two things: he wanted Adelaide Fountaine to love him and he wanted theirs to be a forever love.

THE COMPOUND

Esau stepped into his father's dimly lit room. The old man sat up in his bed, what little hair he had left jutted out at odd angles. His sleepshirt hung in wads around his bony frame. But it was his eyes—wide and glazed with flickers from the bedside candle that sent shivers up Esau's spine. "You called for me, Father?"

He nodded. "Did you see the news?" At one hundred and one years old, his mind and tongue were both still quicker than most of his sons'.

"What part?" Esau asked, careful to keep his tone neutral. Upsetting his father was never a good idea, but especially not when he was so obviously unnerved.

"About the skeleton found in the Darkwater Inn, of course!"

Esau swallowed. "Yes, sir, I did." He offered nothing more, not sure what he should say.

"Are you stupid, son? Do you not see?" His father's voice shook the room. Small remnant of a man, still as powerful as ever.

"I'm sorry, Father. I don't understand." Even at the age of seventy-six, Esau was intimidated by his father. Truth be told, all his children were.

The old man's eyes flashed. "The demon is loose."

1925

"I don't want to go. I want to stay here with you." William clung to Sister Rosemary. If he held tightly enough, maybe he wouldn't have to leave. The thought of going to St. Mary's Asylum scared him.

"You can't stay here, sweetheart. Everybody has to leave when they turn a certain age. Remember, your friend Harold went last year."

"Why can't I just stay with you? I'll be good, I promise." Just thinking about being away from Sister Rosemary made his tummy hurt. He wanted to throw up.

"Oh, my sweet boy, you are good. You aren't being sent to St. Mary's because you did anything wrong. That's where all the young boys go. You'll make new friends, but your best friends, James and George, are going with you. Harold is probably waiting on you there, too."

He sniffed, not wanting Sister Rosemary to see him crying like a little baby. He was seven now, a big boy. Smart, too. All his teachers said so. Even Mother Mary Margaret. "They're all going, too?"

Sister Rosemary smiled. "Of course, and there will be other boys there your age as well. You'll make so many new friends. You'll forget all about me and the other sisters here at St. Vincent, as you should. You might even find a family."

He'd wanted a family for as long as he could remember, a mommy and daddy of his own, not like the one he had. Mother Mary Margaret had told him that his mommy had been killed by a man who let a demon possess him. But his mommy had been a sinner and that's what got her killed.

William was pretty sure the demon-possessed man was what killed her, but he wouldn't say that out loud. Not where Mother Mary Margaret could hear him. She'd rap his knuckles with her ruler for sure.

That ruler hurt!

"You have to remember to say your prayers and mind your manners, sweet William." Sister Rosemary gave him a final hug. "You're going to be just fine."

He still didn't like the idea of leaving her, but if James and George went with him, it couldn't be too bad. They were his bestest friends. And he did miss Harold. It would be great to see him again.

"I made you a copy of the letter that was in your pram the night you came to us." She handed him a sealed envelope. "You aren't old enough yet to understand everything in the letter, but one day you will. I pray you'll keep it safe and not open it until you turn thirteen." She put her hand on the side of his face. "Can you do that for me?"

"Yes, Sister Rosemary. I promise."

She smiled. "Put the envelope in your Bible and keep it safe. One day, when you're old enough to understand, you'll read it and know that you were loved before you came here." She glanced over her shoulder and lowered her voice. "Despite what Mother Mary Margaret says, your mother loved you. Even when she was off doing things . . . well, things she shouldn't have, she made sure you were well taken care of. You only do that for people you love."

He nodded, not understanding anything of what she said, but realizing it was important to Sister Rosemary, so it was important to him.

"Keep it safe. Be good. Say your prayers." She smiled at him again, her eyes looking all watery like his did when we was about to cry. "I love you and I'll miss you."

"Will you come see me?"

She shook her head. "No, I'm afraid I won't be able to come visit, but know that I love you very much and I'll be thinking of you. Always."

6

DIMITRI

"Sorry to hear about the hotel's troubles. Seems over the last year or so, a dark cloud has settled over the Darkwater Inn." Funny, but Malcolm Dessommes's tone didn't indicate any sympathy over the phone.

Dimitri wiped his hands on the rag tucked into the band of his apron. "Well, you know what they say—there's no such thing as bad publicity. Front desk is reporting even more reservations than we can accommodate." Whatever it was about murder and mayhem that attracted people, he'd never understand.

"Thrill seekers, I suppose. Happy to hear the news hasn't impacted the profit of the hotel. Especially since I'm sure you'll soon be interested in selling to me or letting me buy in to be your partner."

Dimitri laughed as he stirred the simmering pot of boiling chicken, onions, and celery. "I already told you I'm not interested."

"*Yet,* my friend. You aren't interested yet."

"I've got to run, Mal. I have to have chicken and dumplings ready for tonight's special."

"I hear you. Just remember I'm only a phone

call away when you're ready to talk dollars and cents."

Dimitri disconnected the call and pocketed his cell phone. Malcolm Dessommes was tenacious if nothing else, he'd give him that.

A sweet voice interrupted his thoughts. "Dimitri? Do you have a moment?"

He smiled at the sound of her voice. "For you, Adelaide? Always, *mon chaton*." He turned to Yvette. "Oversee, please."

His sous chef grinned and nodded.

"Let's go to my office." He placed his hand in the small of Adelaide's back and led her to the back corner of the kitchen that housed the large closet he'd transformed into a little office space. Once inside, he shut the door. She sat in one of the chairs facing his desk, so he sat on the edge of the desk. "What's on your mind?"

"I got a note that you were closing the restaurant during the dinner hour next Friday. That can't be correct."

He let out a little sigh. It was silly to think she'd come see him because she was upset over her father's identity being revealed on the news in correlation to what was happening at the hotel. During work hours, she was all business. He swallowed his disappointment. "It is. The restaurant has been booked for a private event."

"We're booked at full capacity through the end of March. Closing the restaurant during the dinner hour on a Friday night means a lot of lost revenue, Dimitri."

He hadn't considered that. Just another reason he should stick to cooking. "I'm sorry. I should have spoken with you before I agreed."

"It's okay. I just hope that you charged enough for the private party to compensate for the loss of revenue."

Dimitri moved around to his seat behind the desk. "Well, actually, I didn't. It's a charity event." Definitely charity on his end.

"What?" She blinked.

"I agreed to host an artist showing to help support the local arts. I thought it would be good for business." He resisted the urge to squirm under her scrutiny.

"An artist show?" She narrowed her eyes, her annoyance flashing.

A minute passed. Two.

Adelaide let out a long breath. "Are you doing this to help Zoey?" She knew him too well, which even though she was irritated at him at the moment, made him smile.

"She begged and I know she needs this to be a success. It's not just any artist. This is one she's involved with."

"So naturally you want to help her. I get it." She let out another sigh and stood.

He got to his feet and moved around the desk, taking her hands in his. "Don't be mad."

"I'm not mad. That you care and want to help others is one of your most admirable traits."

He squeezed her hands. "Really? And what other traits of mine do you so admire?"

A knock rapped on the door.

Adelaide startled, freeing herself from his hold.

The door inched open and Dr. Chandler Broussard stood in the doorway. "Am I interrupting? I can come back if you're busy."

"No, it's fine. Come on in." Dimitri smiled. "Have you met Adelaide Fountaine, the Darkwater Inn's general manager? Adelaide, this is Dr. Chandler Broussard from the FACES unit in Baton Rouge."

Chandler and Adelaide shook hands.

"It's a pleasure, Dr. Broussard." Adelaide's voice sounded off . . . a little higher-pitched than usual. "Thank you for coming to help out on the case."

"Please, call me Chandler. Dr. Broussard is much too formal." The anthropologist smiled widely at Adelaide, then turned that smile on him, sending little ripples in his gut. "That's why I'm here. I was talking to Beau and we thought maybe you might be able to help with some records the hotel might have kept."

"Oh, you should talk to Adelaide about that. I'm just the cook."

Adelaide shook her head, her gaze going between him and Chandler. "He's being too

96

modest." She looked at him. "Why don't you and Chandler work on the details of what you might have, and I'll send Vicky over to help locate whatever you might need. She found the other records, so I'm sure she could help you with anything else."

Dimitri shook his head. "This is more your thing, Adelaide, and I really need to finish the preparations for dinner." He didn't miss Chandler's smile disappearing—or Adelaide's noticing.

Adelaide again looked between him and Chandler. "I'm sure Yvette can oversee that, right? I mean, we need to do all we can to solve this case." Adelaide's posture had straightened into almost a defensive mode. "For the sake of the hotel, of course."

"I suppose you're right." Of course Adelaide would put needing to solve the case for the hotel's sake above dinner or personal feelings. That was just who she was, and part of what made her an amazing general manager. "Yes, of course." He nodded. "Happy to see what we can do."

Adelaide's smile seemed a little forced. "Perfect. I'll go find Vicky for you." She shook Chandler's hand. "It was very nice to have finally met you, Chandler. Thank you, again, for your help."

"Of course. It's my job. And it was great to meet you, too, Adelaide."

Adelaide gave Dimitri a curt nod, then brushed past him out of the office.

Everything in him screamed that he should go after her, but he had no idea why. Somewhere deep inside his chest, he had the sinking sensation that things between him and Adelaide had just shifted.

And he had no idea what, exactly, that meant.

THE COMPOUND

"Did you hear?"

Jacob looked up from his notebook at his brother Moses. "About what?"

"Father says the demon is loose again."

"What is David planning?" Jacob closed his notebook, but his heart had begun racing. Oh, how he wished he was already sixty-five so he could take the reins of their family. This was the chance he'd waited all his life for.

Moses shook his head. "According to what Saul told Levi, nothing. He wants to wait and see what happens. He has no plan of action."

Jacob's hands curled into fists. He'd always known his older brother was too weak to lead like their father had. "This is unacceptable." He stood and paced. He and David had already locked horns on many issues, so going to his brother wasn't an option. "What does Father say?"

"He has allowed David to talk him into

watching. David says he has prayed and feels that the demon hasn't been released or has no more power here anymore."

"And Father accepts that?" Someone had brainwashed his father. No way would he ever feel like a demon had lost power. Ever.

"No, but Abel, Saul, and Noah all have taken David's side. Father's age has allowed him to be swayed by some of his sons."

Jacob shook his head. "But Father has always, always, been adamant about keeping the evil minions at bay. Now, when the one he despised the most has been set free, he sits back and agrees to do nothing?" This was unspeakably wrong.

Moses nodded. "I know, but they've bent his ear and garnered his blessing to sit by and do nothing unless some sign shows differently."

A slow smile spread across Jacob's face. This, *this* was the moment he'd been preparing for all his life. It was his moment. "Then we'll just have to help show that now, won't we?"

ADDY

What was she supposed to think about Dr. Chandler Broussard?

Addy went back to her office after having instructed her assistant, Vicky, to check in with Dimitri and help in any way. She plopped down into her chair, willing her emotions and thoughts to stop going in a million different directions.

Neither obeyed.

She didn't understand what she felt toward the anthropologist. Her knee-jerk reaction was that she liked Chandler. She seemed nice and more than capable of doing her job, which would help solve the case and help the hotel. But she also seemed to mesmerize both Beau and Dimitri. It wasn't shocking, really, because the woman was quite beautiful and outgoing and clearly very intelligent. Who wouldn't find her attractive and interesting?

That was the crux of Addy's confusion and raging emotions. How was it possible that the two men Addy had feelings for would both gather the interest of Chandler? That was what Addy sensed—the woman's interest and access to both Beau and Dimitri.

That was also what she had a problem with. A very serious problem.

"Hey." Tracey slipped into her office, shutting the door behind her. "I saw the noon news and thought you might need to vent." Addy's best friend always knew the right thing to do and say, and when to show up because Addy needed a friend.

Addy sighed loudly, letting her emotions float away. She grinned at her friend. "Thanks."

Tracey Glapion had been Addy's best friend for as long as Addy could remember. They both had long dark hair and dark eyes. They were both about the same height. Tracey's skin was paler than Addy's, though. Also, she was outgoing and unpredictable unlike Addy's cautious personality, but they balanced each other out. They'd gotten into trouble in high school together, had more fun than they should have, and had taken their friendship into adulthood. After Addy had been raped in college, it had been Tracey's sound advice that had gotten her in with a good therapist to deal with her emotions and heal from the trauma. And Tracey kept Addy's secrets.

"So, your dad got ratted out." Tracey dropped into a loveseat in a sitting area near Addy's desk.

"Yeah, Dad's more than mad, but what can he do?"

"That woman was rude to out him on the news. If she only knew what y'all had been through." Tracey's eyes flashed.

Addy joined her on the couch. "Dad's worried another stalker might pop up, but like I told him, he hasn't gotten any freaky fan mail like that in years. I think he's safe."

Tracey pulled her legs up onto the loveseat and sat crisscross, pulling one of the throw pillows onto her lap. "But you and I both know that your dad isn't worried about himself being a target. He's worried about someone using you to get to him."

"I don't think that's likely. I think the days of

101

stalker fans are over. With the rise of writers publishing their own books and less promotion by publishers for their lead authors, fans aren't as rabid as they once were."

Tracey nodded. "So . . . a skeleton behind a wall? And you didn't even call me? That's kind of my area, Ads." Her perfectly-lined bottom lip puckered out in a pout. "I had to hear about it on the news, and that's wrong on all kinds of levels."

It *was* kind of Tracey's area. Locals claimed Tracey was a direct descendant of Louis Christophe Dominick Duminy de Glapion, the "left-handed husband" of renowned Voodoo Queen of New Orleans, Marie Laveau.

As history told it, de Glapion was a man of noble French heritage. In the 1830s, he was in a *placage* relationship with Laveau. Together, supposedly, they had at least seven children, but only two were reported to have survived—both daughters named Marie, one being the look-alike of Marie Laveau. This Marie purportedly embraced the darker side of voodoo in Bayou St. John. It was from this line Tracey supposedly descended.

"I'm sorry, Trace. Everything just happened so fast and I didn't have time to even think before that Allison Williams ran the story."

"So, tell me the details and I'll see if I forgive you."

Addy grinned and shook her head, but told her

best friend everything, even what her father had told her about the Axeman. "I haven't even had a chance to research that angle."

"Hmm. I seem to recall something about that. I'll do a little digging on my end and see what I can drum up for you." While Tracey owned a New Orleans cemetery tour business, she wholeheartedly believed her ancestors had practiced witchcraft, voodoo, and hoodoo—all subjects that gave Addy the heebie-jeebies. Still, there was no denying there was information in the dark craft, and Tracey was one who could access that information.

While the original Marie Laveau was said to have turned from voodoo practices near the end of her life and dedicated herself to the Catholic church, her look-alike daughter had gone deep into the dark side of witchcraft. Although not confirmed anywhere, it was said that the second Marie murdered her own older sister, the only other living descendant of Marie and Louis Christophe, Marie Philomene Glapion.

It was from the murdered sister's line that Tracey had been born, and she was proud of her heritage. Tracey had even inherited the house on St. Ann Street that was rumored to have been on the site of the original Marie Laveau's home back in the 1830s, and still lived there today.

"So your dad thinks maybe the skeleton was one of the Axeman's victims?"

"Maybe, but I don't think the timeline would fit. The records of the hotel show the only remodeling that would have included masonry in that area, or thereabouts, were in either 1938 or 1958. Dad said the Axeman's last attack was in 1919."

"Hmm. Let me see what I can find out. Maybe it was a copycat murder?"

"It's a possibility, I suppose." Addy chewed the side of her mouth.

"Okay, Ads, what else is going on with you?"

Addy felt the blush hit her face. "It's nothing."

Tracey stared at her, using that uncanny ability to look right into Addy. "Mmmhmm. Spill."

"The anthropologist from LSU that's helping? She's really pretty."

"Okay."

"And I think she's snagged both Beau and Dimitri's attention."

"Oh. My." Tracey pressed her lipstick-red lips together.

Addy shoved her friend. "Don't you laugh at me. Don't you dare."

Tracey held her hands up in mock surrender. "Look, I'm not laughing at you, but honestly, you know both men are gorgeous and special and quite the catch. Why on earth would you be surprised that another woman finds them attractive? And they're men, Ads . . . they would notice a pretty woman, especially if she gave them all the signs that she was interested."

"I know, I know."

Tracey nudged Addy with her foot. "Jealousy isn't fun, is it?"

Addy shook her head. "And if this is what Beau and Dimitri feel toward each other . . . I can't do this to them."

"It's probably time for you to figure out which one you can see a future with and cut the other one loose."

Of course Tracey would hit the nail on the head. "I know, but how do I do that?"

"Look, I know you're working your way back with your faith. Maybe you should really go deep and pray hard about it. I have a feeling you'll get your answer."

Before Addy could reply, a knock sounded on the door, then Geoff stuck his head in. "Oops, sorry. Didn't realize you had company."

Addy and Tracey both stood. "Don't be silly, Geoff. You remember my best friend, Tracey?"

"Who could forget a woman so beautiful?" He smiled and nodded at Tracey.

"Oh, flattery will get you everywhere." Tracey chuckled that deep, throaty laugh of hers. "Nice to see you back at work, Geoff."

"It's nice to be back." He turned to Addy. "Just wanted to update you that we're keeping a security officer posted at the entrance to the renovation area. So many nosy eyes."

Addy groaned. "That reporter." She shook her head. "It's great that we don't have a vacant room left, but it's beyond frustrating that we have to go to such lengths."

Geoff nodded. "I know. I'm sorry, but wanted you to know we've got it under control. We might have a little more overtime for the next week or so to keep the area covered."

"That's fine. Thanks for letting me know. And thanks for taking care of it." Addy appreciated his initiative and decisiveness. Seemed those were traits that not everyone had these days.

"Of course." He turned back to Tracey. "It was nice seeing you again. You should hang out here more often. You brighten up the place." Geoff gave a little tip of his head, then sauntered out of the office.

"Oh, that man is beyond gorgeous, girl. Forget Beau and Dimitri, that man is carved from the same mold of a Greek god." Tracey fanned herself.

Addy laughed. "What about Chuck?"

Tracey plopped back down on the loveseat. "He got offered a promotion that he just couldn't turn down."

"So?" Addy sat back beside her friend.

"So, it's in Lafayette."

"Permanently?"

Tracey nodded.

Addy grabbed Tracey's hand and squeezed. "I'm sorry, Trace."

Tracey shrugged. "Yeah, well, I always wanted what was best for him, and this is. He deserves the promotion. We'd kind of hoped he'd be offered the same position here in New Orleans, but there's no opening for that level." She sighed. "He left two weeks ago."

"Two weeks? Now who isn't telling their bestie important stuff?"

"I know. I just needed to deal with it all myself first, you know?"

"Yeah." Addy leaned over and hugged her. "Are you okay?"

"I'm good. I'm really happy for him. I just don't do that long distance thing. It never works out, and you know how much attention I need on a daily basis." Tracey laughed, even if it was a forced joke.

"Is there any chance he could come back if that position opened up here?"

"Who knows? I don't want to tie him up or me. It's not fair to either of us."

Addy nodded, thinking about how she'd kept not only herself but Beau and Dimitri all tied up.

Tracey gave Addy a gentle shove. "But Geoff. I'm guessing by the vibes I picked up that he doesn't have a girlfriend. Is he dating anyone?"

Addy chuckled and shook her head. "I have no idea."

107

"Well, could you maybe help a girl out and find out?"

"What? You want me to play matchmaker?"

Tracey laughed. "Well, I think you owe me."

"Owe you?"

"Yeah. Owe me."

"Okay, okay. I'll see what I can do."

Tracey stood and pulled Addy up into a quick hug. "Let me know. I'll see what I can find out about the Axeman, too."

"Okay. You take care out there, Trace."

"You take care of you, too. Keep an eye out for crazy stalker fans." With a wiggle of her fingers, Tracey slung her purse over her shoulder and left.

Addy waited a minute before sitting behind her desk. Tracey was right, of course, although she wouldn't let her best friend know that. It was time to make a decision about Beau and Dimitri, and she needed to make sure she was positive about who she wanted.

She opened her bottom right drawer and slowly pulled out her old, worn Bible. Her fingers grazed over the smooth leather. A fluttering of her heart echoed against her chest.

Addy let out a slow breath, bent her head, closed her eyes, and started a silent prayer.

7

BEAU

"Coming up, WDSU's exclusive interview with renowned bestselling author, R.C. Steele." The newscast faded into commercials.

Vincent had given an interview? To WDSU, nonetheless? Beau reached for his cell and called Addy.

She answered on the first ring. "Hey, Beau."

"Your dad gave an interview?"

"What? He just said he was thinking about saying a few things in hopes of avoiding a build-up around some mystery. His publicist called and begged him to use any airtime to promote his upcoming release. I doubt that means an interview."

"Uh, Addy, turn the news on. WDSU."

"You've got to be kidding me." The sound of the same commercials he was watching sounded in the background over the connection.

"That was the lead-in before they went to commercial break."

"They said interview?"

"An exclusive interview."

"Oh my word. I can't believe he didn't tell me. Warn me."

The commercials faded and the face of Allison Williams filled the screen.

"Following a lead that skeletal remains had been found hidden in a two-foot space behind a suspiciously built wall at the Darkwater Inn, this reporter went to the hotel to get details. I never expected to come face-to-face with the elusive bestselling novelist, R.C. Steele. Come to find out, Steele is a pen name for Vincent Fountaine, father of the Darkwater Inn's general manager."

Addy groaned.

"Steele reluctantly agreed to give WDSU an exclusive interview regarding his appearance at the hotel's crime scene."

Beau nodded. "I bet reluctantly is putting it mildly."

Vincent's image joined Allison's on the screen. "Thank you for joining us, Mr. Fountaine. Or do you prefer Mr. Steele?"

"Steele is fine." Vincent wasn't smiling. Matter-of-fact, he looked annoyed and on the edge of angry.

"Are you working on a story that relates to the crime scene at the Darkwater Inn? Are you writing a book that has to do with skeletal remains and an axe found beside the body?" Allison shoved the microphone in Vincent's face.

Vincent pulled back. "As a suspense writer, naturally I'm curious about an uncovered skeleton."

"But are you working on a book about this?"

"No."

Allison Williams's face bunched up as she looked directly into the camera. "Then why were you at the crime scene?" She pushed the microphone back at Vincent.

"Like you, I found it of interest that a skeleton was discovered behind a hidden wall and had an axe beside it. Knowing the history of New Orleans, I was curious to see if perhaps this skeleton had been one of the Axeman's unreported victims."

Allison turned to the camera and spoke directly. "The Axeman was a serial killer that terrorized New Orleans back in the early 1900s. WDSU will be running a series of reports on the serial killer, his victims, and how this relates to the skeleton found at the Darkwater Inn." She turned back to Vincent. "Tell us, Mr. Steele, have you done much research on the Axeman?"

"Not really. I have some old articles that I accumulated years ago, but I only stuffed them in a file cabinet and didn't pay them any more mind, until the skeleton was found with an axe beside it." Vincent shrugged. "I write fiction, not true crime."

"And so you do, Mr. Steele. When will your next book release?"

As Vincent went into his promo pitch for his

new release, Beau sat back in his chair. "Addy, you okay?"

"I don't know." She sighed. "I mean, it's infuriating that Allison Williams ran a story on Dad and on the hotel regardless of what either of us said, but we can't do anything now." She sighed again.

"I know." Beau shook his head, even though Addy couldn't see him. "Marcel and I have feelers out everywhere in the department to find out who keeps feeding information to her. Every time we have a case at the hotel, she seems to know almost as quickly as we do."

"Maybe I should ask around the hotel and make sure it's not someone here who gives her the information." She blew out a loud breath. "I'm so sick of it all."

"It'll be okay, Addy. Our CSU is trying to build a DNA profile from the blood on the axe. All we know right now is that it's a rarer blood type—B negative. We think we might have a partial palm print and a smudged thumbprint. Our tech asked Chandler to assist in trying to clean it up to run it."

"I know Chandler and Dimitri had Vicky pulling records of guests that were at the hotel for the months following the beginning of the renovations of 1938."

"Did they find anything?" Beau hadn't heard anything back from Chandler.

"They were still poring over the records an hour ago when I left. I had to get away from it. I had just gotten up here to my apartment when you called. Now I want to go for a run. Get rid of some of this pent-up frustration."

He stood in response, even though every muscle in his body protested that the plan had been to enjoy a sub in front of the television and forget about the case, hotel, and—yes, even Addy—for a few hours. Funny how quickly a plan could change. "Now that sounds like an idea. Want to meet at Jackson Square? I'll race you."

"You're on, Savoie."

Beau quickly changed into a pair of shorts and tee and sneakers, then drove through *his* city. He'd lived in New Orleans all his life and loved the Big Easy. Even though he loved the city, he had no disillusions of the ugliness lurking in the dim backways and passages. Still, he wouldn't want to live anywhere else.

He parked on Decatur Street and slipped out of his car, taking long strides as a form of stretching as he headed to the square. As always, when he was near the hub of the Quarter, his pulse throbbed. Inhaling deeply, he drew in the essence of the Crescent City. Even with the stench of crime and discord, Beau loved being a New Orleans detective, just like his father before him.

Addy smiled as he moved up to join her at the bronze statue of Andrew Jackson. "About time you got here. What'd you do, stop for coffee?"

He shook his head. "Some of us live a little further away, you know."

"Let's go." She started them off, running toward the circle within Jackson Square. She moved fast, as if she were trying to outrun the issues of responsibility burdening her down.

Two figures moved in the shadow, catching Beau's attention. Probably nothing.

Beau kept up with her, and after a few moments, his muscles loosened and his body leaned into the run.

They rounded the first lap, Beau matching Addy's smooth stride. They ran in silence, their sneakers hitting the pavement in a steady cadence. Theirs was a comfortable silence, created from years of running together and just being together and not needing to fill the space with conversation. It was familiar and unstrained. Beau appreciated the ease in which they related to each other.

Those figures shifted in the shadows again. Beau wanted to turn and get a better look, still, they kept their distance, so he had no reason to approach them. But he kept his guard up.

Another lap, and Addy hadn't slowed. Beau kept even pace with her, letting her outrun her demons. He could only imagine how she felt. As they rounded the square, Addy veered off on St. Ann Street, keeping her speed steady.

"Uh, Addy? Maybe we should stay in the Square." The shadows hid figures too easily out of the square. If Addy was being followed, she'd be an easier target.

"I just . . . need . . . to . . . run . . . straight." She sped up a little and kept heading down St. Ann.

His imagination must be working overtime. There wasn't anyone in sight as they ran.

Beau understood Addy's need to run, even if he didn't like where they were heading in the dark. He kicked up his pace to stay with her. He caught movement of where many pagan devotees who told fortunes and read tarot cards lined the outside of the square. He maneuvered himself between Addy and the street people.

She made the block, turned alongside the wrought iron fence surrounding the square, and slowed a little.

Beau glanced at his watch. They'd been running, not jogging, for over half an hour. No wonder he was a little winded. He slowed even more, trotting a few feet behind her, giving her space, but still close.

She turned left on Chartres Street behind the St. Louis Cathedral and slowed further. Beau let out a breath. She'd most likely end their jog with this block and they could head back to their cars on Decatur.

As she made the turn onto St. Peter Street, the other side where those dealing in witchcraft and the like congregated, he caught sight of two men in black hooded robes. It looked like they wore . . . were those pig and sheep masks they wore?

Before Beau could process their creepy attire, two others in black hooded robes emerged from behind the two masked figures, holding two glass jars.

In that split second, Beau grabbed Addy's arm and tugged her back while coming to a full stop. She jerked back against his chest.

The glass jars burst on the concrete in front of them, where Addy would've been had he not pulled her back. Red liquid splattered on the ground and also splashed up on them both.

The four robed figures ran off down St. Peter Street, disappearing into the night.

Beau held tight to Addy. "Are you okay?"

"I-I'm fine." She shook her hands. "What is this? Is it blood?"

He already had his cell phone out. "Hang tight. I'm calling it in." He kept an arm around her shoulders as he quickly called Marcel and gave him the details. "Call Nolan personally and see if he can come. They weren't wearing gloves so he might be able to get a print off some of the bigger glass shards."

He could feel Addy trembling as he slipped his phone back into the pocket of his shorts. "Marcel will be here soon."

She turned and buried her face in his chest. "Is

this blood? Who would do this, Beau? Why?"

He held her tighter and kissed her temple. He didn't know what was going on, but he'd do everything he possibly could to figure it out.

DIMITRI

"These are all the guest ledgers from the time the remodel was started in August of 1938 and when it ended in January of 1939." Dimitri waved at the stack of a half dozen books Vicky had delivered to the conference room this morning.

Chandler grinned. "I guess it's too much to hope for that there was some flashing note that guest such-and-such went missing, huh?"

Dimitri laughed and shook his head. "We couldn't get that lucky. Adelaide's assistant went through them all and put sticky notes on the only entries that don't have a date the guest checked out. She figured those might be more likely to have gone missing during their stay."

"Smart lady. Sounds logical to me." She took a seat on one side of the table. "Beau said they should get back the notes about missing persons reports during this time sometime today."

The casualty in which she referred to Detective Savoie gave Dimitri pause. "You spoke with Detective Savoie?"

She nodded as she flipped open the first ledger. "I did. Yesterday. Gave him and Addy an update on our forensic artist's work on reconstructing the victim's face."

"What is the status?"

Chandler smiled. "He's glued in the teeth that were loose in the skull, then placed a tiny amount of cotton in the temporomandibular joint and glued the jaw shut. He used cotton and drafting tape to pad the eye orbit and nasal aperture to protect the fragile bones. I believe he'll be placing the eyes and setting the tissue depth marker lengths, and gluing them in place later today."

Dimitri found it fascinating. "Then what?"

"Well, probably Monday morning, he'll build up the clay to the depth of each marker, doing the nose last to avoid damage by bumping. He'll place the hair, basing it on the style of young men around 1940, because we'll split the difference between our guesstimated timeline of 1938 or 1958. After the hair, he'll place the finished skull on a wire armature for neck and shoulders. He should finish it all by Tuesday . . . Wednesday at the latest."

"And then?"

Chandler grinned. "Then we photograph it from every angle, then strip off the clay and return the skull to the coroner's office here."

"Wait, after all that work, you just tear it apart and send the naked skull back?" To go through so much work and then just remove it all . . .

Again Chandler smiled and nodded. "Once he finishes and takes pictures, the New Orleans police can run it through their system and see if there are any connections. If so, we'll run the dental records against the imprints we took and see if we get a match. Beau is hopeful we'll find a match."

"You two seem to communicate easily." Dimitri didn't know if it bothered him because of his and Beauregard's ongoing conflict for Adelaide's interest, or if it had something to do with Dr. Broussard herself.

She transferred information from the ledger into her tablet. "Why wouldn't we? He seems nice enough. So does Addy. They were both very eager to help when I saw them yesterday." She shrugged. "Am I missing something?"

"Oh. No. I just wondered if perhaps there was maybe . . . interest other than professional involved." He drew himself up, mentally kicking himself. He sounded as jealous as he often felt, and he didn't like that about himself.

She grinned. "Uh, no. He's not my type."

He smiled against the heat warming his face.

"Besides, I think there's something between him and Addy."

Dimitri's heart skipped a beat. "Really?" Could it be *that* obvious there was something between Beauregard and Adelaide, but not he and Adelaide? What did that mean?

"Yeah. The way the two of them look at each other. The easy way they are together—at least what I saw of them yesterday." She shrugged and grabbed the next ledger. "I don't know. I just get the sense that there's something between them. I could be wrong, though."

Oh, how he wished she were.

1931

"Happy thirteenth birthday, William." Sister Benedict handed him a box wrapped in plain brown paper.

He tore open the package, disappointment flooding him as he recognized the Westminster Version of the Sacred Scripture.

"I noticed your Bible had some torn pages, so I thought you might like a new one." She smiled.

"Thank you, Sister Benedict." He forced the words and the smile.

She turned and left him in the room alone with George and James. He waited until she left, then dropped the new book onto the bedside table.

"It was nice that she got you something. I didn't get anything on my birthday." George crossed his arms over his chest.

"Stop whining. It's just a Bible."

"Can I have your old one?" James asked.

"No. You can have the new one." He reached for his old Bible, the one Sister Rosemary had given him. "This one is correct."

"Correct?" James asked.

He nodded. "I won't let any demon or spirit enter my mind, even by reading. I tear those pages out so not to give the devil a foothold into my life." Ever since he'd learned about a demon possessing a man who killed his mother, he refused to even read the word *demon*.

"Oh." James stood up and automatically straightened the covers on his bed. He was such a rule-follower. Heaven forbid he leave a wrinkle in his blanket and one of the sisters call him out. They could make him cry with just a look.

"Hey, have either of you seen Harold today? He wasn't at breakfast." Even though Harold was a year older than the other boys, he always ate with them when he could.

Both James and George shook their heads.

One of the sisters rang the bell, signaling it was time for morning classes. James ran for the door. George followed, but waited on William. "Are you coming?"

"I will in a minute."

"Don't be late. Sister Agnes is giving us our spelling test." George rushed after James.

William sat on his bed and opened his old Bible, the one Sister Rosemary had given him. He flipped to the back, to the envelope she had sealed for him six years ago. He'd resisted reading it, keeping his promise to her. But it was his thirteenth birthday today, and he could finally read the letter.

He carefully opened the envelope and pulled out the single sheet of paper. He slowly unfolded it and smoothed it on his lap, then read.

August 6, 1918

To the Daughters of Charity nuns,

I leave to you this sweet seven-month-old boy named William Lowe whom I affectionately call Willie. He is a bright and happy baby, having brought me much joy in the short time that he has been on this earth.

It is with great sadness that I must leave him in your care. You see, he is not my son, although I love him as if he were. I am only eighteen, still living with my own parents, without any means to raise him. I have been blessed to watch and love this child for nearly all seven months of his life.

His mother, Harriet Lowe, was unwed. I'm sorry to report that she refused to state little Willie's father's name on his birth certificate. I came to babysit him soon after his birth, and never knew who his father was. There was never a man who came forward, as far as I know, and claimed Willie as his son.

I'm sure you will recognize his mother's name from the reports and newspaper as the woman who was a victim of the Axeman two months ago. She and her married lover were attacked in his home. Please do not judge sweet Willie harshly because of his mother's sins. He is an innocent boy who had the misfortune to be born illegitimate to a mother who was and continued to be involved with men outside the legalities of marriage.

The Axeman's attack left Harriet with a cut over her left ear, and a partial paralysis in her face. Some have said that this was punishment for her adultery, but I do not know. I leave those judgements to our Sovereign Lord.

Harriet had surgery to correct her injury, only to die from complications arising after her surgery.

I am truly saddened that I must forfeit Willie to your care, for I sincerely love him, but I cannot offer him a life that he so deserves. Despite the tragedy of his short life, Willie is kind and gentle, one of the sweetest souls I have ever known.

I pray that you will diligently search for a family who will adopt Willie into their home, filling his life with love and happiness. These are the basics of what he deserves. Please let him know that although I could not keep him, he was loved so very much.

8

ADDY

"Girl, that almost sounds like someone coming after you with some serious voodoo." Tracey pulled another shirt out of her closet and held it up to her chest and looked in the mirror. She shook her head and tossed it onto the growing pile on the floor.

Addy sat back against Tracey's headboard and stared at her best friend who stood in her closet doorway wearing jeans and a tank top. "Beau said they determined it was pig's blood, but that's almost creepier than if it were human. I mean, who does that?"

"People who think they're witches or trying to do something they have no business trying to do." Tracey disappeared back into her closet for a minute, returning with four more tops.

"The CSU guy said he thought he would be able to get a fingerprint off one of the pieces of glass, but it would be Monday before he could work on it." Addy let out a sigh. "I mean, I know they're trying to get a DNA profile from the axe they found at the hotel, but still . . ." She understood they were busy, but patience had never been her strong suit.

"Hey, I hear you. I'd be creeped out, too, and it takes a lot to creep me out." She held up a royal blue shimmery top. "Think this is too much for coffee?"

Addy grinned. "Too much for a date with Geoff? Nah, he'll love it."

"It's not too dressy?" Tracey studied her reflection. "I mean, it's just coffee. He may not even be interested in me like that."

"Oh please. Trace, he had to ask me for your number, which means he knew I'd pick on him relentlessly about it, but he still wanted your number bad enough to ask. I'd say that means he's interested in you *like that*."

"Mmm." She turned to face Addy. "Do you think it's too soon after Chuck and I called it quits to be seeing someone else?"

Addy considered the question before she slowly shook her head. "I really don't. You made a mature and responsible decision about yours and Chuck's relationship, and I respect you for it. Some people would've tried to hang on, even if they knew the relationship would fail and there'd be a higher chance of people getting hurt." She smiled at the woman she loved like a sister. "I think you're entitled to go out and have fun."

"Yeah, but Geoff is different."

Addy laughed. "Different from what?"

"Other guys I've dated. When he looks at me, it's like he really sees me."

"As opposed to what? Leering at you? You should hang out with better people, Trace."

"Yeah. Starting with my best friend." Tracey scrunched up her nose. "Seriously, it's like he can see into my mind. It's a little unnerving, but kind of neat, too." She shook her head and pulled on the blue shirt. "I'm probably not making a lick of sense."

"Actually you are. I get it."

"Do you? With who? Beau or Dimitri?"

Addy grabbed Tracey's old Winnie the Pooh bear and hugged it to her chest. "A week ago, I would have said both of them."

Tracey rested her hands on her hips. "And now?"

"I would avoid answering." Because deep down, she had a sneaky suspicion that her heart had already made its decision. She just needed it to send the message to her head.

Tracey grabbed the T-shirt she'd just thrown on the dresser and tossed it at Addy. "I thought you were ready to make a decision."

"I am, I promise. It's just that I haven't been able to really spend any alone time with either of them that doesn't have to do with a skeleton found in the hotel's walls or crazies throwing pig blood at me."

Tracey sat beside her and put an arm around her shoulders. "I'm sorry, Ads. It's got to be so hard to always have something happening. It's like you can't catch a break."

"Tell me about it. Just when I think things are slowing down and getting back to normal—whatever that is anymore—something else happens."

"The last couple of years have been a bit of a whirlwind for you."

Addy nodded. "When I got back from Europe, I knew that I wanted to see Beau and Dimitri a couple of times and let my heart decide which I should pursue a relationship with. I'm ready to have a real relationship, not just casual dating. I'm knocking on thirty's door and I'm ready to think about the future and what it could look like for me. But every time I think I can set up time alone with Beau and Dimitri, something happens and my emotions have to be put on simmer."

Tracey squeezed her before standing. "Just make sure your simmering doesn't bubble and overflow. It's a mess to clean up when that happens."

"Like you cook so much that you'd know." Addy grinned.

"I've heard rumors." Tracey grabbed her signature red lipstick and turned to pucker in the mirror.

Tracey's cell blasted.

"If Geoff is calling to cancel, I swear I'm going to cry." She answered the call. "Hello."

Addy crossed her arms over her chest and

stared at her best friend. If Geoff was calling to cancel, Addy was going to have some cross words of her own for him.

"I understand. Are you sure everyone's okay?" Tracey's already porcelain skin paled even further. "Yes. I will. Thanks." She set her phone on the dresser and moved to the bed. She sat down next to Addy.

"What is it? You're scaring me, Trace."

Tracey took both of Addy's hands. "That was one of Chuck's crew from the station here. There's been a fire."

"Chuck?"

Tracey shook her head. "No. And, Ads, I need you to hear all the details before you freak out, okay?"

Addy's heart sped. Was it Beau? Dimitri? If it wasn't Beau, why wasn't he calling her? "What is it?"

"It's your dad's house."

Addy moved to jump up, but Tracey tightened her grip on her hands and kept her in place. "First, your dad is okay. He's at the hospital being treated for smoke inhalation, but he's okay."

"What happened?"

Tracey shook her head. "A neighbor saw the light from the flame and called 911. The fire department arrived and got your dad out. He was unconscious in the living room. He's okay, though. He regained consciousness in the ambulance and is alert and responsive in the emergency room."

Addy pushed off the bed and stood. "I have to get to the hospital." She couldn't even think. Where were her car keys? Had she even brought a purse?

Tracey slipped her cell into her pocket. "Come on, let me drive you. You're in no shape to drive."

Addy nodded and headed to the front door. Her legs felt like they were made of rubber. "I just can't believe this."

"Honey, there's more you need to know."

More?

Tracey continued before she could ask. "Your dad asked for Beau when he got to the hospital. He said someone hit him over the head and set the house on fire with him in it."

BEAU

"Okay, let's go over it again." He still had a hard time grasping the implications of what Vincent was telling them. If it had been anybody other than Vincent, Beau would wonder if the bump on the head rattled his memory. But this was Vincent . . . the man who'd stepped in and acted as a surrogate father when his own had died in the line of duty. The man who was smart as a tack and didn't mince words.

The small examining room space of Tulane

130

Medical Center had been too confining and loud to take a detailed police report from Vincent. Luckily, Marcel had been able to flash his badge and get Vincent into a private triage room. He'd been sucking the oxygen for almost half an hour now, and the doctor had just let him stop. Now to see if he could talk without coughing up a lung.

Vincent took a drink of the water from the bottle the nurse handed him. She glared at Beau and Marcel. "If he starts to cough or have trouble speaking, you'll need to step out."

"This is a police matter—" Marcel began.

"This man is my patient and that takes precedence." She wasn't going to budge on this one.

Beau nodded. "We'll take it slow and let him go at his own pace."

She hesitated, then gave a curt nod. She smiled at Vincent. "Keep sipping on that water. The doctor will be in shortly to look at your throat again and make sure there isn't any damage from the smoke."

Vincent smiled up at her. His face was smeared with dark soot, looking like bruises. They'd put the stitches in the back of his head where he'd been hit, and now it was covered with a gauzy bandage. "Thank you." His voice sounded froggy, cracking but not wavering.

"Push the button if you need me." She turned and walked briskly out the door.

Marcel pulled a chair up close to the bed while Beau stood nearby, notebook in hand.

The door burst open.

"Daddy!" Addy spoke at the same time she flew into the room and hugged her father hard. "Are you okay? How bad are you hurt? Oh my goodness, your head. What happened?"

"I'm okay." He kissed her cheek.

"Your voice!"

"Hey, give him a little breathing room, Ads." Tracey shut the door behind her. Now there were four of them in there with Vincent.

Addy stepped back, but still clung to her father's hand. "Why didn't you call me?" She turned her glare on Beau as Vincent took another drink of water. "Why didn't *you* call me?" Addy didn't wait for a response, just turned back to her father. "What happened?"

"That's what he's about to tell us." Marcel rolled his eyes at Tracey.

Good thing Addy didn't see it.

Beau cleared his throat. "We're about to take his statement."

"Don't you dare imply that I need to leave or I'll twist off on you, Beauregard Savoie!"

"Shh. Just go sit with Tracey and you can stay." Vincent patted her hand.

Without argument, Addy did as her father instructed.

Vincent took another drink of water before he

looked at Beau. "I'd finished cleaning up the kitchen from dinner and went into the living room to do a little writing. I turned on the stereo and settled in my recliner. I had my MacBook open and was writing when I noticed a shadow flicker across the screen." He cleared his throat, paused for a second, then took another drink.

He cleared his throat again. "I turned to see if maybe a car's headlights had caused the shadow when a dark figure stood behind me. I felt the Mac slide off my lap as I turned, then I saw the figure lift something over his head. A pain shot down my head and everything went dark. Next thing I know, I'm in the back of an ambulance."

Beau wrote in his notebook as fast as Vincent spoke, then read over what he'd written while Vincent took another drink of water. "About what time would you say this was?"

"Around eight fifteen, eight twenty."

"This shadow flicker," Marcel interrupted, "I'm not following."

Vincent let out a slow breath. "My Mac laptop screen isn't matte. It's shiny. So any movement catches my attention. Sometimes it's a headlight of a car coming through the curtains on the front windows. If someone walks behind me and there's backlight, it'll cause a shadow. It's very distracting. This time, a person moving behind me caught my eye."

"I see." Marcel nodded.

"When you say a 'dark figure,' what do you mean?" Beau asked. "Dark hair? Wearing a dark shirt?"

Vincent took another sip of water before croaking out his answer. "Dark-colored shirt. Hoodie, I think, because I remember seeing the dark material over his head."

"His? You're sure it was a man?" Marcel asked.

"Pretty sure. The build reminded me of a man. Wider shoulders than a woman." He cleared his throat. "I was sitting so I can't gauge if he was taller than me. I'd guess he was just under six foot, but that's not real accurate." He took another drink of water and cleared his throat again.

"What about the face? White? Black? Any facial hair?" Beau asked.

Vincent shook his head. "I only saw him for a split second before he zonked me, but nothing comes to mind." He took another drink of water. "Now that I think about it, I almost think I couldn't even see a face."

"Like the face was covered and you couldn't see it?"

"No. More like the face was entirely blacked out. Sunken further back from the edge of the hood." He shrugged. "I know that really doesn't make a lot of sense. Maybe it was the angle because I was sitting below him. I don't know. Like I said, it was all really fast before it was lights out for me."

Beau's gut tightened. Black hooded figure . . . face obstructed. Was starting to have an all too familiar ring to it.

"Can you remember anything else?" Marcel asked.

Vincent cleared his throat. "When I came to, I was already on a stretcher in the back of an ambulance. They sat me up and put gauze on the cut on my head and started feeding me the oxygen while I sat there and watched my house burn." Tears welled in the older man's eyes. "All those memories of you growing up . . ." He stared at Addy and shook his head.

She moved to his side and put an arm around his shoulders. "The memories are in our hearts, Daddy, not in that house." But tears flowed down her face. "I'm just so thankful you're okay." She kissed his cheek and sat beside him on the narrow bed.

"I know, Addybear. It was just hard to watch it." His eyes cleared and he snapped his fingers, then looked at Beau with wide eyes.

"What?" Beau gripped his pen tighter.

"I saw something in the woods behind the house when I was in the ambulance. The dark figure." He shook his head. "No, there were two of them." His eyes widened more. "It wasn't a hoodie. They wore long black-hooded robes."

Addy gasped and lifted her hand to her mouth.

"What?" Vincent asked.

135

Beau spoke before Addy could explain. "Can you recall anything about those faces? At the edge of the woods?"

Vincent stared off into space, clearly struggling to focus.

"It's okay if you can't." The last thing Beau needed was for Vincent's mind to try and fill in the gaps because his subconscious felt pressured to know.

Vincent shook his head. "Nothing. It's not like they were faceless, as odd as that sounds, but more like it was just a black void. That doesn't make sense either, does it?"

A man in a white coat opened the door and joined them. "Well, is there a party going on in here I wasn't invited to?" The doctor smiled, but had to weave around Tracey and Marcel. He glanced around the room. "I need to examine my patient before discharge, so if you all could wait out in the waiting room . . ."

Everyone moved toward the door. Vincent gave Addy another kiss before she shut the examining room door behind her and joined them in the hall. She punched Beau's arm. "Why didn't you call me immediately?"

His bicep stung where she'd hit him. She might be slight, but the woman could pack a punch. Clearly. "I got the call and Marcel and I rushed over here. I didn't know it was your dad until I got here. Once I did, I was trying to get information and make sure he was all right before I called you."

"How did you find out?" Marcel asked.

"That would be me." Tracey raised a finger as they opened the double doors out of the triage area into the waiting room. "One of the firemen who responded to the call is a friend of mine and knew I was friends with Vincent and Addy. He called to give me a heads up, and Addy happened to be at my house when I got the call." She dug out her cell. "Hexes! I forgot I was supposed to meet Geoff ten minutes ago. He probably thinks I stood him up. Excuse me." She headed outside the emergency room entrance, dialing her phone.

"Geoff?" Beau asked Addy.

She shrugged. "They have a coffee date, but I'm still mad at you. How couldn't you call me as soon as you knew it was Dad?"

"I'm sorry, Addy. I had to do my job first, which was make sure he was okay, then try and figure out what happened and who did it, so I can catch them and make them pay." He led the trio to the vacant row of chairs off to the back wall of the waiting room.

She hesitated only a moment before she dropped onto the chair beside him. "The black hooded robes? Is this connected to the guys who threw the pig's blood at us?"

"I don't know." But his gut had that sinking feeling that they were linked.

"Why did you cut me off when I was going to mention the guys who threw the jar of pig's blood at us?"

"Because we can't have your father's recollection tainted with something you say that he, even subconsciously, infuses into what he thinks are the facts," Marcel explained.

"Oh."

Beau nodded. "Look, we're going to do our best to figure out what happened and to get the person or persons who did this, but you've got to let us do our job."

She nodded just as Tracey came back in. "Geoff understood." She smiled as she sat on the other side of Addy. "He said to tell you that if you need anything, he's available for whatever you need."

"Geoff's a good guy." Addy nodded.

Tracey stopped smiling. "Look, Ads, I called my friend after I got off the phone with Geoff. He said that your dad's house didn't burn all the way down, but it has a lot of damage. Emphasis on *lot*. No way can your dad stay there tonight and probably not for a while. I don't know how long it'll take your dad's homeowners insurance to send somebody out or anything, but you should probably make other arrangements. My friend said that because your dad said someone set the fire, it's listed as a crime scene and the arson investigator won't allow anyone to go into what's left of the house until he clears it."

138

"He can stay with me," Beau said.

Addy shook her head. "Don't be silly. He can take my bed and I'll sleep on the couch tonight, then I'll get him a suite tomorrow. I do happen to be general manager of a hotel, you know."

Beau kept his mouth shut. For once, he was very glad that Addy lived at the hotel because it sure appeared that she and Vincent were somebody's targets. He didn't know whose or for what, but he sure intended to find out.

9

DIMITRI

"Good service this morning, Pastor." Dimitri shook the preacher's hand.

"Glad you enjoyed it, Dimitri. How're you doing?"

Dimitri nodded. "I'm good. See you next week." He headed out of the sanctuary and toward his car.

The early March sun beat down on the asphalt parking lot. A gentle breeze kicked a few stray leaves across the lot.

"Imagine running into Dimitri Pampalon here." Zoey grinned as she held her toddler son on her hip. He held a wad of her dark red hair in his fist. "How're you?"

A tall, thin guy with a head full of dark, wavy hair stood awkwardly beside her car just behind her.

"Hey, Zoey. I'm good. How're you?" He reached out and tickled the toddler's belly. "And how're you, Mister Sam?"

"He's being quite the handful today. He gave the nursery workers quite the workout, I hear." She took a step toward the man. "Dimitri, I'd like you to meet Solomon Youngblood. He's the artist we'll be featuring on Friday night." She smiled at him brightly, like she used to smile at the men in the bar at the hotel. "Solomon, this is Dimitri Pampalon. He'll be hosting your showing at the Darkwater Inn and also is the chef who'll be cooking something scrumptious to serve."

Dimitri reached out and shook Solomon's hand. "Nice to meet you." The guy's hand was so limp that it could hardly be called a "handshake."

"You, too." Solomon's gaze dropped to the church's parking lot. Social graces apparently weren't high on his skill set. It couldn't be his age. While probably only a few years younger than Dimitri's thirty-four, he acted more like an insecure teenager.

Maybe it was that quirky artist thing.

Zoey seemed to feel the awkwardness, too. She shifted Sam from one hip to the other. "Solomon's a very gifted artist. His paintings will blow you away. They're so moving. Emotional. Deep." Her eyes plead with Dimitri to say something.

He struggled to remember what she'd told him about the artist. "I understand all of your paintings have a religious tone?" He hoped he was remembering right.

"Yes. That's the only way I can exhibit my work." He glanced at his watch, then looked at Zoey. "I must leave. Father won't like it if I'm late." He leaned over and gave her a kiss on the cheek, then ducked his head as he turned back to

141

Dimitri. "It was nice to meet you. Thank you for hosting my show this weekend."

"Of course." But before Dimitri could say any more, Solomon jogged off and turned the corner. He looked back to Zoey. "Are you sure a show is the best idea for him?"

She opened her car door and lifted Sam into his car seat. The toddler wiggled and squirmed as she struggled to get his arms into the harness. "I know he's a little awkward around people, but that's just because of his family."

"What's wrong with his family?" Dimitri made faces at Sam behind Zoey's head.

The toddler laughed and made waving motions to Dimitri.

Zoey clicked the belts in place, handing Sam a plastic army man and a couple of superhero figurines. She shut the back door and turned to face Dimitri. "They're just . . . strange. Best I can tell from what Solomon has said is they're kind of religious freaks and his whole family lives together in like a commune or the like. Even his dad, who is like over a hundred years old."

Dimitri chuckled.

"No, I'm serious. His dad is really at least a hundred years old."

"Wow."

She nodded as she played with her keys. "He's quite overbearing, too, from what I understand. Most of Solomon's brothers aren't even allowed to leave their home. The only reason his dad lets Solomon out is because he says it would be a sin to keep his God-given talent from the world."

"Sounds a little nuts." Actually, more than a little nuts, but to each his own. Dimitri wasn't one to talk. His own father was overbearing and could be downright cruel on many occasions.

Okay, on most occasions.

"I haven't met his dad. Haven't met any of his family, to be honest."

"And you're dating this guy?" Dimitri leaned against the front of Zoey's car.

She blushed, but smiled. "He's sweet. Treats me with such respect. Never makes me feel like I'm a second-class citizen because of what I once did to support myself and Sam. And that's something else—he's nice to Sam and doesn't make me question my choice to be a single mom."

"Sounds like he makes you happy."

"He does. It's nice for a change to not have to guess his motives. For once, I'm the one who seems to have the upper hand in a relationship."

Dimitri just smiled. "I'm happy for you."

"Thanks. So, you can understand why I want the show to go well for Solomon. He really needs the boost of confidence, as well as proof to his father."

"I understand that all too well."

"I know you do." She grabbed Dimitri's hand and squeezed. "So thank you."

Sam began fussing in the back seat. Zoey opened the driver's door and smiled at Dimitri. "It's time for his morning nap. I better go before he starts wailing like there's no tomorrow."

"Bye, Sam." He waved at the toddler before patting Zoey's arm. "I'll see you Friday."

She smiled and nodded before slipping behind the steering wheel.

Dimitri watched her drive off before heading to his own car. Maybe he should do a little checking up on Solomon Youngblood before his show at the restaurant. The guy's behavior went beyond a little odd. Dimitri wanted to know what he was in store for.

And, if he were being honest, to make sure Zoey was okay. There were a lot of crazies out there, and one could never be too careful.

ADDY

"Daddy, I don't think it's a good idea for us to go to the house." Addy folded the blanket her father had used last night. She'd fought for him to take her bed, but he'd adamantly demanded to sleep on the couch. In the end, he'd gone into a coughing fit and she hadn't wanted to stress him more, so she'd let him have the couch.

He was getting a suite today, whether he liked it or not. But first, she had to talk him out of going to the house to see what was left.

144

"Addy, it's my home. I have to go see how much is salvageable." He slipped on his sneakers, one of the few personal belongings he'd made it out of the fire with.

She'd gotten him some sweat pants and tees from the gift shop last night, toiletries from the hotel's housekeeping department, and Beau had delivered a bag late with new undies and socks.

"I understand, but the doctor told you to take it easy for a few days. That's a big knot on your head under those stitches. You're supposed to rest a lot. Put your feet up."

He finished putting on his shoes and stood. "I can't rest not knowing. It's not like I'm going to go do any lifting or anything. Besides, I need to get my truck."

"You definitely aren't supposed to be driving, Daddy. Especially not while you're taking the pain medication on top of the head injury. I'll have one of the porters drive your truck over."

"Addy, I'm not an invalid. I have a bump on my head." He grabbed the keys he'd had in his jeans pocket when he'd been dragged out of the burning house. Luckily his wallet had been in his back pocket. "I need to go get a new cell phone, too."

"Dad, you have a bump and a cut with eight stitches. I think you should lay around for at least a day."

"You can either drive me over, or I'll get a ride.

Either way, I'm going." He stood with his hands on his hips, wearing the pinched look of a bulldog.

She wasn't going to win this argument either. Addy sighed. "Fine. I'll take you to the house, but you aren't driving your truck back. I'll have someone get it for you. Deal?"

He nodded. She held out her hand for his keys.

"You'll take me to the mobile store, too? I can't be without my phone."

"Yes, I'll take you there, too." Which would be her excuse to get him away from the house. She grabbed his keys. "Let's go."

She stopped at the valet stand on her way out and gave her father's keys to one of the guys, giving them instructions to collect Vincent's truck.

Moments later, they were in her car, on the way to the house she'd called home all of her life.

His knee jiggled the closer they got to the house.

She didn't know how to prepare for what she might see. If they'd been able to get in and get her dad out, surely the house hadn't burned to the ground. If there was only a black pile of rubble where her home had once been . . . well, she didn't know how she could take that.

Her entire childhood and all her life milestones were wrapped up in the house. Baking cookies for Santa with her dad, who let her use as much frosting as she wanted. Dyeing Easter eggs and staining her fingers purple—and her dad's pink. Sitting with Dad in the living room scribbling girlish stories in her journals and drinking chocolate milk while Dad wrote his professional books drinking strong coffee.

She drove silently as she let more times flood her memory. Getting ready for her first date, and her dad scaring the snot out of Timmy Pepper when he came to pick her up . . . slumber parties with Tracey, who didn't care that Addy's mom was always drunk . . . she and Trace practicing "kissing" with their lipstick on the bathroom mirror.

All the pictures and cherished mementos were in the house, like postcard collections from all the vacations and trips she took over the last three decades. She'd moved out, yes, but so many of her photographs had been left at the house. Her permanent home.

Her heart ached to think that her special place—home—might be gone. Many of her fondest memories included Beau: sharing PB&Js on the back porch when they were no more than seven or eight, camping in her backyard with her dad when they were barely ten, countless holidays—Thanksgivings and Christmases and Easters . . . so many reminiscences.

The house that had been her refuge when she'd been sexually attacked in college . . . it welcomed her home and gave her safety and comfort.

She slowly made the turn onto their street. Addy reached out and took her dad's hand. "No matter what we find, we know it's going to be okay. We'll get through it just like we do everything: together."

He squeezed her hand, then let it go. "You got that right, sweetheart."

She gripped the steering wheel until her hands cramped, but kept her eyes glued out the front windshield.

Oh, merciful heavens!

She eased the car to park beside a marked fire department's car that sat alongside her father's truck at the turn of the driveway. She remembered to actually put the car in park before she turned off the ignition and step outside.

The stench of smoke still smoldered in the air. Addy's heart lodged in the back of her throat as she took in the sight of the charred ruins. Her eyes lit on where the living room used to be. The metal springs from her father's recliner were blackened and lying on top of piles of ash. There wasn't even a frame of the chair he'd been sitting in when he'd been knocked unconscious. It was nothing short of a miracle that his neighbor had seen the flames so quickly after it'd been set, called 911, and that the fireman had been able to find and save Vincent before he'd been burned alive.

"Oh, Daddy."

Addy sucked in air, closed her eyes, and sent up silent prayers of thanks for the hedge of protection that had clearly been around her father last night. Only that protection could have kept her father alive.

She was grateful—would forever be filled with such gratitude that her father's life had been spared. She couldn't imagine not having her father in her life every day.

"It's okay, Addybear. We're okay." His voice cracked as he took hold of her hand and held it tightly.

She turned and hugged him, tears burning her eyes as she clung to him.

He kissed the crown of her head.

"Who are you and what are you doing here?" The rough edge of the man's voice pulled Addy away from her father toward the stranger.

"This is my home." Her father glanced at the rubble and shook his head. "Or it was." He held out his hand to the man. "Vincent Fountaine, and this is my daughter, Adelaide."

The man shook her father's hand. "Mel Watson, arson investigator. I understand you were the one who reported to the police that you believe the fire was set."

Vincent nodded, his hand going to the bandage on top of his head. "I don't believe it, I know it. Have the bump up here and eight stitches to prove it."

Mr. Watson shook his head. "I did find that an accelerant was used. From my initial investigation, I'd say that a lot was used. Almost overkill, in my professional opinion." He stared at Vincent. "Whoever set this fire meant to destroy the house and everything inside. Not just that, but they wanted quick results."

"Well, I'm gonna go out on a limb and say they wanted me dead, for whatever reason, since they knocked me out and left me in my chair."

Addy pressed her lips together. The intent was clear, and it made her want to vomit. Who would want to kill her father?

"I'm sorry, sir." Mr. Watson waved toward the house. "I'm also sorry for this. Although the front is pretty much a hundred percent destroyed, the back of the house has some damage, but there is much that is salvageable."

Addy glanced back at the house. Their bedrooms were in the back of the house, and that's where many of their irreplaceable mementos had been. Maybe . . .

"Could we go look back there? I mean, we just want to see what personal effects we can recover." Addy took a tentative step toward Mr. Watson. "Please? We promise not to touch anything unless we get your permission first."

"Actually, ma'am, I've finished my observations. I just have to go write up my report. I was about to tell the young officer there that he could release the scene. You're free to go and touch anything you'd like, but I'll warn you to be extremely careful. While most everything is cooled, there are glass shards and other items that can cut or hurt you."

"Oh. Okay. By the way you asked what we were doing here, I thought maybe we couldn't be here."

Mr. Watson smiled at her. "It's my experience that many times the arsonist will return to the scene so he can admire the results of his handiwork. I question everyone."

"I see." That made sense, but it was kind of sick, too, to set a fire and then want to go see the damage you caused. Well, the people who had done this clearly were sick, so this shouldn't surprise her.

"Have you contacted your home owners insurance yet?" Mr. Watson asked.

"Not yet. Will their settlement be delayed because this will be ruled an arson?" her father asked.

As the two men talked, Addy cautiously headed around the property to the back of the house that still stood. She would have never guessed from where she'd stood at the front of the driveway that there was significantly less damage back here. She cautiously stepped over some debris as she walked into the room that had been her father's bedroom. The large closet in the corner still stood, even the wood door.

She stepped into the closet. Soot covered most all of the clothes that still hung on the rods. She pushed her father's clothes to the very back of the closet and found a zipped, plastic protective bag hanging up. Addy gently pulled it forward and unzipped it with shaking hands.

Inside was her grandmother's white beaded-and-lace wedding dress, the one her father had kept all these years for Addy—as pristine white as the last time she had seen it. Fresh tears welled in her eyes as relief washed over her. Of all the material items that could've been lost, she would have grieved losing her paternal grandmother's wedding dress the most.

"It's okay?"

She turned, gently holding the bag, and faced her father. "It's fine."

He smiled, and his eyes shimmered as well.

They held each other's gaze for a moment, then he sniffed. "I think I'm going to grab some of my clothes. Looks like most of my stuff is okay."

"I'm going to put this in the car." She headed back to the driveway. Her day had started with such dismay over the destruction—now she was filled with such gratitude. Her father was alive and the one irreplaceable heirloom was safe.

Thank You, Jesus.

10

BEAU

"Have you seen Gene or Kenny?" Marcel stopped at Beau's desk with coffee as soon as his partner had made it into the precinct. He passed one of the two paper cups to Beau, then perched on the edge of Beau's desk.

"No, do they need help on a case?" The two guys his partner had mentioned were newer homicide detectives, still learning some of the ins and outs of working a murder case.

Marcel grinned. "They got a double homicide this morning that seems . . . well, possibly connected to our case. Captain Istre advised them to speak with us."

"What?" That made no sense at all. "Did Captain forget our victim was most likely murdered back in 1938 or 1958?" He took a sip of coffee. "By the way, did we send Addy the missing persons reports from those years to cross-reference with any guests that were at the Darkwater Inn during that time?"

Marcel nodded. "I had them sent over yesterday and Addy's assistant, Vicky, said they'd get right on them. I sent 1938, 1958, and 1959, just to make sure we covered all possibilities."

"Good." Beau took another drink of his coffee. "Now, what about Kenny and Gene's case?"

"According to Kenny's report, they were called to a residence in Tremé area this morning for a double homicide. A couple in their late fifties— Joey and Theresa Maggio, were found dead in bed by their son. He had come to the house to take his mother to a doctor's appointment." Marcel stretched his legs out and crossed his arms over his chest. "The couple was killed with blows to the head from an axe, and the bloody axe was left on the floor by the bed." He grinned. "Sound similar?"

No way! "You've got to be kidding me."

Marcel shook his head. "I wish. Captain sent Gene and Kenny to talk with us." He stood and moved to his desk across from Beau's. "I guess we'll be overseeing the case."

"Not our case." But the similarities . . . no way could it be the same killer. A copycat. Beau shook his head. That blasted reporter and her *exclusive*. "Did you get any leads on our leak to Allison Williams?"

"I've got a couple in the secretary pool who said the reporter's called and asked for comments or information, but nothing on someone actually giving her anything."

She had to be getting inside information from somebody. "No way would a copycat have killed anyone with our case's same MO without that woman's report." Something else occurred to him in a flash. Beau snapped his fingers. "The attack on Addy in the park and on her father at his house!"

"What?"

"Both incidents happened after the report about the skeleton. We'd suspected that they were likely connected, and I think they're connected to our case."

Marcel sank back in his chair. "Man. Talk it out with me."

Beau nodded, his mind working to track it all. "Okay, the report comes in about the skeleton. We go and start the case. Walt's office calls in FACES." He grabbed a pen from his desk and tapped it as his mind worked out the timeline while he spoke. "The next morning, Vincent goes to the hotel with Addy because he caught on the connection between our skeleton and the Axeman attacks, although it looks like the timeline for that connection doesn't match."

"Right. The Axeman attacked in 1918 and 1919, and our skeleton was most likely killed and put in place in the hotel in 1938 or 1958."

Beau jotted on a scratch piece of paper. "But we didn't know that at the time Vincent went with Addy to the hotel."

"I follow you." Marcel took a drink of his coffee.

"And that reporter showed up that same time and publicized Vincent as R.C. Steele as well as being Addy's father. Then the reporter mentioned the skeleton and the Axeman in her interview. In that same interview, Vincent said he had research on the Axeman and stuff in a cabinet at his home." Beau wrote faster as his thoughts raced. "Then later that night, Addy gets blood thrown at her. Last night, a day later, Vincent gets knocked out and his house burned down with him in it."

Marcel made a clucking noise. "You think someone burned down his house to destroy the Axeman research he mentioned?"

"Do you have a better working theory?"

Marcel shook his head. "No. Sure seems like someone doesn't want anything about the Axeman to be brought back into the public eye. Why?"

Wasn't that the question? "Maybe a descendant of the Axeman doesn't want it to come out and their connection to the serial killer?"

"Could be, but since the Axeman was never caught, would be pretty hard to prove a family connection."

"True." Beau stared at his notes. Nothing made sense, but the answer had to be here somewhere. They just hadn't made the connection yet. "Maybe if we get more info from Kenny and Gene it'll give us a little more insight."

Before Marcel could reply, his email notification sounded. He clicked, then grunted.

"What?" Beau set his coffee off to the side.

"It's from Nolan. He says they've completed

the DNA profile from the axe found at our scene. He's sent it to the FBI to run through CODIS and NDIS."

Beau nodded. The National DNA Index System, and the system for analyzing and communicating data, Combined DNA Index System, were both administered by the FBI. "Any idea how long it'll take to get a response from the feds?" Beau wasn't too keen on having the FBI involved in any aspect of his case. His experience with them hadn't been exactly positive.

"Nolan didn't say, but he'll follow up with the FBI."

"I'm not real hopeful, considering how long ago our victim was murdered, but it's worth a try. Does Nolan say anything about the palm print?"

Marcel shook his head. "But that would be a long, long shot, man. Palm prints only started getting recorded in the systems in the early 2000s, so I'm doubting we'll have any match for our case's timeline."

Beau tossed his pen on the desk and leaned back in his chair. Every time he thought they had a lead, the timeline didn't match or the evidence wouldn't be supported. Dead ends. He was truly stumped on this case, which didn't happen very often. Then again, most of his victims were murdered recently and not eighty or so years ago.

What were they missing?

"Nolan says the prints they pulled from the

glass shards weren't clear enough so they can't run them in the database."

Another dead end. Beau dropped the paper coffee cup into the trash, still about a fourth full. He needed to do something . . . they needed a break in the case. "I think I'll head over to the Darkwater Inn and see if they've made any connection between the missing persons reported and guests of the hotel."

Marcel nodded. "I think I'll go check in with Gene and Kenny, just to see if there's anything that might give us a lead."

"Good deal. Call me if you find anything and I'll do the same." Beau stood, then unlocked his drawer and placed his gun in his holster. He didn't really want to talk with Dimitri, but he was getting desperate for a new direction in the case.

He'd talk to the devil himself if that's what it took to make sense of all this.

DIMITRI

Dimitri sat up straight and rolled his shoulders. He, Adelaide, and Vicky had been poring over the list from the police of missing persons in 1938, 1958, and 1959. Each of them had taken a year. He had 1938 while Adelaide had 1958 and Vicky had 1959. If there was a connection here, they were going to find it.

"I think I'm going to go take a break and check emails." Vicky stood and stretched. They'd been at it all morning.

"Take an early and long lunch." Adelaide smiled at her assistant. "We're almost to the end of the lists anyway. I'll finish up."

"I'm not going to argue with you." She stuck a sticky note to mark her place on the list. "That's where I left off." With a little waggle of her fingers, she left the conference room.

"Are you getting hungry?" Dimitri might not be able to do much to impress Adelaide these days, but feeding her was his forte.

She checked her watch, then shook her head. "Not just yet. I figured I'd eat something with Dad later. I need to make sure he eats and takes his medicine." She stood and stretched her arms over her head. Hunching over reports and ledgers for so many hours had tightened all her muscles.

"I'll make something special and have it sent up." Dimitri smiled. He wanted to go and rub her neck and shoulders, but hesitated. Ever since the skeleton had been found, he'd felt a . . . he didn't quite know what to call it. The best way he could describe it was a slip between him and Adelaide. A distance between them, ever so slightly. He didn't like it, but didn't know what to do to get back the easy feeling he used to have with her.

She smiled back at him as she twisted. "Thanks, Dimitri. That'll be nice. And thank you for letting me put Dad in a suite here. If his homeowners doesn't cover all the cost of his stay, I'll pay the difference."

He shook his head. "Don't be ridiculous. He's your father. I wish you'd just let us comp the whole stay for him."

"I appreciate that, I do, but Dad won't hear of it."

"I understand, but just so we're clear, there will be no charge above what his insurance allows."

"Thank you. The adjuster is supposed to call Dad today when he completes his inspection. Thank goodness he didn't give a time he'd be at the house to look at it, or Dad would be sitting there waiting on him."

Dimitri smiled. Adelaide didn't realize how much like her father she was.

She returned to her seat. "I think I'm going to go over a few more pages before I check my messages and return any calls or emails I need to before lunch."

He nodded.

"But if you need to go ahead and go, I totally understand. I can do this on my own for a few hours."

As if he'd leave her to this task alone. "I think we're almost done, to be honest. I'm on the last page from the 1938 missing persons list."

She shook her head. "I've only got two pages left in '58. Nothing matches. Nothing even close."

Desperation filled her voice as big as a Mardi Gras float. "I really thought there'd be a match."

"Me, too. Maybe there's one on these last pages." He smiled at her. "Race you through the end."

She nodded and bent back over her list and ledger. She absently tucked the lock of hair that brushed her face behind her ear.

He couldn't help staring, but the strongest sense of loss rose from the pit of his gut and tightened in his chest. Dimitri couldn't explain it, but the feeling was deep . . . profound. He gave himself a mental shake and went back to the last page of the police's reported missing persons list for 1938.

None of the names matched any on the ledger. A total waste of time. He could have been placing the order for Friday night's event food, or maybe showing Yvette the new—

His thoughts skidded to a halt as he read the note on the missing persons list: Harold Pampalon.

"Nothing." Adelaide slammed the ledger shut and set the list to the side. "Looks like I got finished with my list first, so I'll start on the last pages of 1959." She looked at him. "What? Did you find a match?"

"No, not a match."

"But something?"

He stared at the name, trying to mentally go through the list of his ancestry that he'd seen in the family history file. "December 1938."

Adelaide continued to silently stare at him, waiting for him to continue.

"One Harold Pampalon was reported missing by his father, Louis Pampalon."

"Was there an update listed? Adelaide moved around the table to look at the police list. Some of the names did have comments beside them. So did Harold's. Adelaide read aloud, "No efforts on the case made due to the testimony of friends that Harold had left."

Dimitri heard Adelaide read the words. He read along with her, but it still didn't make sense. Who was Harold Pampalon? He couldn't recall ever having seen the name before. Had it been on his family tree in the file?

"Do you have any idea who he was?" Adelaide asked him.

Dimitri shook his head. "I'm going to go look over the file you had Vicky pull for me and see if he's in there. I don't remember the name."

"Me either." She chewed her bottom lip as she lifted the paper. "I'll ask Beau to see if he can pull up anything else from the police about this report."

"I hope there's something."

"Dimitri . . ."

He looked at her, even as he began to shake his head. "I know what you're going to say, and I don't think so."

She held up a hand in a stopping gesture. "I understand where you're coming from, I do, but you and I both know there is a person who pretty much knows your family history inside out. At least from the time this hotel was built."

"No. I don't want to see him, and I'm pretty sure he doesn't want to see me."

"You don't know unless you go."

He snorted. "Please. The last thing the man said to me was that I was a waste of Pampalon blood and if he ever saw me again, it'd be too soon." He shook his head again. "Besides, I don't think he's put me on the visitor's list, Adelaide."

"Beau could get you in to see him, even if you aren't on the list." Her voice was low. Calm. Tone unwavering. "The worst that could happen would be that he refuses to talk to you, and that's where you are now, so it's not like it's a big loss."

Dimitri stared at the table. He wanted answers, of course, but he didn't want to see his father. Claude Pampalon had made sure everyone in the courtroom at the sentencing had known exactly what he thought of his son. He'd accused him of setting up everything so that he could get control of the Darkwater Inn.

Adelaide was wrong—there was so much more for Dimitri to lose. His self-respect, of course, but also the tentative control he had on his temper when it came to Claude Pampalon.

1933

"I'm not going anywhere else. I'm my own man." William stared at his two best friends, George and James. Night had just set over New Orleans, and they were supposed to be saying prayers before lights out.

"What are you gonna do?" James, the smallest of the three, stared at William with his eyes wide.

"The whole moving St. Mary's and changing its name . . . it's stupid." William watched to make sure he had both of his friends' full attention. He shifted from his kneeling position, still holding his rosary. "They're going to lose paperwork and stuff. You know they will."

George nodded as he rolled one of the beads between two fingers, but James just kept staring by the nightlights casting shadows in the dorm rooms.

William glanced around to make sure none of the other boys were listening before sitting on his bunk. He couldn't trust any of them, only George and James. "I'm going to get out of here during the move."

"What?" Even George had wide eyes now as he stood, glancing over his shoulder toward the door.

"Where are you going to go?" James asked, still in his kneeling position.

These two . . . so easy. William didn't let his smile show as he set his rosary on the metal table between the beds. "Look, I'm fifteen now. We all know that we aren't ever going to get adopted out of here, and once we turn seventeen, well, the home will basically kick us out anyway." At least, that's what he'd heard. He had no intention of hanging around to find out if that were true. He'd rather leave on his own terms than in whatever way this boys' home intended.

"But where will you go? What will you do?" James sounded so whiney, making William wonder if he should rethink his plan.

"What have you got planned?" George smoothed the pillow on his bunk beside William's bed and sat back on it.

"I'm going to live my life." William puffed out his chest a little. Yeah, he might be a smaller guy, but he more than made up for that with his brains. He knew that.

"How? You have no money." George slipped under his covers.

James followed suit on the other side of William. "Yeah."

William shook his head. "Don't you guys read the paper?" When both of his friends shook their heads, he sighed. "The Works Progress Administration is doing all sorts of stuff, repairs and new stuff, in City Park. They've been talking about hiring all types of people."

"But those are engineers and stuff, William, not fifteen-year-olds," George replied.

"They said in the paper that they were looking to hire on even uneducated young men to do the clean up behind the workers." William snorted. "I'm educated. Smart. All the teachers say so."

George nodded.

William went ahead with revealing his plan. "I'm going to get hired on. From what I read, they provide lunch, too. I don't eat much more than that. At least not until I start getting paid." He'd thought it through. This was his only chance. He knew it was time. God had told him it was.

He and God, they'd been having some intense conversations lately. Oh, not the prayers the old biddy nuns tried to force him to recite from memory. Those were meaningless. Lip service, he knew that. God had shown him that.

God had shown him that he had a purpose, too. God would reveal it soon, but William had to do his part. He had to leave. Had to trust that God would provide and show him what he was supposed to do.

But he didn't want to do it alone. "Guys, you two are my best friends, so I'm only telling you two." He waited, flipping his head and gaze from one to the other. "If you want to get out of here and be your own man, too, I'll let you go with me." He pinched his lips together and held his breath, but forced his expression to remain the same.

Neither George nor James spoke at first. James looked across William to George.

How dare the little goof look to George? William was the leader here. Always had been, always would be. He squared his shoulders. "Unless you two are too chicken to come with me. I just thought I'd give you a chance to be a man, but if you would rather stay here under the skirts of the nuns . . ." He shrugged as he let his sentence fade.

"No, I want to go with you." George nodded. "I can work. I'm strong."

William silently let out the breath he'd held. "Good." He smiled at George, happy that he wouldn't be going alone.

"Where will you live?" James asked.

William turned to the youngest of them. "The papers are always mentioning abandoned houses and flats right down the road. We can squat in them. Rotate so we don't get caught." He caught the frown of both James and George, so pressed on. "Or if it's pretty out, we can camp out in the park, sleeping under the stars."

George nodded, back on board.

"It'll be like an adventure." William smiled at James.

The young one hesitated, then looked at both

William and George. "Okay. I'll go with you, William."

William smiled. "I'm not William anymore. I'm changing my life, becoming my own man, so I'm going to change my name, too. I'm going to be Will. Will Youngblood."

11

ADDY

"Hey, Beau, do you have a minute?" Addy spoke from beside his desk, clutching the folder with the police lists of missing persons.

"Hey. Of course." He shot to his feet, clearly surprised to see her.

She laughed. "Marcel was talking to an officer up front when I came in, so he told me to come on back. I hope that's okay."

He smiled and motioned for her to sit in the chair next to his and Marcel's desks. He waited until she sat before he did. The little gentlemanly gesture warmed her, and she wasn't exactly sure why it touched her so. But it did, and she smiled back at him. She set the folder on the corner of his desk.

"Did you find a match?"

She shook her head. "Not of a guest, but we did find a connection between a missing person and the Darkwater Inn."

"Do tell."

Addy quickly filled him in on finding a Pampalon name on the list. "Dimitri is going to look through all the records he can, but a Harold didn't sound familiar to him."

"Let me see what I can find out." He lifted the phone and called one of the officers who worked in records. After giving her the file number from the list, the name, and a promise to buy her a *real* coffee—not anything from the precinct—he hung up. "What?" He stared at Addy.

"What *what?*"

"Why are you smiling at me like that?"

The heat tinged her cheeks and she dropped her gaze to his desk and shrugged. "You're just so nice. Even when you're asking someone to basically do a task that is part of their job, you always ask so nicely."

Now it was his turn to blush a little. "I guess I just try to treat people the way I want to be treated."

"It's nice. Not many people do that anymore." But Beau always did. She'd never seen him be rude or short with anyone in the department. It spoke of his overall general personality.

One she liked.

She shook her head. Now wasn't the time or the place to have these thoughts. "I suggested Dimitri go visit his father and see if Claude knows anything."

Surprise washed over his handsome features. "I can imagine Dimitri wasn't too thrilled with that idea."

She smiled and shook her head. "You know he wasn't. He said that he was pretty sure that

170

Claude hadn't put him on the visitor list, but I told him you could probably get him in to see his father if he wanted."

"I could. If he wanted that."

"I'm hoping his curiosity will win out over his hard feelings against his father." She ran her finger along the side of his desk. "I mean, I understand how he feels. No one could ever accuse Claude Pampalon of being a decent human being, but he *is* Dimitri's father." She looked at Beau. "Who knows? Maybe prison has changed him. Softened him."

"That's not exactly how prison usually works, Addy. It usually makes people a little harder and rougher around the edges."

"I can hope though, right?"

"You can always hope." His smile didn't quite reach his eyes. He clearly didn't believe there was much chance of Dimitri's dad changing.

Maybe he was right.

"How's Vincent?"

Addy grinned. "Oh, Daddy is Daddy. Avoiding taking his medication because he says he doesn't need it. Irritated that he's having to stay at the hotel, but I think secretly he's enjoying himself. He's got a replacement phone and I took him to the Apple store this morning, so he has the newest and greatest MacBook. When I left him after lunch, he was having a grand time setting everything up."

171

"That's Vincent all right. I talked with the arson investigator. They've definitely ruled it arson, but have no clues or leads on who's responsible."

"What about the guys in the dark robes with hoods? Aren't they the same ones who threw those jars of pig's blood at us?"

"We can't be sure. We really have nothing to go on. No prints could be pulled from the jars. CSU says they were regular Mason jars like the hundreds carried at the local grocery or superstores in town. There's no connection to them and what your father says he saw."

"Says he saw?" She leaned forward in the chair.

"Come on, Addy. I believe him, but he was under quite a bit of stress, having just regained consciousness and sitting in the back of an ambulance on oxygen, watching his house burn down. His testimony would never stand up in any way."

It was all so unfair. "Have you heard anything from Chandler?"

He nodded. "Their forensic artist is almost done with her 3D rendering of what they think the person looked like at the time of death."

3D? "How?"

"Apparently it's a complex process where they measure points and stuff and then put clay over the skull. They have the hair from what they recovered here, so they will add similar fake hair to complete the look. Once they get it all done, they'll take pictures and send them to us to run through the database."

"That's really cool." That's what she'd expect to see on the crime shows. "I guess it'll look like the victim then. That'll be a little weird. Seeing somebody we've never seen before except as bones."

"It's pretty amazing what forensics can do, that's for sure."

She eased back in her seat. "Chandler's pretty intelligent."

He nodded. "She is." Beau didn't offer anything else.

"She's pretty, too."

He stared at her until she wanted to squirm in her seat, but she sat ramrod straight.

"Yeah, she's pretty. Not as pretty as you, though."

Her heart melted, and it had nothing to do with the flaming heat in her face.

"Anyway," Beau was sensitive enough to change the subject, "we should get those pictures back tomorrow, or Wednesday at the latest."

"Wow. I guess I thought it'd take much longer. Something with that much detail and all." She couldn't imagine the artistic ability someone would have to possess in order to create a likeness from a skull. Pretty amazing.

"You'd think, right? I'm anxious to see it. Not that we'd recognize anybody from back then, but it's still neat to think we could get an ID based on it."

The phone on his desk rang. "Detective Savoie." He grabbed a pen and a scrap of paper. "Mmmhmmm."

Addy couldn't help herself, she stood so she could read as he wrote.

Harold Pampalon reported missing by parents— Louis & Eva on Dec 25, 1938. Friends said he was going to St. Louis. Asked them to go w/ him. Checks at hospitals and John Does—no results.

Thank goodness she'd been reading his chicken scratch all her life because his handwriting was atrocious.

"Nothing else? No further updates?" Beau tapped the pen on the desk as he talked on the phone. "I see. Of course. Thanks. Let me know when you want that coffee." He chuckled. "You got it. Thanks again." He replaced the phone into its cradle and looked at her. "Nothing else was done on the case. It wasn't marked closed, but they figured it was just another young adult running off to get out from underneath his parents' thumbs."

She nodded, but Addy struggled to rein in her emotions. Maybe it was because of Chandler . . . maybe it was because of the stress of knowing she needed to choose between Beau and Dimitri . . . or maybe it was that her father had almost been killed and she'd been so relieved to save

174

her grandmother's wedding dress, but whatever it was causing it, Addy couldn't deny the streak of jealousy she'd felt when Beau had been on the phone with a female police officer.

That had never happened before.

"Addy?"

She focused on Beau. "Sorry, my mind went off."

He chuckled. "So I saw. Anyway, that's all we have on the old case. Not that I really expected something, but we tried."

But something didn't seem right. "Beau, what kid runs off on Christmas Day? I mean, that's the biggest time for families, right? Why leave town on that day, of all days?"

"I don't know. I can't answer that. But apparently they spoke with friends—plural, so it was more than one—and the story held water. I mean, if not, there would have been more of an investigation."

"You think?"

Beau grinned. "I don't know much about how the cops worked missing persons in those days, but I'm pretty sure the Pampalon name carried weight, even back then. Probably even more so. I would bet that the cops did everything by the book to make sure they didn't overlook something that would indicate foul play."

"I guess." She sighed.

"If you want, I'll pull the records and get the

name of his friends who were interviewed, but I'm not sure what good that would do since I'm sure they would be deceased by now," Beau offered.

She shook her head. "No, you're right. So while it is intriguing, that still leaves us nowhere in figuring out who was buried in the wall of the Darkwater Inn."

"No, I'm afraid it doesn't." He smiled as he stood. "Do you think Vincent is up to some company this evening? I thought I might stop by and check in with him."

"Please do." She stood and let Beau lead her to the front door of the precinct. "I want him to take it easy for the seven days until he gets the stitches removed. As restless as he already is, the next five days are going to be hard. I'll take any help in distracting him that I can."

Beau grinned. "Let me pick up pizza then. We can get in a heated argument about the latest books-turned-movies that you know he wants to pick apart."

"Sounds perfect. Thanks."

BEAU

He should feel guilty for the surge of happiness that hit him when he'd realized Addy was jealous about Chandler, but he didn't. Not at all.

If she was feeling jealous over him, didn't

that mean she was possessive? And if she was possessive, that had to mean she was still involved with him emotionally. With everything going on, they hadn't had an opportunity to go out. Tonight would be nice, just hanging out with her and Vincent in their comfortable, familiar way.

Maybe if he was lucky, he'd be able to sneak in a kiss. Or two. Or ten.

He grinned as he headed across the lobby of the Darkwater Inn, pizza box and six pack of root beer in hand.

"Detective Savoie."

He stopped and sighed, waiting until Dimitri caught up with him. "I think we're well past the formalities, don't you?" He didn't wait for an answer. "What can I do for you, Dimitri?"

"I was wondering if I might have a word, but I see perhaps now isn't the time." He nodded toward the pizza box.

It was probably a personal offense to a chef like Pampalon to have a take-out pizza in his hotel. Beau swallowed the smile. "What can I help you with?"

"Today as Adelaide and I were going over the list you sent us and comparing that to the hotel's ledgers, I came across a family name I didn't recognize."

He nodded. "Harold Pampalon." Beau caught the barely-detectable microexpression of surprise, then disappointment. "Addy told me. She dropped by the precinct to see if I could find out any more information on his disappearance. I'm sorry, but there was nothing besides the note that the police had interviewed some of Harold's friends. They stated Harold had said he was going to St. Louis and asked them if they wanted to go."

"I understand, and appreciate your checking. However, I was wondering more if you could . . ." Dimitri wiped imaginary lint off his immaculate jeans. "I checked all my ancestry records and I can't find a Harold Pampalon. I was wondering if, perhaps . . . Adelaide thought maybe you could help me be able to visit my father in prison."

The enormity of what it cost Dimitri personally to ask such a favor hit him. "Of course. Happy to do it. How about tomorrow afternoon?"

"That soon?" Surprise filled every nuance of Dimitri's face.

"Might as well go sooner rather than later, yes? It can be a nice distraction for you, what with everything going on here."

Dimitri nodded. "Yes. Thank you. Tomorrow afternoon will be fine."

"Great. I'll call the prison and get it set up, then I'll give you a call and let you know the time. Okay?"

"Yes. Thank you." He nodded toward the pizza box. "You know, I could have made you a pizza with much fresher ingredients that would taste a whole lot better." Dimitri grinned. "I'm just saying."

Beau laughed. "I'm sure, but this is Vincent's favorite and I'm trying to help Addy keep him in line with the doctor's orders. He can be a handful." He smiled at Dimitri and turned toward the elevators.

He stepped inside and told the elevator attendant to take him to the floor of Vincent's suite. He hadn't meant to be rude to Dimitri, but he didn't want to stand there and continue a conversation with the man he was vying with for Addy's romantic attention.

Pampalon might own a hotel and have money and be charming, but Beau had known Addy longer. They had a history. Their pasts were intertwined with the highs and lows of heart-breaks, celebrations, disappointments, accomplishments, and family ties. Beau had every intention of making sure Addy knew that he loved her and always would.

Once this case was over.

He knocked on the door to Vincent's suite, and Addy swung the door open. The hectic look on her face told him a thousand things at once, but nothing more telling than her father's hollering behind her. "If that's housekeeping, tell them I do not want anybody to turn down my bed. I'm a grown man, quite capable of fixing my own sheets."

Beau winked at Addy and walked past her into the parlor. "Well that's good, because I have no intention of touching your bed, old man."

"Beau, my boy." Vincent's eyes widened. "Is that what I think it is?" He stood from the couch. "It is. I could kiss you." He headed to the table.

"Please don't, but you're welcome." Beau laughed, loving this man who had been his surrogate father since his own had died when he was twelve.

Addy got three glasses and filled them with ice before bringing them to the table. "Since he brought you pizza and root beer, do you promise to be nicer now?"

Vincent waved her off. "After dinner, if you're nice, I'll let you see my new MacBook. That puppy is awesome."

Beau sat next to Addy, across from her father. He put a piece of pizza on his own plate, then one on Addy's.

"Guys, I think I'd like to say grace aloud tonight, if you don't mind." Addy's eyes were rounder than usual.

"Of course." Beau couldn't believe this. He knew why Addy had drifted from her faith—her horrible experience with Kevin Muller—and he had been praying God would call her back . . . well, he couldn't be more elated.

By the look on Vincent's face before he bent his head, the feeling was mutual.

"Dear God, thank You for this food. Please use it to the nourishment of our bodies, and our bodies to honor You. And thank You for keeping my dad safe. Amen."

"Amen," Beau and Vincent said in unison.

Beau got one bite in of his second slice of pizza before his cell phone went off.

Addy and Vincent both chewed slowly and stared as he checked the display and answered. "Hey, Marcel, what's up?"

"Murder."

He sat back. "We're not up in rotation."

"Nope, Gibbons and Witz are the ones who drew the case."

They were seasoned detectives, especially Gibbons. "I fail to see why you're calling me then."

"Captain wanted us to run by. Seems the murder is one Lance Bassemier, killed in his home on Laharpe Street. Wanna guess how he was killed?"

"An axe, which was left at the scene?"

"You got it. Anyway, I'll text you the address and meet you there."

"Okay." Beau disconnected the call and took a final swig of his root beer.

"A murder with an axe?" Vincent asked.

"Daddy! You know you shouldn't eavesdrop on Beau's business calls."

"It's okay. I'm sure it'll be on the news later.

Allison Williams seems to know things almost as soon as the police do."

"I saw the report she gave on the five o'clock about a couple being found dead," Vincent offered.

Beau nodded, not offering any more details as he stood.

Vincent stood, too. "Now that I think about it, she didn't mention if they were found shot or stabbed." He rubbed his chin. "I'm gonna go out on a limb and guess they were killed with an axe that was conveniently left at the scene."

"Oh, no." Addy grabbed Beau's plate and empty glass and took it to the kitchenette. "Please tell me there's not someone out there killing people with an axe."

"It looks like it. This will be the third victim today." He grabbed Addy's hand and held it tight before kissing her temple. "Y'all stay in the hotel, okay?"

"Us? We're fine. You're the one out there working the case."

"But it all seems to be connected to the hotel . . . and to the two of you." He stared hard at Vincent until Addy's father gave a slight tilt of his head. He turned back to Addy. "Just be alert, okay? Put my mind at ease."

"Of course." She laid a hand against his chest. Surely she could feel his heart almost beating its way out to her. "You be careful out there, Beau. I mean it."

He put a quick peck on her lips. "Yes, ma'am. For you, anything."

12

DIMITRI

Dimitri toyed with the plastic edge of the visitor's badge clipped to his suit jacket as he licked his lips. The smooth plastic against his fingers seemed out of place contrasted with the harshness of the prison.

Cha-clink!

The sound echoed off the quiet walls of the federal penitentiary, causing his spine to stiffen as the electronic door of bars disengaged and slid apart at an agonizing snail's pace.

The guard tapped his shoulder again and gestured toward the private visiting room usually reserved for visits between attorneys and inmates. Beau had gotten Dimitri this privacy with his father, and Dimitri was suddenly more appreciative than he ever imagined. "I'll wait right out here to take you back whenever you're ready."

Dimitri nodded, then hauled in a long, ragged breath, let it out slowly, and proceeded into the room. His pulse hammered. He discovered his feet were reluctant to move, as if *he* were the prisoner condemned to spend years behind bars, not the man he called his father.

Inside the prison walls was nothing like Dimitri had ever imagined. The air reeked of urine and feces, masked only by the overbearing odor of cheap disinfectant. He swallowed against the urge to turn and run, then steadied himself by glancing down. Cracks streaked along the dank, dismal gray floor in a repetitive pattern, causing a strange sense of normalcy invading his perception of the unexpected. The dreary, yet foreboding atmosphere overpowered his senses more than the stench.

He sat in the cold, unyielding plastic chair on the side of the wooden table closest to the outer door. To make a quick getaway if need be? Maybe. Possibly. Likely. The room boasted no windows—no chance of sunlight, or hope, to pierce the stagnant atmosphere of the isolated four walls. Musty air hung in the room like a cloud of hopelessness.

Footsteps echoed down a hall, then the door swung open and Claude Pampalon glared at his son.

"What are you doing here?"

Dimitri stood suddenly.

The guard who'd escorted Claude hesitated at the doorway, as if gauging if it was safe to leave the two men alone.

"I needed to talk to you."

A moment passed between them, then Claude shrugged. "Why not? At the very least, it'll break up the routine here." He moved to the opposite side of the table and sat. "Talking to you in here is better than sitting in the community room out there."

"We'll be right out here." The guard stepped out into the hall, closing the door behind him, but standing beside the guard who'd brought Dimitri in. Both of them could see through the window filling the top half of the door.

Dimitri sat back down. Now that his father was before him, he didn't know what to say. How to start. Where to start.

"Must be something important for you to actually come here." Claude's eyes narrowed. "What did you do to my hotel?"

"Nothing. We're actually finishing up some remodeling Adelaide ordered. We'll be able to add more rooms, which we need since we're staying at capacity pretty much all the time." At least, that's how Adelaide explained it.

"But those skeletons in the walls, huh?"

Who had told him?

Claude laughed. "It's prison, son, not the dark ages. We do get newspapers and newscasts here."

"Oh. Right." He hadn't really thought about that. He'd hoped to get through the visit without the interrogation that was sure to come next.

"I'm assuming the police haven't identified the remains yet?"

"Not yet. We've narrowed it down to the early

186

to mid-1900s when renovations were done to the hotel."

"But no matches yet." Claude didn't ask.

Dimitri shook his head.

Claude sighed and sat back in the chair. The plastic popped a little. "If you came to ask me if I know anything about it, I don't. Surely you can't imagine something that happened when I couldn't have been older than a child would be my fault."

"Of course not." Dimitri shifted in the uncomfortable chair. "But while we were going through old documents, I came across a name in our family that I've never heard before. Harold. Harold Pampalon. Do you recognize it?"

"Uncle Harold."

"What?" How had he never heard of a man his father deigned to use a familial term in reference to?

"Harold was my father's older brother."

"Then how come I've never heard of him?" Was his father just messing with him? Making up some story just to break his routine of boredom?

"Because he ran away from home when my father was an infant and was never heard from again."

That detail matched everything he'd learned, but . . .

"You see, my grandparents had tried to have

children when they were younger, but couldn't. Medical testing back in the early 1930s wasn't what it is today. If a couple didn't have children, no one really understood why not. Most either went childless, but some who were wealthy enough to afford it, adopted children. My grand-parents, Louis and Eva Pampalon adopted Harold as a young teen."

Dimitri didn't know what to say. He just leaned back in the chair and stared at his father.

Claude nodded as he continued. "How I understand it is that Louis and Eva, childless and getting older and realizing they needed an heir to bestow the Darkwater Inn to, they opted to adopt. But not a baby. No, I was told that Eva didn't want a newborn that wasn't hers, so they adopted an older child. Harold."

Fascinating.

"They sent him to the best schools, trained him in the hotel . . . basically giving him the best opportunities in life, much like I did for you." Claude smirked at Dimitri. "But then, like you, Harold repaid them by running off from them."

Dimitri straightened in the chair. "I didn't run off from you, Father. I told the truth. You were the one doing nefarious and illegal activities, putting not just yourself, but also the hotel at risk." He stared at Claude across the table. "If anything, you were the one who caused this separation."

"Interesting that you decided to care about the fate of the hotel at that moment, despite my years of trying to involve you. Rather convenient, I'd say."

This was starting to sound all too familiar. "I didn't come here to rehash it all with you."

"Why did you come, young Dimitri? Ah, yes. Harold. Fine." Claude relaxed in his seat. "At any rate, no one knows why Harold ran away, but my father always said he was told it was because of him. Because Louis and Eva were finally able to have a son of their own, Harold was fearful he would be pushed aside in favor of my father, Henri."

Which, if Dimitri were being honest, sounded like the way it would've been in his family, the way it always went. Generations were hung up on the Pampalon name and producing heirs to carry on the hotel legacy.

"Father said that there are a few pictures of Harold holding him as a child in an old photo album, but I never saw them. Frankly, I never looked because it didn't concern me."

And the cold and calculating Claude had resurfaced. Prison might have started chipping away at his self-righteous attitude, but there was still a long way to go.

"At any rate, if you're truly curious about our family history, all of Father's papers are in the safe in my bedroom at the house. There might

189

be adoption records or papers in there." Claude smiled that cocky smirk of his. "Oh, wait, you don't have that combination, do you?"

As usual, his father dangled something in front of him only to yank it away. But this time, it didn't matter. "I don't need a combination, Father. The police opened it when they served their warrant to search the house for any additional stolen pieces of art. That safe has been open since before you were imprisoned." He stood. "At least it wasn't a total waste of time to come here. I'll look for those papers."

Claude shot to his feet. "Sit down and let's talk some more. Tell me what's going on with the hotel." The desperation to avoid minutes of loneliness almost got to Dimitri.

Almost, but not quite. "Once the remodel is completed, I'll have it appraised."

Claude nodded. "Good. Good to have the worth of the hotel kept up to date."

"Especially because Malcom Dessommes keeps calling with offers to buy. I wouldn't want him to underbid." With that, Dimitri turned and opened the door. He stepped into the hall and nodded at the guards.

"You can't sell my hotel! Dimitri! Don't you walk away from me. You can't sell my hotel! The Darkwater Inn is mine!"

Dimitri never turned back, not even glancing over his shoulder. He started down the hall the way he'd been brought in, effectively ignoring his father.

It felt fabulous.

ADDY

"Thank you for being willing to go through all this with me." Dimitri opened the large box. "I don't trust just anybody to go through whatever my father deemed worthy of keeping in his safe."

She was flattered, of course, but honestly, there wasn't much else that she felt at the moment. What did that mean? She watched as Dimitri unpacked the box. "I still can't believe how much stuff Father had crammed into his wall safe."

"To be fair, he is the owner of the Darkwater Inn and probably has a lot of papers in his home safe that are duplicates of what we keep in the hotel's vault." Addy smiled as she sat in one of the conference room chairs. She hadn't expected to be back in this room sorting through papers so soon after finishing yesterday.

"Well, it was a big safe." He pulled out expandable folders, portfolio keepers, and stacks of papers.

She still found Dimitri handsome as ever, and he was certainly sweet and sexy, but . . . she couldn't quite explain that something inside her had changed, but she didn't feel the same *pull* towards Dimitri that she once had.

"A *really* big safe."

"Oh, my." She'd expected Claude kept a lot of private documents, of course, but this . . . Dimitri was right—this was unbelievable.

"Yeah." He finally set the last packet of papers on the table and moved the empty box to the floor. "I don't even know where to begin."

The task *did* look overwhelming, but Addy knew they could tackle it. One pile at a time. She pulled the first expandable folder toward her. "Let's just take everything as we come to it. We should be able to scan each pretty quickly and determine if there's any reference to Harold." His great-uncle. The information seemed insane, yet, also not. Not that that made any sense either.

Nothing in her life was uncomplicated, it would seem.

"Okay." Dimitri pulled a pile of loose papers toward him and began skimming.

Addy let out a sigh and opened the expandable folder. It might be they were chasing a dead-end, which would be something Claude would do—setting his son up with meaningless tasks just to prove a point, but chances were good that if there was any information on Harold's adoption, it would be in this mess.

But not in this slot of this folder. All these papers were in reference to the Pampalon house and estate.

"I really appreciate Beauregard setting it up for me to see Father privately."

Addy put papers back into the folder. "He said he figured you'd rather avoid the ordeal of the regular visiting room."

"I did, and I'll have to thank him."

She pulled out the next group of papers and began scanning, even as her heart pounded. Why? This was just Dimitri.

"Adelaide?"

She glanced up. "Did you find the papers already?"

"No." He set down the papers he clutched. "I want to talk to you."

She set down the papers she'd held as well, the tone of his voice telling her this was important. "Okay."

"You know how much I care about you. How wonderful I think you are and what an amazing woman you are. Right?"

Her chest tightened, but she nodded.

"I hope you know that I truly want what's best for you."

The rush of blood pulsating filled her ears, numbing her thoughts. She slowly nodded. "I know all that, Dimitri, just like I hope you know I want what's best for you. I think you're wonderful and amazing as well."

"I do." He smiled. "I just wanted you to know that no matter what happens between you and me, or you and Beauregard, I am your friend."

She let out a slow breath against a very dry mouth. She swallowed several times before she could speak. "I appreciate that." Where was he going with this? How should she respond? How had her life become so complicated?

"I just wanted you to know that."

She forced the smile she flashed at him and lifted the papers again. She'd felt sick at the thought of him ending a romantic relationship with her . . . but on the other hand, she hadn't felt a sense of loss. What did that say about her? What did it all mean?

"And I wanted you to know that despite it all, I think Beauregard is a good man, as well as being a good detective."

But the mention of Beau's name . . . no, this definitely wasn't the time or place. "He is." She forced herself to look at the stack of papers she held. They referenced the autos and boats in the Pampalon estate—titles, deeds, etc. She jammed them back into their place, only slightly wincing as the divider shoved against her cuticle, and pulled out the last group from that folder.

"Adelaide?"

She really didn't want to have this conversation about relationships with him . . . here . . . now. Okay, she didn't want to have it period, but if he wasn't going to let the matter drop, what choice did she have? She glanced across the table at him. His eyes were on a couple of sheets of paper he held, his face pale. It wasn't about them . . . "What is it?"

"These are the adoption papers of one Harold James."

She dropped her stack of papers onto the table beside the folder. "Details?"

Dimitri nodded. "A male baby, born on October 31, 1917 to parents Robert and Samantha Holmes at Charity Hospital here in New Orleans. He weighed six pounds, six-and-a-half ounces and was eighteen inches long."

Addy rested her elbows on the table and continued to stare across at him.

"He was adopted through St. Mary's Asylum for Boys to Louis and Eva Pampalon on April 1, 1931."

Addy dropped her palms to the table and shook her head. "Wait a minute, this boy was born on Halloween and was adopted on April Fools' Day? Then runs away on Christmas?" She couldn't believe the irony. "This poor kid was doomed from the beginning."

"Apparently so. And an informational sheet from the hospital is here. It confirms the information on the birth certificate: date and time of birth, name of parents. Blood type. Attending physician's signature." Dimitri handed her the papers and flipped through the ones that were under it in his stack. "There's nothing more here on Harold."

Only three sheets of paper, a birth certificate, hospital record, and an adoption certificate, and that summed up a whole person's life? No, that couldn't be. He had to have lived. Gone to school. Done something. Anything.

She read his birth certificate again, then lowered the papers and stared at Dimitri. "Why did his parents give him up for adoption? He was two years old then."

"That's a good question." He shrugged. "Maybe they fell on hard times and couldn't afford to provide for him."

No, that didn't make sense. "I don't think that's it. The great depression wasn't until the stock market crash of October 1929. This was a good decade before then, when times weren't so hard. Most people were able to live comfortably before the bottom fell out."

Dimitri shook his head and tented his hands over the table. "I don't know. Maybe the orphanage would have records. I'm sure they kept more details than what was put in the adoption papers."

She read the adoption certificate. "He was adopted through St. Mary's Asylum for Boys here in New Orleans, but they didn't take babies. He must have transferred there." She shook her head. "I've never heard of it. I mean, I know the St. Vincent's Orphanage over on Magazine Street had a lot of babies back in the day. It's been converted to a guest house you can stay in now. Maybe they know where to look for records like that?"

Dimitri nodded. "Maybe. And I'll put in a call to the Archdiocese of New Orleans parish. St. Mary's had to have been a Catholic orphanage and I'm sure the district would know where such records are kept and if they are available."

"Smart." She nodded. She flipped the page to the hospital record. "And maybe we could check with Charity Hospital, too. I mean, it'd be a long shot, but . . ." she stared at the information, something nagging on the edges of her mind.

"What?"

She chewed her bottom lip. Something . . . she should pick up on something . . .

"I doubt the hospital would have any information about an adoption that happened on a child that was delivered there two years previously."

Not the adoption . . . something else.

"Although, maybe the hospital had some notes if the child was deformed or needed future medical care, which could be a reason the parents would give him up for adoption. Adelaide?"

The attending physician's name . . . date . . . time . . . blood type. That was it, blood type! "The hospital recorded Harold's blood type as B negative!"

He stared at her from under wrinkled brows. "Yeah?"

"Dimitri, the blood on the axe found here by the skeleton is B negative. The same as Harold's."

"And he went missing on Christmas Day in 1938, during which time the Darkwater Inn was being renovated."

She grabbed Dimitri's arm. "Our skeleton is none other than your great-uncle Harold."

1935

"I wanted to share something with you two." Will watched James and George as he spoke. Both looked at him, even as they continued to eat the sandwiches he'd stolen off the cart at lunch today. "I've been given special instructions by God."

Both of his friends nodded. Ever since they'd left the orphanage and struck out on their own, they had been missing mass. Will had let them know that he was in commune with their holy father to lead them and to give these young souls direction. Now was the time to tell them of the first stage of the plan. "He's instructed me to start a group of devoted followers of His to do His holy work."

James let the last bite of his sandwich drop to the napkin.

George swallowed. "What work?"

Will smiled. "I don't know exactly what yet, but God's shown me it will be important. We will be following His leading."

"So what do we do?" James asked.

"We need to start behaving in the way that is pleasing to Him. He has shown me where I've been failing Him. There is much evil here in this city, and it is His desire to reduce that here. We are to call ourselves the *Cretum Deus*."

"What does that mean?" George took a drink of water.

"It is a literal translation of *God Decreed.* That's what our group will be—decreed by God. We will follow His truth, His wisdom, His leading. Without fear and without wavering." Will ignored his own hunger pains. "We must not let God down with our first task that He gave me last night."

"What's that?" James leaned forward, closer to Will.

"We are to gather more young men to join us in our quest to do God's work as He relays it to me."

"Guys, not girls?" George asked.

"Not just yet. The Lord will eventually call us to bring women into our fold, to do their part in His will, like cooking, cleaning, bearing us children to continue doing God's work." Will tried not to frown, but he felt his facial muscles tighten. "But it's important to remember that women are not important. God has shown me that. He clearly has little disregard for females other than to obey men and produce sons to continue His holy work. It is because of my own mother's failure to keep herself from sin that I didn't have a father."

"But a demon possessed a man and killed your mother, right?" George pressed.

Will held in the sigh as he slowly nodded. "Yes, because God will allow Satan to use sinners to do evil if they aren't true followers. That's what all who enter the *Cretum Deus* must be—true followers of God."

"How will we know that?" James asked.

Will looked at his friend. "God will let me know if they aren't and they will be dealt with."

"It sounds okay and all." George wadded up his trash and stuck it in his pocket to use to start a fire later, just like Will had taught them. "But how are we supposed to get and keep followers and true believers? We barely survive ourselves, now that it's getting cooler out and the work at the park is slowing. We hide out and sleep in the park or break into one of the abandoned buildings when the weather's bad. That doesn't exactly entice anyone to want to join us."

"Does the Bible not say in the book of Luke, 'And he said to all, "If any man would come after me, let him deny himself and take up his cross daily and follow me." ' It doesn't say to follow God only if there is a place to live, plenty of food to eat, and all the comforts man prefers. It clearly says that man should deny these luxuries and follow God's leading. That's a true believer, and that's what we want and need."

James nodded. "That's what the Bible says all right."

Will smiled. James had studied the word of God daily and knew much from memory. Probably more than Will himself, but Will had God speaking to him in dreams, so reciting Scripture wasn't necessary. "We should begin our task tomorrow. 'Gathering the sheep,' as God has told me."

Again, James nodded. "I'll ask all the guys I work with tomorrow if they are believers and followers of God."

Perfect. "If they say they are, have them come see me here." Will already felt like the leader he'd been called to be.

"You aren't going to work at the park with us?" George asked.

Will shook his head. "As you said, the work is slowing, and I'd rather you and James be able to work. Besides, I will need to question each of the men you and James send to me. To see if God accepts each one into the *Cretum Deus*."

"That will put us short on wages coming in though." George pointed out the obvious.

"No, because each man who joins will turn over their wages to the group. We'll purchase food and needed items and dispense to our members." Will shifted to keep the balance on the wobbly old chair he sat upon in the abandoned house they were using for the time being. "Eventually, we should be able to save enough to rent a place for us all."

Before George could argue any more, James's excitement came through. "I'll start gathering the flock tomorrow. I'm so glad I came with you, William—I mean, Will. Even though I was scared, I prayed and knew that God wanted me with you."

Will smiled. "I prayed before I asked you two to come. If God wouldn't have wanted this, I would have never invited you." He smiled wider. "Make no mistake about it, guys, the Lord has a very specific plan for our lives and He's starting to unveil it to me in stages. Following His leading to go out on our own was the first step, trusting Him to meet all our needs. This is the second step in His plan. I know He's going to use *Cretum Deus* to help rid the world of evil."

"How can you be so sure?" George asked.

"I was brought into this world through the sin of my mother. She was taken from me because of her sin and because another person allowed a demon to take control of him. God has been carefully leading me in this direction all my life. Now He's calling me to action." Will shot his stare between his two friends' faces. "Calling us to act on His behalf."

13

BEAU

"Good morning, partner." Marcel grinned as he sat at his desk, flashing his pearly whites at Beau. "Ready to take a ride?"

"Why, what's going on? Why are you in such a good mood?"

"There was another attack this morning. Amelia Schneider, four months pregnant, was attacked in her home by a man with an axe."

"That's sick, Marcel, even for you. To be in such a good mood over a murder. And of a pregnant woman, too." He couldn't believe his partner was so cheerful after such horrors. Maybe Marcel had finally just gone off the deep end. He might need psychological help.

"Ah, I said she was attacked. I never said she was murdered." Marcel grinned.

"What?" Could this finally be a break they needed? Not that it would solve the skeleton case, but the other three murders could very well be solved with such a lead.

"Right. Mrs. Schneider is currently at the hospital being checked out with her doting husband in tow, awaiting two of the best detectives to arrive and question her."

Beau jumped to his feet. "What are we waiting for?"

Ten minutes later, they were pulling into the parking lot for the hospital's emergency room. Marcel flashed his badge to the ER check-in nurse, and within moments, they were in the cramped little examining room with the victim and her husband, who sat on the bed beside her. Beau dismissed the two uniformed officers to the hallway until they were done. No way was he going to let whoever had attacked Mrs. Amelia Schneider get another opportunity.

Marcel introduced them to the couple, then dove immediately into the interview. "Please, Mrs. Schneider, we know this is terribly upsetting, but our goal here is to catch the man who attacked you, so please, tell us what happened."

Beau pulled out his notebook and pen.

"I was watching the morning news while Wally took a shower." She laid a hand on her baby bump that had a belt monitor hooked up to a low-beeping machine. "Mornings are harder for me because of the morning sickness, so I can't start cooking breakfast too early or I get sick."

Her husband took her hand and patted it. "We've gotten into the habit of Amelia watching the news and having some water and a cracker or two while I take a shower. After that, we usually have enough time to have breakfast together before I head in to work."

"So you were watching the news?" Marcel prompted.

She nodded. "I caught movement from the corner of my left eye, and turned toward the front door, and all I could see was a figure in a dark, hooded sweatshirt wielding an axe. I screamed, but then I felt such a sharp pain on my head . . . and I don't remember anything else until Wally was pressing one of our kitchen towels on my head, rocking me in his arms, and telling me the ambulance would be there soon, to just hold on." Tears filled her eyes.

Her husband leaned over and kissed her, then turned back to them. "I wasn't sure what I heard at first. I thought it might be the television, but something told me to check on her. I threw on my jeans and went into the living room. I saw Amelia and called her name."

"Did you see anyone in your house besides your wife?" Beau asked. He normally wouldn't interrupt a witness's account, but he needed to get a mental image of what had happened in the order it happened.

Wally Schneider nodded. "I called out her name when I saw her on the floor with blood on her head. I thought she'd fallen, but then I saw a figure in all black wearing a hood run out the kitchen door. I hollered after him and would have given chase, but Amelia was down and bleeding and I had to help her. I called 911 and they told me to put a clean towel on the cut on her head. They stayed on the phone with me until the ambulance arrived."

"Are you sure the person was wearing a hood?" Marcel glanced at Beau and a thousand words passed between them silently.

"Positive. He was on the other side of the kitchen bar, so I couldn't see his legs so I have no idea what kind of pants or shoes he wore, but he was definitely wearing a black shirt with a hood. And the shirt wasn't tight. It was very loose."

"Almost like it could be an outer garment?" Beau asked carefully. He would never lead a witness, but the connection was so obvious. He just had to be sure.

Wally shook his head. "It wasn't tight like the hoodies everyone wears these days. It was almost flimsy, like maybe a windbreaker or something that was several sizes too big."

Like a robe.

Beau paused and stared at his partner. It was close enough for him. He gave a slight tilt of his head.

Marcel gave a quick nod back before turning to Wally again. "So, the guy ran out, then what happened?"

"Like I said, he ran out of the kitchen door, I called 911 and did what they told me to help Amelia. I grabbed a kitchen towel, and that's when I saw the axe lying on the floor by the kitchen door. That freaked me out because I saw that reporter on the news the other day, talking about the old Axeman serial killer. Is this another Axeman?"

"After you got the towel on your wife's head, then what?" Beau knew that distraction was the easiest way to avoid answering direct questions he didn't want to answer. Couldn't answer.

He was right. Wally continued his recollection. "The ambulance got there right after she came to. We got here, the doctor finished stitching her up, and then the police officers arrived. We're just waiting on our OB to get here." He patted the belt-thing wrapped around her stomach. "The nurse said once he looks over her stress test results and if everything is okay with junior, we'll get to head home."

Not without police stationed outside their door. "For your own protection, until the assailant is apprehended, we will have officers outside of your home."

"Why? Do you think he'll come back?" The fear was very evident in Amelia's voice. She clutched her husband's hand.

"No, but we want you to feel safe." Marcel had a very soothing and comforting tone at times like these. "This is mainly for your peace of mind."

"Oh. Okay."

The nurse entered and looked straight at

208

Marcel. "Her doctor just arrived. He'll need to examine her in just a moment."

"Of course." Beau pulled one of his business cards from his pocket and handed it to Wally. "If you remember anything else, just give us a call."

DIMITRI

"Got a second?" He hesitated at Adelaide's office door.

She looked up from her desk and smiled. "Sure. Come in." She started to stand.

"Don't get up." He crossed the space to sit in the chair in front of her desk. "I just wanted to update you on what I found out after our figuring out the skeleton is most likely my great-uncle Harold yesterday." He pulled out his folder with everything he'd acquired on the man, and opened it.

"Good. I was wondering if you discovered anything else."

He nodded. "I spoke with the archdiocese office for Orleans parish. After much conversation, and a long wait for a return call from this morning, I got an email with the information I wanted."

"Well, tell me." Adelaide laughed.

Dimitri smiled. "Well, you know how you commented on big events in his life happening on holidays?"

She nodded.

"It continues. He was born on Halloween in 1917 as we know, but he was turned over to St. Vincent's Infant Asylum for adoption on Halloween 1919."

"No way!"

He nodded. "I know. That's why I called the archdiocese office back this afternoon, just to confirm the dates."

She shook her head slowly as she leaned back in her chair. "This is unbelievable. I mean, I can't even fathom. It's unreal."

"I know, but they confirmed." He glanced back down at the open file sitting on the edge of her desk. "The reason he was left at St. Vincent's for adoption is because his parents died in the big flu epidemic."

Adelaide lifted her hands. "Sorry, don't know about that."

"I didn't either, at first. I did a little online searching and then I remembered learning about it. In the fall of 1918, an oil tanker arrived at the port in New Orleans. On it were like five or six men who were sick with Spanish influenza. Even though the state health board barred the ship from coming into port, some of the men were taken to Belvedere Hospital. And the epidemic started."

She nodded. "I remember learning something about that. There was like record-breaking numbers of deaths, right?"

"Yes. Estimates are in the 3,500 range. They'd

gotten it under control a bit in early 1919, but another round hit in the fall, and the death toll rose again. The country got hit hard, but Pittsburgh, Philadelphia, and New Orleans had the highest number of deaths."

"So Harold's parents both died from the flu?"

He nodded. "Sadly, that's why he was given over to St. Vincent's. Of course, the archdiocese office says that many children were left there if their only adult family members were sick, and many were later reclaimed once they were well."

"But not Harold?"

Dimitri shook his head. "Both of his parents died. Incidentally, they're buried in St. Louis Cemetery Number Three."

"So he was available for adoption then. He was, what?—two years old?"

"Exactly two."

"Why wasn't he adopted? I mean, it's not like he was an older child who are statistically harder to place."

"The lady I spoke with indicated they had many, many children taken in at St. Vincent's in 1918 and 1919 because of the influenza out-break. Many families had illnesses in their own homes. Some who weren't affected were leery of adopting a child whose parents had died from the flu, worried the child might contaminate them."

Compassion settled over Adelaide's delicate and beautiful features. "That's horrible."

"It is, but what could they do?" He shook his head and looked back at the file. "It was policy then that when the babies and toddlers turned seven, they were sent to asylums befitting each gender. In this case, Harold was transferred to St. Mary's for boys."

"That poor child."

Dimitri nodded. "I've put in calls to the Touro Infirmary, the hospital where, according to the archdiocese records, Harold's parents died."

"Why?"

"I just want to find out as much as I can about his family. What if he had family he could have gone to?"

"While heartbreaking, there's not much that can be done now, Dimitri."

He shrugged. "That's true, but I just want to know, for my own curiosity."

"I understand."

Dimitri sighed. "Anyway, Harold was transferred to St. Mary's in 1924, on no holiday." He smiled across the desk at Adelaide.

She grinned back. "Progress, I guess."

"Not exactly. Remember, he was adopted by the Pampalons on April 1, 1931."

"April Fool's Day."

He nodded. "At the ripe old age of fourteen or so."

Adelaide chewed her bottom lip. "Interesting that they would adopt a child so old, isn't it?"

"They needed an heir."

"What? Surely you're kidding."

Oh, how he wished he was. "According to my father, his grandparents—Louis and Eva, believed they were unable to have children and were aging. They realized they needed an heir to bestow the Darkwater Inn to, because heaven forbid the Pampalon name not be carried on." He shook his head, recalling his father's story. "Apparently Eva didn't want to adopt a baby. No newborn that wasn't her own flesh and blood, so they adopted an older child. Harold."

Dimitri had wrestled with this last night and this morning. "I'm not sure if they adopted him at fourteen because it would be easier to teach him, or if they could get free labor at the hotel out of him. I don't know. Either way, according to Father, they sent him to school and groomed him to take over the hotel."

Adelaide ran her top teeth over her bottom lip. "Yet seven years later he runs away? From this?" She gestured toward the building. "Why?"

"Louis and Eva Pampalon had given birth to my grandfather, Henri, in 1937, the year before Harold ran off." He considered Claude's attitude, and clearly that of Louis, who would adopt a teen boy to make sure the legacy of the Pampalon name continued. "Maybe he was made to feel that

Henri, a Pampalon by birth, would be the legal heir. It's possible he was made to feel inferior." Dimitri could so relate.

"Perhaps." Adelaide propped her elbows on her desk and rested her chin in her hands. "He was twenty-one years old when he disappeared. Don't you think that's a little old to run away?"

"He was a legal adult. Maybe that's what he was waiting for—to reach a legal age."

She dropped her hands to the desk and shook her head. "Back then, the legal age was eighteen, not twenty-one. It still bugs me about it being Christmas Day."

Dimitri grinned at her frustration. "Maybe he didn't like what he got as a Christmas present?"

She threw a paper clip at him, laughing.

"Hey. Sorry to interrupt." Beauregard strode into the office as if he had every right to do just that.

Adelaide's stayed firmly in place as she turned her attention to him. "Hey, Beau. Guess what? Never mind, you'll never guess, so I'll tell you. We figured out who the skeleton is."

"Really? Who?"

She nodded at Dimitri. "Tell him."

Dimitri shifted in his chair to look Beauregard in the face. "Harold Pampalon, my great-uncle."

The detective pulled out a piece of paper from the folder he carried. "Here's what he looked like." He turned the paper toward them and showed them a picture before setting it on the edge of Adelaide's desk.

Dimitri gasped. He flipped through his folder and pulled out the photograph of Harold Pampalon and an older man in front of the hotel, written on the back *Louis and Harold, Darkwater Inn, 1937*. He set it on the desk beside Beauregard's picture.

It was of the same man.

Adelaide stood and walked around to stand between Dimitri and Beauregard in front of the side-by-side pictures. "Oh, wow. They're nearly identical."

"This is the 3-D rendering from FACES?" Adelaide asked.

Beauregard nodded. "Chandler sent it over less than an hour ago."

"I'm amazed at the clear resemblance." Dimitri couldn't believe someone could reconstruct a face that *was* the person. The talent was awe-inspiring. "It's definitely Harold, born Harold James, died as Harold Pampalon."

"That means he didn't run away on Christmas Day." Adelaide nodded. "I knew nobody would run away from their family on the biggest holiday of the year."

Adelaide's heart was almost too kind.

"I guess that means the big question is, who killed him and why?" Beauregard pulled out his cell phone and took a snapshot of the two pictures together. "Now that we have a confirmed identity, we'll start backing up and going through Harold's past and see what we can find out."

"We can probably help you." Adelaide smiled up at Dimitri and put her hand on his. "Well, Dimitri can. He's been getting all the information on his great-uncle from the time of his birth until he went missing in 1938."

Her touch, while as gentle and familiar as before, felt . . . different somehow. Almost *too* familiar. Comfortable. It didn't seem to pull at his gut like her touch usually did. Odd. Must be all the talk of death and destruction.

Beauregard nodded at him. "I'd appreciate any information you could share. Would save us some time."

As he looked up at the detective and Adelaide's matching smiling faces, something inside of him knew they were meant to be together.

Dimitri wasn't quite sure if that devastated him, or if it was just a big disappointment.

14

ADDY

"Daddy, your coffee's ready." Addy set his cup beside the plate of fresh fruit she'd brought to his suite. "News is about to start."

Vincent shuffled from the bedroom into the parlor holding a hand towel. "Honey, can you make sure I dried the stitches good enough? I don't want the doctor to have any reason not to remove them tomorrow afternoon." He sat down in front of the plate and cup.

She took the towel and dabbed at the healing gash on the top of his head. It was the first time she'd seen his gash without a bandage. It looked . . . well, it was a thin cut, but . . . was it possible the guy in the black robe had hit her father over the head with an *axe?* She gasped.

"What?" Vincent twisted and grabbed the towel, looking up at her.

No sense getting him worked up. Not until she could talk to Beau about it. "It looks fine. I'm actually surprised at how fast it's scabbed over."

"Yeah, well it itches like the dickens." He reached for the coffee.

"That's good. It's an indication it's healing." She used the remote to unmute the television for the morning's newscast, then grabbed her own mug and sat at the table beside her father.

It had become their routine to have breakfast together with the news every morning since the fire. Although she had been having supper with her father at home every Thursday night, it had been really nice starting off the day with her dad.

Her father grabbed the remote and turned up the volume. "Here's that annoying reporter."

Addy struggled not to scowl as Allison Williams filled the screen. "Police won't confirm that the murder of Joey and Theresa Maggio on Monday morning is connected to the murder of Lance Bassemier Monday afternoon, but all three victims were found brutally murdered in their beds. A fourth attack occurred just yesterday morning. The police haven't released details, but this reporter can confirm it was a woman who survived the attack."

The newscast faded into commercial break.

"That woman is such an ambulance chaser. The families of those poor victims are probably in the final stages of planning their loved ones' funerals, and Allison Williams is giving out the mental image of people bloody in bed." She shook her head and pushed away her plate. The strawberries just didn't look too appetizing at the moment. "It's actually despicable. And then to announce one of the victims survived! Why, that's just telling her attacker that he didn't finish

218

the job. It puts her in such danger. Allison should be fired, or held accountable if that woman is attacked again." Beau was probably having a fit.

Vincent pressed the rewind button on the remote.

"Daddy, please tell me you don't want to hear this again."

"Shh. Just a minute." He pushed the play button.

". . . murder of Joey and Theresa Maggio on Monday morning is connected to the murder of Lance Bassemier Monday afternoon, but all three victims were found brutally murdered in their beds. A fourth attack occurred just yesterday morning. The police haven't released details, but this reporter can confirm it was a woman who survived the attack."

Vincent turned off the television and jumped up from his seat. He disappeared into the bedroom.

"Dad?" Addy stood. What was happening here?

He returned to the parlor with his new laptop. He sat down, pushing his plate away with the computer and opened the MacBook.

"Daddy, what's going on?"

"Just a second. Let me make sure I'm right."

She'd learned long ago that when her father was following a hunch or a plot twist or anything of the like, he wouldn't be rushed in explaining himself. Addy took a drink of her coffee and snuck a glance at the clock. She still had twenty or so minutes before she needed to be at work. Good thing she lived in the hotel, so she didn't have to worry about the weather or traffic.

"There. I'm right!" Vincent sat back in the armless chair of the dining table. He pointed to the laptop. "See for yourself." He grinned, clearly pleased with himself.

She moved around so she could see the monitor. A web page was loaded with names and dates from 1918. "Um, what am I looking at, Dad?"

"Those are the victims of the Axeman."

"O-kay." She shook her head. "I don't follow."

He sighed and turned the computer back to read. "First victims were Joseph and Catherine Maggio. Next was Louis Besumer." He nodded and grinned. "And Harriet Lowe, who survived the attack."

But she didn't understand. She shook her head. "You're going to have to explain it to me, Dad. I don't see the point."

"The first two people attacked on Monday morning were, according to our least favorite reporter, Joey and Theresa Maggio." He tapped the computer screen. "Joseph and Catherine were attacked in their bed and there was an axe left on the floor. The news said Joey and Theresa were found in bed. What do you want to bet there was an axe left on the floor there?"

"Come on, Dad. That's a reach, don't you think?"

"Louis Besumer and his lover, Harriet Lowe, were also attacked, but survived." Her father rubbed his chin. "Monday evening a Lance Bassemier was attacked in his home. Louis Besumer . . . Lance Bassemier. And a woman was attacked that same day." Vincent wagged a finger at Addy. "What do you want to bet her name is close to Harriet Lowe? And that both she and Lance were attacked with an axe that was left at the scene?"

She had to admit, it sure seemed more than a coincidence, but someone repeating the attacks of the Axeman? Now? Why? It was a hundred years since his attacks. There was no way Harold could have been the Axeman's victim. But why was the axe in the space with him? None of it made sense.

"There's a connection, honey, I feel it. I'm going to do some research so I can give it all to Beau. Can I email it to you when I'm done and have you print it out for me?"

"Sure, Daddy." She stood and carried her plate and mug into the little sink area, thankful for housekeeping. She needed to get to the office. "I've got to go. Call me if you need anything or if you leave." She gave him a quick peck on the cheek.

"Yeah. Okay. Have a good day, honey." But Vincent was already opening a new Word document.

"I'm serious, Daddy. If you plan to go anywhere, let me know. Don't forget what Beau said."

He stopped typing to look up at her. "I heard you and I will. I haven't forgotten. I could say the same to you, too."

"Deal. If I leave the hotel, I'll let you know." She smiled and gave him another kiss. "Love you, Daddy."

"Love you, too, Addybear. Have a good day."

She headed out of the suite, the reassuring tapping of his fingers on the keys making her smile as she made her way to the elevator.

"Hello, Ms. Fountaine," Richard, the elevator attendant, said as he held the door for her. "Lobby?"

"Yes, please." She smiled and pulled out her cell phone as she exited and headed to her office. As she unlocked her door, she dialed Beau's cell phone.

"Hello, Addy." He answered on the first ring.

She flipped on the lights and made her way to her desk. "Hey, Beau. Listen, I know you're busy, I saw the news this morning."

He sighed long and loud. "I swear, that woman needs a gag."

"Oh, I agree. Anyway, today was the first day I really got to look at my dad's head injury without the bandage." She felt a little silly continuing.

"Is it okay? Is he all right?"

"He's fine, ornery as ever." She booted up her computer.

Beau chuckled. "That's Vincent."

"Yeah. Anyway, as I looked at the gash, it kind of looked about the length and size of the niche in Harold's skeleton we found." Funny how she already had switched to referring to him by name now.

"Yeah?"

"I'm just wondering if it's possible that my dad was hit with an axe." She tapped her fingers on her desk. "I mean, I know if an axe was left, it most likely burned up in the fire, so we really can't say, but the wound looks like—"

"Yes."

She stilled and grabbed a paper clip from her desk and absentmindedly began straightening it. "What?"

Beau sighed. "Yes, it very well could have been made by an axe."

She paused. He'd sure answered quickly, and with confidence. "You already thought of that, didn't you?"

"We needed to get an idea from the doctor for our report. As he was giving us details of the injury, Marcel asked and the doctor confirmed that an axe or hatchet would be consistent with the gash he'd sustained."

"And you didn't tell us?" She bent the now-straight paper clip until it snapped.

He inhaled slowly, making an almost hissing sound. "We can't prove or disprove what caused it because of the fire. I can't just make assumptions, Addy."

"But you could have told us it was possible."

She thought about what her dad had been so excited about. "Beau, was an axe found at the scenes of the attack on Joey and Theresa Maggio and Lance Bassemier?" She threw the two pieces of the paper clip into the trash can under her desk.

He hesitated. "I can't give out such information about an open investigation."

Which likely meant yes. "The woman who was attacked and survived . . . was her name anything close to like Harriet Lowe?"

"Again, I can't discuss an ongoing investigation, Addy. Why all these specific questions?"

"Dad has a theory that the attacks are someone repeating the attacks of the Axeman from 1918."

"A copycat killer?"

"Dad said this morning that the names of your victims are way too similar to that of the Axeman's victims, and in the same order."

"Interesting."

"Yeah. He said he was going to do some research today and email it to me to print out so he could give it to you."

"I'll look forward to it."

"So you don't think he's off on a tangent?" She reached for another paper clip. Her heartbeat quickened. Surely her father's theory had to be wrong. Someone wasn't running around New Orleans, replicating murders from a serial killer.

Beau didn't respond.

"Beau?"

"I can't discount anything at this point, Addy." The enormity of his words were weighted down with the heaviness of his tone. "Not when it comes to these cases."

Oh, no. Then it was possible someone was repeating the Axeman murders. She'd have to read her father's research, just to be prepared.

"I wish I could tell you more, Addy, I do, but I can't. The captain is already on the warpath because of Allison Williams's reports. He's out for blood until we can find whoever is giving that woman information."

"I understand." She did, but that didn't mean she wasn't scared.

Her other line beeped. She glanced at the display. "Hey, Tracey's calling."

"I'll call you later, okay?"

"Okay, bye." She switched over to Tracey. "Hey, girl, what's up?"

"Geoff asked me to go to an art show at your hotel on Friday night."

"That's great." She'd forgotten about the show Dimitri was throwing for one of Zoey's artists. "It's a date-date, right?"

Tracey laughed. "Of course it's a date-date,

girl. So, what kind of artist? I need to plan what I'm going to wear and that depends on the type of artist."

Addy shook her head and tossed the straightened paper clip onto her desk. "I honestly don't know. Dimitri set it up for Zoey and that's about all I know at this point." She grabbed a scrap of paper and jotted a note to be sure and let the guests know the restaurant would be closed tomorrow night.

"Well, then ask Dimitri, will you?"

Addy grinned. She wanted to know more about the artist anyway. "Sure. I'll ask him this morning and call you back."

"Thanks, love. Appreciate you. Gotta run." The line went dead.

Shaking her head, Addy stood and slipped her cell into her pocket. Typical Trace. She was actually a little envious of her best friend. Tracey appreciated that life was but a fleeting moment, and tried to enjoy every moment she'd been given. Her love of life drew people to her like a magnet.

She grabbed her note and headed toward her assistant's office. Might as well get this workday started.

Erika, one of the front desk managers, met her in the hall with a large box wrapped in flowered paper with a big, yellow bow on top. "Ms. Fountaine, this just arrived for you."

"Wow, that's something." Addy moved to take the box from her.

"I can set it inside for you, Ms. Fountaine. It's heavier than you'd expect."

Addy opened the door to her office. "Thank you for bringing this."

Erika set the box on the little table in the settee area to the left of Addy's desk. "It's not your birthday, is it?"

Addy shook her head as she looked over the beautifully wrapped package. "There's not a card."

Erika helped her look. "I guess they wanted to be anonymous."

Visions of the jar of pig's blood danced before her eyes. "Do you know who delivered it?" Addy didn't recognize the wrapping paper. She reached for the bow and looked because some of the local stores put their sticker on the bow.

No sticker on this one.

"I don't know, Ms. Fountaine. We were busy, just Misty and I working the counter, and I didn't get a good look at the delivery guy. He was just a guy with a box and said it was for Adelaide Fountaine. I didn't even think to ask him where he was from. Is something wrong?"

"No. It's fine. I would just like to know who to thank is all." Addy forced a smile. "Thank you for bringing it back."

"Yes, ma'am. I'll ask Misty if she recognized

the guy or anything and let you know if she did."

"Thanks." Addy waited until Erika had left, then stared at the box.

It was beautiful, certainly, but without a business marking or a card . . .

Addy shook her head. It was probably just an oversight. The card probably fell off in the delivery person's van.

Carefully, she slid the bow from the box. No explosion, no blood seeped out. She shook her head. She was just being silly. Addy pulled the lid off and pushed away the plain, white tissue paper to reveal a flower-shaped wooden box.

She gently removed it from its careful packaging and set it on the settee table. It *was* heavy, probably real wood, but was only about six inches by six inches. Now she wondered if she should have called Beau before she opened the box. If there was something in there, she'd contaminated any evidence.

But . . . curiosity pushed her to open the smooth and shiny lid.

An upbeat ragtime tune filled the air as she looked at the empty interior, eloquently lined with black satin. She shut the lid, letting silence pervade her office again, and turned the music box over. No marking of creation or anything for that matter, just the metal key to wind up the music box.

She opened the lid again. The tune was jazzy,

typical for old New Orleans, not the modern-day zydeco tunes. Addy preferred the old jazz, but had to admit, she didn't recognize this particular tune. She grabbed her cell from her pocket and opened the music-identifying app. It came back with an old jazz tune.

That didn't seem quite right. She accessed a different tune recognizing app and tried again. The result was a different performer of old jazz.

She went back to the first app and tried again. A third, different composition was the result.

Addy chuckled. Probably too old for identification, as some of the true jazz tunes were, so the apps just pulled something close.

She shut the lid. It still didn't answer who it was from. Who would send her such an odd—yet kind of nice—gift?

It was probably from Dimitri. He liked to send her gifts, and this was quite a display. She should thank him for it. She needed to ask about the art show tomorrow anyway. For Tracey.

Yet she didn't want it to be from him. Well, she did, because that would mean she was right and there was no reason to be alarmed. But she didn't, because he'd been acting strangely lately, which was understandable, considering everything.

More importantly, she'd started feeling differently toward him recently. Like the butterflies in her stomach whenever he was near her weren't active anymore. She still found him handsome and kind and wonderful, but . . . it was as if any romantic feelings she'd felt for him had gone away. Vanished. When she thought of what made her heart beat faster, all she could think about was Beau.

She sucked in air and put her hand over her mouth. Had she really just thought that? Did this mean what she suspected it did?

Addy let out a slow breath. She needed to talk to Dimitri. As hard as this would be, honesty won with her every time.

Even if it meant hurting people she cared about. And maybe, just maybe, hurting herself as well.

1936

Will rose from the altar. Why was God continuing to be so silent to his prayers? He needed guidance and needed it now.

One of his followers had told him last night that the building they'd been squatting in for the last month or so had been sold and the new owners would be taking possession of the place by the end of the week. Will had to act fast.

Winter had befallen New Orleans and the wind cut through them all. Will needed to find a new place for *Cretum Deus*, which now had almost eighty believing males. About twenty women had been accepted by Will to care for these men's needs.

All of the followers would look to Will for provision of shelter. If he didn't provide . . . well, he had to find a way.

"Will, I need to ask your permission for something." James stood in the doorway of their makeshift altar room.

He turned and moved to his chair. "What is it?" He couldn't take another problem at the moment.

"It's about the young woman I told you about last month, Etta. She's a widow and had been a friend of one of the girls who came to live with us not too long ago."

A woman. With all the complicated decisions he had to make, James comes to him with an issue about a woman. He sighed. "What about her, James?"

"Well, you see, I think I've fallen in love with her and want to marry her."

What? Will narrowed his eyes as he stared at his friend. "We don't marry in *Cretum Deus*. You know that."

"I know, but I love her."

"Love? What do you know of love, James?" This was absurd.

"I love God."

"That's a holy love. A reverent love. They don't compare." What was this nonsense?

"I love you. I love George."

Such a wimp. "We are like your brothers, James. We grew up together, and we're bonded by our belief in God and following Him through *Cretum Deus*. We are true believers, so of course we love one another."

"I want to marry her, Will."

For the first time—no, the only time—James was going to have to stand his ground. Over a woman?

James must have recognized the simmering fury rising in Will, for he began to prattle on. "She's a widow, Will, and she has a big house. If I marry her, I'll have ownership of the house, and of course, I'd make sure to sign that over to you for *Cretum Deus*. We could live there. It's huge, at least a dozen bedrooms. We could have a permanent home, Will. Just think about that. And if I marry her, we'd have children. These children would be raised in *Cretum Deus'* ways. True believers. A legacy to ensure our ways would go on through the generations. To make sure there were always true followers of God to do His will. His works."

Will held up his hands to silence James's ramblings. While the thought of marriage was beneath him, he couldn't help but wonder if this was God's answer to his prayers for shelter for the group. Dare he turn his back on such an opportunity if it was the method of God's provisions?

He closed his eyes and kneeled. God didn't respond, but Will kept his prone position as he considered the notion. The home was a definite plus. If she was a wealthy widow, then he, through James, would control all her assets, which would mean they could branch out further.

Children. He'd allowed the men to have relations with the women brought into the group. They had desires and if certain needs were met, the members were much more malleable to do Will's bidding. But the women were under strict instructions to ensure no children would result from those relations. If they were to allow such, the women would be gotten rid of. Will had made sure they all knew this before they were accepted into the group's folds, not into the group itself. Women weren't worthy of that.

However, James did have a point, surprisingly. He did need to think about the future of the group. He had been assured by God that he would lead the *Cretum Deus* for many decades, but he did need to think about what would happen after that. He was only eighteen, but a man had to plan. He had to raise sons, and rear them correctly. And they had to be legitimate children. True children of *Cretum Deus*.

Will opened his eyes and stood. He motioned for James to come to him.

"Did God answer you?" James almost whispered.

Will nodded. "You have permission to marry this Etta that you love."

James's smile lit up his whole face.

"But with a condition."

The smile froze on James's face. "What's that?"

"You may not consummate your marriage until Etta bears me, as leader of *Cretum Deus*, a son."

15

BEAU

"We have another murder. One Jacob Roman found dead this morning by his wife. Want to guess what the murder weapon was?"

Beau sighed and shook his head. "An axe?"

Marcel nodded. "Gibbons and Witz got the case." He tossed the report across the desks. It landed on the space between them. "This is starting to get all too familiar."

Beau flipped through the pages of the report. "Someone is going through a whole lot of trouble to lead us in the direction of the Axeman with the use of those axes."

"Yeah, and it's frustrating that the axes are the victims', so we can't even trace someone who bought so many." Marcel grabbed his water bottle and twisted off the cap. He gulped down half of it.

Beau tossed the report back to his partner. Nothing outstanding had been noted. No prints, no forensic evidence determined yet, no eyewitness accounts . . . nothing that could lead any of the three teams of detectives to a suspect. There was nothing to go on, and it was beyond frustrating. "Why do all these people have axes?

I mean, I have a house, and I don't have an axe."

Marcel tilted his water bottle towards his partner. "And how does the killer know they have axes?"

"That's a good question." Beau thought about what Addy had mentioned about Vincent's theory. "Let me look at something." He opened his web browser and ran a search for victims of the Axeman. As he read, he found himself nodding. Addy's dad might have hit on something. "Listen to this, the original victims of the Axeman were, in order of attack, Joseph and Catherine Maggio, Louis Besumer and Harriet Lowe, Anna Schneider, Joseph Romano, Charles and Rosie and Mary Cortimiglia—Mary was only two years old, by the way—Steve Boca, Sarah Laumann, and the last victim, Mike Pepitone."

"He killed a two-year-old child?"

Beau nodded as he opened his notebook. "Now here are the names of the people who've been attacked with an axe over the last week: Joey and Theresa Maggio, Lance Bassemier, Amelia Schneider, and now Jacob Roman." He glanced over the desk to Marcel. "Sound familiar?"

Marcel nodded. "That's slick, man."

"I can't take credit. Vincent Fountaine figured out the connection." Oh, boy, he'd love that he'd been right.

"Maggio and Maggio. Besumer and Bassemier. Schneider and Schneider. Romano and Roman."

Marcel leaned back in his chair. "Are you saying the next victims will be a family involving a child with a name similar in some way to Cortimiglia?"

"Maybe. Probably." He stared at the list again. "Why isn't there one for Harriet Lowe?"

"What?"

Beau tapped his pen against his notebook. "There's a match, similar last name and matching gender, in order, for four of the five original Axeman attacks with the ones from the past week. Yet, there isn't one for Harriet Lowe. Why not?"

"I don't know, but we should probably figure out who she was." Marcel sat up and tapped on his keyboard.

Beau ran a search on her—too many results. He amended his search to *Harriet Lowe Axeman New Orleans*. He bypassed the find-a-grave pages because they probably didn't have much useful information. He clicked on one page and read the details of her attack aloud:

"On June 27, 1918, Louis Besumer and Harriet Lowe were attacked while sleeping in the home owned by Besumer, located on corner of Dorgenois and Laharpe Streets. Mr. Besumer was hit in the head with an axe, which resulted in a skull fracture, while Ms. Lowe was hit just above her left ear. A Mr. Zanca, driver of a bakery wagon who was coming to make his daily routine delivery, knocked on the home's door. Mr. Besumer opened the door for Zanca, who quickly summoned help from police and paramedics even though Mr. Besumer didn't want them because they would find out about his mistress. Mr. Besumer recovered but Harriet Lowe died at the hospital after surgery to repair her face. Ms. Lowe had given statements that were not accounted for because of her delusional state following the attack."

Marcel jumped in. "I can't even find a date of birth for her. Her death is recorded on August 5, 1918 at Charity Hospital."

"Very odd." He smiled across the desks at his partner. "Maybe our records department can get some more details. If you emailed the request to a certain lady friend of yours, we might actually get a rush response."

"Yeah, yeah, yeah." But Marcel's fingers flew over the keyboard. "Okay, it's sent."

Beau kept checking the other pages. "The reports of what happened to her are pretty much all the same on all the sites. It's kind of sad."

"Well, yeah, anybody getting conked on the head with an axe and dying is sad, Beau."

He rolled his eyes at his partner. "No, that she was attacked at her lover's house, who didn't even want to call an ambulance or the police because he didn't want everyone to know he was cheating on his wife. And then to survive the attack but die later from the surgery to fix the damage the Axeman did? That's sad."

"Yeah, it is sad. I wonder if she was married. Nothing in the report stated it."

Beau leaned back in his chair and laced his fingers together behind his head. "I've got a gut feeling that it's important that a replicate of her attack was omitted."

"How?"

He shrugged. "I don't know, but I just have that feeling." He dropped his arms and sat up. "Addy finally asked the question of if it was possible her dad was hit with an axe before his house was set on fire."

Marcel crossed his arms over his chest. "What did you tell her?"

"The truth. That it's possible, but with the fire destroying physical evidence, we can't assume either way."

"I think it was. I think that was the copycat's first attack."

"Why?" Beau knew they'd already discussed this before, but it never hurt to walk through the case again. Maybe they'd missed something.

"The only thing that sets Vincent Fountaine out from anybody else is that he's a famous writer and he was at the hotel the day the news of the skeleton was reported."

Beau nodded. "Vincent said he had research

239

on the Axeman at his house. The next day, he's attacked and his house is burned down."

"His head wound could have easily been made by an axe. His description matches what the guys were wearing who threw blood at Addy."

Marcel straightened in his seat. "You know, I've been thinking about that. Who do you know who wears black hooded robes and masks?"

"Uh, kids during Halloween."

Marcel chuckled. "Yeah, but it's not October."

"Okay, where are you going?"

"Cults."

Beau rolled his eyes again. "Most of the cults here don't wear masks. Fangs to pretend they're vampires, yes, but masks? Usually not."

"Some do though, right?" Marcel typed on his keyboard. "You said the masks looked like a pig and a sheep?"

"Yeah. Creepy." But it wasn't the actual masks that were creepy. It was more the feeling just the figures filled Beau with. An ominous, dark feeling that sank in the pit of his stomach. That was the only way he could describe it, even though he knew it didn't make a lot of sense.

"Well, it seems the pig and the sheep are prominent figures in some religious cults." Marcel scrolled down a webpage and read aloud. "Celtic lore views pigs as symbols of abundance. Many Native American tribes associated the pig as a symbolic link to abundance, fertility and agriculture. Even in early Christianity, pigs were often symbols of wealth."

"Yet they hid behind a mask?"

"Now, the sheep is traditionally a symbol of sacrifice, and also of purity and innocence. In early Christian groups, and still in many cults today, sheep are symbols of renewal, victory of life over death, and innocence. Even in the Bible, sheep are considered the perfect victim which should be sacrificed to God."

Beau ran a finger along his upper lip. "That's true. Abraham was told to sacrifice his only son, but God provided a sheep to sacrifice instead."

"Let me check something." He typed, then clicked. "Okay, in our database, there are several cults here in the greater New Orleans area that use an animal as a symbol." He looked up. "There are only three that use either the pig or sheep versus the other twenty-something who have bats and rats or goats or whatever as symbols."

Beau shook his head. "Why does everybody think that New Orleans is filled with vampires? I get that we have a strong history of witchlore and voodoo and hoodoo, but when did we become the vamp capital?"

"Too many movies and television series set here that depict the fanged ones."

"And all romanticized to stir up the young people." Beau shook his head. Every year, the death rate rose of people who were killed by crazy teens and young adults who thought they were in some cool vampire family. It was a sad reflection on the city that Beau loved so much.

"But, I'm not seeing any connection between these three religious cults to the Axeman or Harriet Lowe, or even the Darkwater Inn." Marcel leaned back in his chair. "Every time we think we might have a new direction to go, we get shut down."

"Captain isn't going to be happy that he has three sets of detectives working on cases that are connected, and we can't get one decent lead."

Marcel pointed at Beau. "You're the senior detective out of all six of us."

"Gee, thanks for that." He moved to his browser and typed in "Axeman New Orleans" and searched. "Okay, maybe we need to know more about the original Axeman so we can figure out why someone's copycatting his attacks." He accessed the old database of the New Orleans newspaper. "Maybe the reporters then were just as determined as Allison Williams and had some stories about the serial killer."

"Just got an email back on Harriet Lowe. Her date of birth was September 10, 1889. She was born to a single woman who was recorded as being a widow. Initial review is that she was an only child."

Beau glanced at his partner. "That's it?"

"My girl is doing more digging, but she wanted us to at least have that," Marcel said.

"To let you know she was giving you preferential treatment, huh?"

Marcel just grinned.

Beau shook his head and went back to his newspaper archives. "Hey, the Axeman actually wrote a letter to the New Orleans paper."

"Really?"

"Yeah, it was published in the paper on March 13, 1919. Check it out."

Marcel got up to look at the screen.

Hell, March 13, 1919

Esteemed Mortals of New Orleans:

They have never caught me and they never will. They have never seen me, for I am invisible, even as the ether that surrounds your earth. I am not a human being, but a spirit and a demon from the hottest hell. I am what you Orleanians and your foolish police call the Axeman.

When I see fit, I shall come and claim other victims. I alone know whom they shall be. I shall leave no clue except my bloody axe, besmeared with blood and brains of he whom I have sent below to keep me company.

If you wish you may tell the police to be careful not to rile me. Of course, I am a reasonable spirit. I take no offense at the way they have conducted their investigations in the past. In fact, they have been so utterly stupid as to not only amuse me, but His Satanic Majesty, Francis Josef, etc. But tell them to beware. Let them not try to discover what I am, for it were better that they were never born than to incur the wrath of the Axeman. I don't think there is any need of such a warning, for I feel sure the police will always dodge me, as they have in the past. They are wise and know how to keep away from all harm.

Undoubtedly, you Orleanians think of me as a most horrible murderer, which I am, but I could be much worse if I wanted to. If I wished, I could pay a visit to your city every night. At will I could slay thousands of your best citizens (and the worst), for I am in close relationship with the Angel of Death.

Now, to be exact, at 12:15 (earthly time) on next Tuesday night, I am going to pass over New Orleans. In my infinite mercy, I am going to make a little proposition to you people. Here it is:

I am very fond of jazz music, and I swear by all the devils in the nether regions that every person shall be spared in whose home a jazz band is in full swing at the time I have just mentioned. If everyone has a jazz band going, well, then, so much the better for you people. One thing is certain and that is that some of your people who do not jazz it on Tuesday night (if there be any) will get the axe.

Well, as I am cold and crave the warmth of my native Tartarus, and it is about time I leave your earthly home, I will cease my discourse. Hoping that thou wilt publish this, that it may go well with thee, I have been, am and will be the worst spirit that ever existed either in fact or realm of fancy.

The Axeman

Marcel slowly shook his head. "That man was crazy."

"Right?" Beau printed the page for the file. "This is unbelievable. I can't believe they never caught someone so arrogant." He clicked to the next page.

"Most criminals who are that brazen almost want to get caught."

"There's more craziness. According to this report, after the first murders—Joseph and Catherine Maggio, a mysterious chalk message was found a block away from the scene of the crime, the Maggio's home on the corner of Upperline and Magnolia Streets. It was written in a childlike handwriting, and read: "Mrs. Maggio will sit up tonight just like Mrs. Toney." No one knows what it meant or who left it there, but most suspect it was the Axeman himself."

"This whole thing is so bizarre. I mean, really."

The hairs on the back of Beau's neck stood at attention as he continued reading from website reports. "It was reported that a bloody axe was left behind in several of the victims' yards. After word of this hit the media, several other people came forward to say that similar axes had been left in their yards as well. The questions were was the Axeman targeting those others? Had he begun to break into their homes, but stopped for some reason? Or was he trying to strike fear into residents of New Orleans?"

"You know, we haven't let it slip out about the axes yet. I wonder if there are any that have been found in someone's yard. If they were reported, no one would have thought to alert any of us homicide detectives because they wouldn't know of any connection." Marcel pinched the bridge of his nose.

"Or they weren't even reported because they don't think it matters. I mean, think about it, if you found a tool in your backyard, you'd probably just stick it in your toolshed or ask your neighbor about it, if you remembered the next time y'all cooked out."

Marcel nodded. "You're right. There's no way for us to know unless we go public with the information."

"But we don't want to do that because it could cause mass hysteria. Allison Williams already has people in a frenzy. Imagine how everyone will react if we tell them someone's out there, duplicating the Axeman attacks."

Marcel's cool demeanor slipped.

"What?"

"What was the date of that letter the Axeman wrote to the paper? March thirteenth?"

Beau checked his notes. "Yeah, that's right. He said anybody playing jazz at that day and time would be spared. Why?"

"Hang with me here . . . he said he'd be coming through New Orleans when?"

Again, Beau checked his notes. "At precisely twelve fifteen the next Tuesday night."

Marcel typed on his computer. "Okay, back in 1919, March thirteenth fell on a Thursday, which would put the following Tuesday as the eighteenth of March."

"I follow you so far. What's the connection?" He might not know where his partner was going, but every muscle in Beau's shoulders and neck had bunched into tight wads.

Marcel let out a long, slow breath. "It stands to

reason that if someone *is* replicating everything of the Axeman, the method and similar victim names, I would think that date, March eighteenth, would be important since it meant something, obviously, to the original Axeman. Right?"

Beau nodded. That all made sense.

Marcel locked stares with his partner. "Beau, today is March fourteenth. The eighteenth of March is Monday."

16

DIMITRI

"I'm sorry I had to bring Sam, but his babysitter has a stomach bug." Zoey set the toddler on the floor of Dimitri's small kitchen office and put a diaper bag filled with toys in front of him. "I had to call in to work, but I knew you needed to finalize everything for Solomon's show tomorrow." She straightened.

"It's okay. Mister Sam is a fan favorite." He smiled down at the little boy pulling toy cars and board books out of the bag. He loved children, he did, but he really had no desire anymore to have one. The relationship with his father was the main reason, but as he'd looked back through earlier generations, he could clearly see that the pressure to be perfect and have a legacy . . . to live up to some sort of expectation of a family name . . . he couldn't imagine putting that kind of stress on a child. Not when he'd lived under that himself all his life.

Dimitri would like to think he'd be different, but what if his father had thought the same thing at one time? Or his grandfather? Great-grandfather? What if all the Pampalon men hadn't planned to be so demanding but had changed as they got older or when they had their children? Could Dimitri take such a chance?

"Thanks. I just want this show to be perfect. It's really important for Solomon's career. We might not get another chance to have a show. His father is so overbearing. I think I told you that before. Anyway, he agreed to the show, but lately, Solomon says he's been acting like he'll change his mind. His brothers are all fighting over who should be in charge since his father's so old."

"In charge? Like of the family business?" Dimitri smiled as Sam ran a toy car over the floor.

Zoey shrugged. "Kind of, I guess. Their dad is a religious freak, and I'm not knocking faith, you understand. He just has some very strange ideas that he's pushed into the family."

"Like what?" He wished he would've done that research on the young artist that he'd intended. Time just got away from him.

"Well, I think Solomon said he has like over a dozen older brothers, but when I asked him about any sisters, he said his father didn't keep track of his daughters." She bent to sit Sam down again since he'd started to toddle around. "I've met his brother Isaiah, who seemed normal enough, but has to escort Solomon around when he comes to the gallery. Like a chaperone, even though Solomon is thirty years old."

"That is weird." Not just weird in an odd way, but in an almost creepy way. Who didn't even keep track of their daughters?

She nodded. "Solomon and Isaiah both come across as extremely intimidated by their father. Like excessively so." She grabbed Sam just before he tossed one of his books into the trash can.

"Where do they live?" Dimitri reached out and touched the softness of the boy's cheek. Sam giggled.

"They all live in that big old house in the warehouse district."

"The whole family lives together?" Dimitri had barely been able to live with his father. He couldn't imagine living with over a dozen other men. "All his brothers? And I'm assuming women who may or may not be his sisters?"

She nodded. "I know. It's so weird. Solomon's dad is a hundred and one, seriously, he's really one hundred and one years old. Solomon's brothers range in ages from like seventy-nine or eighty down to Solomon, who's the youngest. They all live there and there are women there, because I've heard Solomon mention their names."

"What do they all do? For a living, I mean." Dimitri bent and handed another car to Sam, who took it and plopped to sitting and rolled the car over his legs. He laughed again. "They have to have some way of supporting themselves. Even living together to cut costs, they still have monthly expenses."

"They don't really have jobs, at least not from what Solomon says. He said there are a lot of other men in the group who work and donate to the group. I guess it's like a religious donation because they're kind of like a church group."

"Zoey, that doesn't sound like any church group . . . that sounds like a cult." Now Dimitri really wished he'd done research. He would take care of that today, before tomorrow's showing, to see what Zoey had gotten herself into.

"Come on." She grinned and gave his arm a gentle shove. "Cults are the people running around with upside down crosses tattooed on their faces and shouting that their leader is the new messiah."

Dimitri handed Sam the board book that had slipped out of the toddler's grasp. "You said that Solomon and his brothers, and obviously the other people in the group, are intimidated by his father. They give their money to the group. Sounds like they just might consider his father a messiah. Or his father might tell people he is. Or merely imply it."

She shook her head. "No. I mean, cult people are all crazy. They stockpile guns and ammunition and stuff. Solomon says he's never even seen a gun."

"Not all cults are survivalists, Zoey, or believe in stockpiling arms."

"I just can't believe Solomon would join a cult of any kind. He's not like that. He's kind and gentle and sweet."

"If he was born into the cult, he wouldn't have joined, and he wouldn't necessarily think of it as a cult of any kind. It would've been all he'd ever known." Dimitri set on the edge of the little desk and allowed Sam to pull himself up using Dimitri's pant legs. "And he can be kind and gentle and sweet—most cult members who are just the followers are." Solomon's father would most likely be the leader of the cult or one of his older sons.

Zoey shook her head. "I just can't believe that."

"Think about it for just a minute. They're exclusive. A large group of them live together. The actual family itself really doesn't work, depending instead on *donations* from the other members. The father figure is domineering and intimidating. He can *allow* or *deny* someone permission to go and do something, like have an art show. They're very religious, although keeping that religion pretty much to themselves. Come on, Zoey. You're smart. Look at it logically."

Tears pooled in her eyes. "Oh, Dimitri, can that be true?"

"It's okay. You're okay. I could be wrong."

But he knew he wasn't. Deep down, he knew Zoey could be in danger. "But maybe you should have a hard conversation with Solomon. Maybe tomorrow night after the show." So he could be there . . . just in case.

"What if he denies it? Or worse, what if he doesn't see it either? Like I didn't."

"Well, then, you just ask him to explain the oddities. That is, if he's important to you."

Zoey nodded. "He is. He's the first man who has treated me like a lady, even after he found out I had a son and what I used to be." She ducked her head and licked her lips. "He makes me smile. Makes me feel special." Tears pooled again. "What if he did it on purpose just to further his career to get out from under his father's—family's thumb?"

Dimitri hugged her tight. "Shh." He patted her back until her sniffles subsided, then let her go. He grabbed a napkin from the desk and wiped under her eyes. "I don't think any man would do that, Zoey, but if he did, well, that part has nothing to do with his family being a cult. That's just a sorry excuse for a man right there."

"Mamamamama." Sam reached for the bag with his toys, but couldn't reach it.

She grinned and bent down and gave Sam a kiss, then set him on the floor and slid the bag in front of him again.

"I think you should talk to Solomon. It's

obvious you truly care about him. If there's a chance he feels the same about you, then you owe it to your future happiness to broach the subject." And if she did that after the show tomorrow night, he'd be around to make sure things stayed on an even keel.

"I guess."

"At least you would know where you stand." It wasn't like Zoey to be so unassertive. He'd seen her stand toe-to-toe with some of the shrewdest businessmen in New Orleans and not be the least bit fazed.

"While Solomon hasn't come right out and said it, I think part of the reason he hasn't taken me to meet his father is because I have Sam." She put the toddler back down by the bag and handed him a plastic car. "Or maybe he doesn't want to have to explain my past."

Dimitri put a hand on her shoulder. "Hey, we all have pasts. You're a good mom and you take care of your son and are raising him with all the love you have. You take him to church and are raising him in faith, so you're doing an amazing job."

She smiled.

"Oh. Hi, Zoey." Addy stood in the doorway, her gaze falling on Dimitri's hand on Zoey's shoulder. Then her gaze fell to Sam who toddled toward her, flashing his few teeth. Addy squatted in front of him.

ADDY

"Hi, handsome. What's your name?" Zoey's little boy was a doll, opening his arms to Addy. She pulled him to her and stood.

Zoey smiled. "That little booger is Sam, who was supposed to play quietly so I could go over tomorrow's show with Dimitri." She ran a hand over Sam's golden hair. "His babysitter had a stomach bug, so he's with me today."

Addy grinned as Sam played with her necklace. "Well, why don't you and Dimitri do what you need to, and I'll play with Sam?"

Zoey's eyes widened. "I couldn't ask you to do that."

Addy smiled wider as the cute little toddler snuggled her neck. "It'd be more for me than you. I could use some sweet innocence time."

"Well . . . if you don't mind?" Zoey glanced at Dimitri.

He nodded. "It shouldn't take us long to go over the menu and a few other items. We'll be right in the kitchen."

Still holding Sam, Addy moved to sit behind Dimitri's desk. "We'll be fine."

"Thank you." Zoey planted a kiss on the top of Sam's head, then followed Dimitri out of the little office.

Sam didn't even fuss as his mother left. He clapped as he held Addy's necklace.

"Oh, you are a sweet boy, aren't you?" Addy couldn't help but kiss his sweet, chubby cheeks. She inhaled. He smelled like baby lotion and sunshine.

Something in her ached. She hugged Sam and closed her eyes. She could imagine herself in a few years with a child of her own. Sitting at her father's house, having dinner, Vincent and Beau smiling . . .

Addy bolted her eyes open wide. *Beau*. That's who she saw herself with whenever she thought of her future . . . a family.

As she sat Sam gently to the floor and grabbed one of his books to read to him, she knew in her heart what it all meant. And knew what she had to do.

Today. Now.

Oh, this was going to be hard. One of the hardest things she'd ever done. She breathed in deeply, as if she could calm her pounding heart just by willing it to slow down.

As she took a moment to smile at Sam as he played, Addy realized her heart had been leading her to this for some time now. She cared for Dimitri, and always would, but her heart? Her heart had a lifetime connection with Beau.

Twenty minutes, a half dozen silent prayers for wisdom, and five books read later, Zoey and Dimitri returned to the little kitchen office.

"I'm so sorry we took a little longer." Zoey

began stuffing books and toys into a diaper bag.

Addy stood and hugged Sam. "It was no bother, really. I enjoyed being with him." She handed him to Zoey. "He's the most precious thing."

Zoey smiled as she took Sam and slipped the diaper bag strap over her shoulder. "Thank you." She turned to nod at Dimitri. "I'll see you tomorrow."

"Let me know if your sitter is still sick. I'd be happy to watch him for you." Addy smiled, meaning what she said.

"I will. Thanks." Zoey and Sam left.

Dimitri moved to sit behind his desk. "That boy's a cutie."

She shut the door, then sat in the chair before his desk. "He is that."

Dimitri's eyes went to the closed door, then back to Addy's face.

Panic filled her like rising floodwater. She inhaled through her nostrils, exhaling slowly through her mouth.

"Adelaide, what is it?" Dimitri's handsome face was filled with concern.

How could she hurt him? What kind of person was she? She licked her lips. Tracey had been wrong—dating two men, even being totally up front about it, hadn't been the right thing to do. How hadn't she realized that no matter what, all of them could get hurt?

"Are you okay?" He came from behind his desk

and sat in the chair beside her, taking her hand and squeezing it.

She nodded, not trusting herself to speak just yet. Her blood rushed in her ears, her pulse pounded deafening.

A moment passed. Maybe he was giving her time to collect herself . . . maybe he knew what was about to come . . . maybe he was being the gentleman he always was, but he sat silently, holding her hand.

Dear Lord, please give me the words.

She licked her lips again. "Dimitri . . ." Just saying his name filled her eyes with tears. She blinked. Hard.

He squeezed her hand again. "What's wrong, Adelaide?" He rubbed his thumb over her knuckles. "Are you okay?"

She shook her head. "No, I have something I need to tell you." She let out a breath. "I need you to know that you are a very special man and you are very dear to me."

He sat still, not speaking, just holding her hand.

Her mouth was so dry, it felt like the Mohave Desert. "Please know that I never meant to lead you on. I've enjoyed getting to know you on a romantic level. You're an amazing man. Romantic. Handsome. Generous. Loving."

"But not someone you could see yourself with for the rest of your life." His voice barely cracked.

She desperately wanted to cry, but forced back the tears. She was the one ending it . . . she had no right to make him feel worse. It felt like a part of her was dying. "I'm so sorry, Dimitri."

He pulled her into a hug. "It's okay, Adelaide. Really."

She held him tighter than she ever had before. Maybe she'd been wrong. Maybe she'd been too hasty.

Addy closed her eyes and inhaled, letting herself just feel. Dimitri's arms tightened around her and his heart thudded next to hers. Warmth filled her. She exhaled.

Dimitri pulled away, just the space of a breath. His lips grazed hers.

She wrapped her arms around his neck and kissed him back. He deepened the kiss, pulling her tight against him. The kiss was as mind-blowing as always, but this time . . . this time she felt like she was cheating on Beau, and that had never happened before.

Addy pulled away. No doubt now that she hadn't made a mistake.

Dimitri rested his forehead against hers and ran his thumb along her jawbone. "Oh, Adelaide. Thank you for your openness and honesty." He kissed the tip of her nose.

"I'm so sorry, Dimitri."

He smiled slightly and released her. "Don't be. I, too, have felt something wasn't right between us. There hasn't been a sense of permanency. A feeling of forever."

She nodded, relief calming the butterflies in her stomach. "You, too?"

He nodded. "We will always remain friends, though."

"Of course." She smiled back at him. "And our working relationship has always been separate and great."

Again, he nodded. He took her hand and kissed it. "You are an amazing woman, Adelaide Fountaine. Beauregard is a lucky man."

Her muscles bunched.

He shook his head. "Don't feel guilty for loving him. You both deserve every happiness in the world." He sobered. "I mean that. Truly."

"I know you do." She rested her hand against his face. "Thank you, Dimitri."

1938

"I finally found him." James rushed into Will's office wearing a wide smile, George on his heels.

Will looked up from his book, every nerve ending in his body at attention. There was only one person he'd had both James and George looking for over the last three years.

"You found the man who proclaims to be the Axeman?"

"We did." James handed over a folder. "Robert Holmes."

Will opened the file and stared at the black and white photograph of the man staring back at him. His eyes were cold. Empty. Lifeless. He laid on a slab, obviously in a morgue with his nameplate on his chest. "He's dead?" Will looked from James to George.

George nodded. Under Will's direction, he'd been trained as an investigator, his sole focus in finding out who the Axeman really was. "As you can see in the file, while there isn't cut and dry evidence Robert was the Axeman, or the police surely would have announced it, the documentation all lines up." He approached and sat in the chair in front of Will's desk, flipping over the photograph to the first page.

"Every night of the attacks, Robert's wife,

Samantha, said her husband hadn't been in bed during the time. Her neighbor reported seeing blood stains on several of the shirts hanging on the line to dry." He flipped the page to the next.

Several drawings and pictures of doors with holes in the bottom were on the sheet.

"The way the Axeman entered his victims' homes was usually a panel on a back door of a home was removed by a chisel. Well, Robert was a woodworker, so he had several chisels and knew how to use them." George started to reach to turn to the next page.

Will pulled the folder toward him and shut the folder. "Just tell me."

George sat back in the chair. "Well, everyone always wondered what prompted the Axeman to start killing."

"He was possessed by a demon, that's why." Will knew this. *Knew* it.

George nodded. "Yes, well, probably because he began to go a little mad. You see, according to his wife, Samantha, everything was fine until they had their son. He was a colicky baby, crying all the time, and that seemed to drive Robert mad. He couldn't sleep without the aid of help. His immune system was lowered. There are countless reports Samantha made to her neighbors regarding her husband's crazy ideas."

"If she told so many people, why didn't the police question him? Or arrest him?"

"Because Samantha said Robert began to believe he was one of Satan's generals."

Yes! He knew it! God had shown him all too clearly. Will nodded, even as his heartbeat raced. "This is the Axeman." Glory be, merciful heavens . . . he'd found the man who'd weakened enough to let a demon possess him and killed Will's sinful mother.

"Was. He and Samantha both died in the flu outbreak in the winter of 1919, which is further evidence that he was, in fact, the Axeman because the attacks stopped in the fall of 1919."

So the demon had descended back into the bowels of hell? That was it? No action needed? Surely God didn't call him to form the *Cretum Deus* and seek retribution for all the Axeman had stolen from Will. Surely this couldn't be the end—Wait—

"You said they had a son?" Will knew that many times the sins of the father were passed down to the son. Chances were high that the demon might have left Robert near the time of death and entered the child. Bloodlines were strong and once the door was opened for evil, it could be passed down from father to son.

James nodded. "I did some research and found that they had a son, Harold, who was born in 1917."

"What happened to this child? This son of the Axeman?" Who could have the demon within him, just waiting to be called forth by the Evil One.

"Will, it's Harold." James smiled. "Harold Holmes from St. Vincent and St. Mary's."

17

BEAU

"Captain, I'm going to strongly suggest we have extra officers out in the Quarter this evening." Beau sat alongside Marcel in Captain Istre's office.

The captain shut the file Beau had handed him. "You really think this copycat is going to act tonight? Attack a family with a young child?"

Beau glanced at Marcel, then nodded. "We do, sir. It follows the pattern. He's attacked on Monday morning, late Monday night, which he probably considered Tuesday, on Wednesday, and then yesterday."

Captain Istre nodded and ran a hand over his thinning hair. "I'm almost shocked that there hasn't been a news report connecting all these attacks. Is Allison Williams sick or something?"

"We've been putting out notices all through the department that we know there's a leak to Allison Williams here, we're actively searching, and that you would deal with the person responsible." Marcel grinned. "Guess that was enough to scare whoever it was to keep their trap shut."

"Good."

Beau inched to the edge of the seat. "We also

suspect that the copycat is a relative or in some other way connected to Harriet Lowe, one of the Axeman's victims. Hers is the only attack not duplicated by the copycat."

"What do we know about her?" the captain asked.

"We just got the background report back we requested. We know that she was an only child, never married, but—and we're waiting for documentation on this—we believe she had an illegitimate child who would have been less than a year old at the time of her death." Beau pulled out his notebook to continue.

"Having no family, her child would have been left with St. Vincent's orphanage. According to the report, one William Lowe, aged seven months, was left there in August of 1918. He was transferred to St. Mary's Home for Boys in 1925." Beau flipped the page. "In 1932, changes began to happen at St. Mary's, and in 1933 it moved to Marrero and its name was changed to Madonna Manor."

"What happened to Lowe?"

Marcel picked up the story. "That's just it—there's no record of William Lowe after St. Mary's moved and changed its name. From the reports we received, apparently it was fairly common for boys around that age of fifteen and older to run away. As they were moving, they weren't monitored as closely as they should have. During that particular move, three boys—including William—who had been at St. Mary's were never counted once it became Madonna Manor."

"So they just disappeared?"

Beau nodded. "It would seem so, sir."

"So we have no way of tracing this William to see who his family became as a man? His children? Grandchildren?"

Marcel shook his head. "No way to know who might be crazy enough to decide to copycat the murders that took their ancestor's life."

"We have a call in to the archdiocese to see if anyone there can remember this William Lowe and what might have happened to him." Beau stuck his pen in the spiral loops of the notebook.

Captain Istre shook his head. "Why start the copycat attacks now?"

Beau sat back in his seat. "Well, this year marks the one hundredth anniversary of the final Axeman attacks."

"Oh, that's just lovely. We get through Mardi Gras and Twelfth Night, and now we have the anniversary of the Axeman attacks. Great. Just great."

Beau fingered the edge of his notebook. "There's a chance it's even worse, sir."

The captain tossed his pen on the desk and leaned back in his chair, lacing his fingers behind his head. "The hits just keep on coming."

"There's a possibility a cult is involved." Beau

glanced at his partner sitting beside him.

Captain Istre sat forward, tenting his hands over his desk. "Excuse me?"

"Hear us out." Marcel held up a finger.

Beau watched the captain's face as Marcel explained about the robes and masks.

Marcel pressed back in his seat. "Now, the only documented cults in the area that focus less on the fanged ones and more on religious themes are *The Disciples* and the *Cretum Deus*."

"Both of these cults have been known to wear dark, hooded robes and animal masks. Specifically the pig and sheep masks." Beau thumbed through his notebook. "Both of the cults have been around for years and years, both are reported to put great emphasis on dates and anniversaries, and both have had reports regarding animal blood and rituals."

That last part really was freaky. Especially since it seemed that Addy and her dad were targets. Some of the reports of the ritual killings of animals were gruesome, even to a seasoned cop. Every protective fiber in Beau seemed to be on high alert. He just couldn't discern if that was because he cared so much, or if his detective's hunch had kicked in.

"Is there any chatter on the streets about either of the cults planning anything?" Captain Istre picked up a rubber band and began wrapping it around his fingers, then popping it.

269

Marcel shook his head. "Not that we've heard. I called in some of the guys in narcs and special units and asked them to keep their eyes and ears open."

"If it is one of these cults and they are planning something, surely someone would've heard a whisper at least." The captain stretched the rubber band between his hands.

"We've put the word out so if there are any whispers, we'll hear about it." Beau shut his notebook. "I'm still going to ask that we up patrol in the Quarter, especially this weekend since the eighteenth is Monday."

"You think that's the copycat's deadline?" the captain asked.

Both Beau and Marcel nodded. "We'll see if we can find a reason to visit the cults as well," Beau offered.

The captain hesitated. "We're already exceeding estimated overtime this month, and we're barely over halfway through."

Beau's chest ached. They *needed* extra patrol . . . he could feel something big was about to happen.

Captain Istre set down the rubber band. "Look, I'll tell each shift to order the patrol units to be visible and moving all through their beat the entire time. No parking and doing reports or monitoring. All units will be moving through the Quarter, every shift this weekend. That's the best

I can do without something more specific to go on."

Disappointment sat like a rock in the pit of Beau's gut.

"If you find out anything, anything at all that can be confirmed, I'll order in more patrols."

Marcel stood, nudging Beau's foot with his own. "Yes, sir. Thank you, Captain."

Beau stood and nodded, but words wouldn't form. This was a mistake. He could feel it deep in his bones. Something big and terrible was going to happen before Monday.

He followed his partner out of the captain's office and across the floor to their desks. "Man, we need to find something."

"I hear ya." Marcel dropped to his seat while Beau did the same behind his desk. "Let me contact someone at the FBI office. She might have something on one of the cults. At least we might get some info."

Beau nodded and let his notebook drop to his desk with a resounding thud. "If only the victims of the copycat were somehow connected, we might be able to get a bead on who might be his next victim. But a couple with a kid under the age of three in a city of nearly four hundred thousand people?"

He stared at his closed notebook, mind spinning. There had to be a connection that he just hadn't seen yet.

Marcel pressed the mute button on his cell while he kept it to his ear. "We need to figure something out, because if my gal can't give me any insight, we're back to having nothing."

Beau shook his head, processing his thoughts. All they had to go on was the similarity to the last name. The family who the Axeman killed was the Cortimiglia family.

He ran a search for that name in the database. That yielded no results. He ran a search on similar names in the greater New Orleans area. Two results loaded: Angelica Cordamaglia and Matt Scordamaglia.

Angelica Cordamaglia was sixty-eight years old and lived in the Garden District. She had no record, except for two parking tickets from a couple of years ago, and those she'd cleared within thirty days of issuance. She was widowed and her only child, a daughter, lived in California.

On the only other result, Matt Scordamaglia was a mortgage broker who lived on the outskirts of the Quarter. Although only thirty-six, he'd been divorced twice. Both times, the wife had filed for divorce and cited adultery as a prevailing reason. Neither of the marriages had produced children. He'd been arrested three times for solicitation of a prostitute, each time paying a fine and getting off with a slap on the wrist, as most in the city did. He had a couple of DUIs, as well as a drunk and disorderly charge, all had been processed. No open warrants or outstanding charges. He was a scum, for sure, but that didn't make him a target for the Axeman copycat.

DIMITRI

"You were right. About everything." Zoey's big, round dark eyes glistened with tears.

Dimitri handed his culinary spoon to Yvette and led Zoey from the kitchen to his office. "Sit down, you look like you're about to fall down." He eased her into a chair.

She was paler than usual and her eyes were bloodshot. He handed her a bottled water from the small fridge he kept in the tight space. "Now, what are you talking about?"

"Everything about Solomon's family. At first, he brushed off my questions, but finally, he started answering. The more he answered, the more I realized that his family was a cult. I told him that and he freaked out, but then, as I explained it like you had with me, he began telling me more details that proved the fact."

Dimitri sat in the chair beside her. "Like what?"

"Like his father is the leader. He has no idea how many females are in the group or which ones are his sisters because his father deemed them unimportant. But his brothers? They all have different mothers. Solomon said that his father has *never* married. Not once in his one hundred and one years, but he has fifteen sons, even though three of them are dead. And their mothers? All of them were or are married to like the bigwigs in the group."

That was crazy.

Zoey took a drink, then her words continued to fall over one another. "Solomon says that before his mother died years ago, she told him that the only way someone could get married in the group was they had to give his dad a child first. She said that she loved one of the men in the group enough that she bore Solomon just so she could marry the man." Zoey shivered. "Solomon said his mother was only twenty-two when she had him, and his father was seventy-one! That's gross."

Gross, but also not so uncommon in a cult. "What else did Solomon say that made him agree it's a cult?"

"One of his brothers, Samuel, caused a stink years ago—before Solomon was even born. From what Solomon was told, his father exiled Samuel and no one has heard from him since. Ever. It's like he disappeared."

Sounded like he made an escape. Or was dead . . .

"Another of his other brothers, Ezra, called his father and brothers out and told them they were not living the way Jesus would have them. He said he was going to leave and tell everyone how warped the family was. Do you know what happened to him?"

Dimitri shook his head, dreading hearing, but knowing he needed to.

"He was mysteriously attacked and paralyzed. He won't speak of the accident or what caused it."

No way could Zoey get involved with this. "What does Solomon say?"

"He's scared, Dimitri. Totally petrified. He's one of the few who gets out and is able to see the real world and knows that his father has limited them all. He wants to get away, but after what happened with Samuel and Ezra, he's terrified."

Dimitri didn't blame him. "So what's his plan?"

Zoey took another sip of water. "His father's so old, he keeps thinking he should die soon. He says every time the old man gets sick, all the brothers get together and pray, and every time he gets well. Solomon says his father tells them that's because he's still doing God's work." She shrugged. "For Solomon and his brothers who doubt his father's ways . . . well, if he wasn't doing God's work, don't you think he'd have died by now?"

Modern medicine had certainly extended lifespans in recent generations. "So, if his father was dead or out of the picture, everybody would what, just disband?"

"It gets complicated here, too." Zoey pushed

her long, dark, red hair out of her face and over her shoulder. "It seems some of the brothers are true believers of everything their father has taught them, while some of the others, like Solomon, have come to realize their dad is pretty warped. The rule in the group is that when one of the Youngbloods turn sixty-five, they step into the leadership role, under their dad's authority, of course." She took another drink of water.

"Solomon says that right now his brother David is in charge, and David understands his father's way isn't necessarily the right way. Solomon says David is very peaceful and tries to keep everyone calm with each other."

Dimitri nodded. "Well, that's moving in the right direction." There might be hope yet.

"But, one of the ones who follow their dad's ways is about to turn sixty-five next year. He's supposedly very much like his father. Rigid and actually, according to Solomon, even more unforgiving. He has a violent streak and an explosive temper."

"Oh." Dimitri didn't know what to say. He wanted to tell Zoey to stay far away from the whole lot of them, but he had a feeling she wasn't going to. Not if her heart was already involved with Solomon. "So what does Solomon want to do?"

She took the last gulp of water, wiped her mouth with the back of her hand, and tossed the bottle into the recycling bin in the corner. "I told him he had to leave. I told him I couldn't be with him if he stayed."

An ultimatum. Hmm. Might work. "What did he say?"

"He understood, and he agreed. He said he's subconsciously known for years that he needed to get away and that falling in love with me—he actually told me that he loved me—" Zoey grinned and blushed. "He said that because of me, he knows he can't wait. Can't wait for his father to die or to see what happens with his brothers. He needs to get out while he can, even if he's scared."

Dimitri nodded. "Sounds like he's made the right decision. For you two, but also for himself." He smiled, knowing that Zoey had to be relieved, but he still had his doubts. His first concern, of course, was Zoey and little Sam's safety and well-being. "So, what's his plan, if you don't mind my asking?"

She took his hand. "He plans to leave tonight, just not go back home after the show."

Oh, this might not be a good idea. "Won't he have his chaperone tonight?"

She nodded. "But he'll ditch him and come stay at my house. At least for a little while until he can get some money. That's another reason this show tonight is so important. If we can sell at least four pieces, if he budgets well, he should be okay financially for a month or so until he can start earning a regular income from his art."

"Oh, Zoey. You can't do that. Your place will be the first place they look. That's putting yourself and your son at risk."

Tears filled her eyes again. "I don't have another choice. Now that he knows the truth and wants to get out, I can't *not* help him. There's nothing else for me to do."

Dimitri's stomach dropped to his toes at the thought of something happening to Zoey or Sam. He let out a long breath. "No." He couldn't put Solomon up at the hotel. They were at full capacity, but also, he couldn't put everyone at the Darkwater Inn in possible danger. "He can stay with me at my house. They won't think to look for him there."

Zoey's smile lit up her entire face. "Are you sure, Dimitri? I mean, I appreciate it and want to jump on your offer, but I want you to be sure. I mean, it's your safety and your house, right?"

He nodded, already regretting the offer but knowing there wasn't any other viable option at the moment. "I'm sure."

Leaning over, Zoey flung her arms around his neck and hugged him tight. "Thank you, Dimitri. Solomon will be so relieved to know he won't have to go back to his father or *Cretum Deus* again."

1938

"William? William from St. Mary's? It is you, isn't it?" The young man stopped in front of him, just as was planned.

Will faked his confusion, then grinned. "Harold? Harold Holmes, is it really you?"

"It's Harold Pampalon now." He ignored Will's outstretched hand and gave him a side hug and clap on the back. "Oh, man, I can't believe this! I always wondered what happened to you. Even tried to look you up a couple of years ago but had no luck."

"You, too. One day, you just were gone from St. Mary's. It was like you disappeared. The nuns said you were adopted, but they wouldn't give much information." Will took a subtle step backward. The demon had to be hiding inside Harold. If it recognized the worker of God that Will was, no telling how it would react.

"We have to catch up. Are you busy right now? Can we grab a cup of coffee?"

Will grinned. "I actually am free at the moment."

"Great. Come on. Let's go to my hotel." He began to lead Will down the street.

"You're staying at a hotel?" He hoped his voice carried the ring of confusion he'd worked hard to perfect over the last two weeks.

Harold laughed. "No, my family owns it. Come on." He clapped Will on the back again.

Will quickened his stride, trying not to recoil at his touch. He couldn't be sullied by the demon. "So that's who adopted you?"

"Yes. A great couple, Louis and Eva Pampalon. They're wonderful. I can't wait for you to meet them. And I have a little brother who was just born last year. I never thought I'd find a kid cute after living in the asylums, but he's swell. What about you?"

"Oh, I wasn't adopted. I left St. Mary's when they moved. James and George, too. We became each other's family."

"Wow." Harold opened the door to the Darkwater Inn, letting Will enter first. "So you guys are all together, huh? That's great. I just can't believe this. It's so fortuitous." He led the way to the small diner-like counter. He motioned to the man behind the counter. "Two coffees."

"Yes, sir, Mr. Pampalon."

Will clenched his jaw. He should have the respect like Harold. He'd earned it. He hadn't been demon spawn.

"So you and the boys are still together, huh? What do you do?"

"I've become a religious leader of sorts."

Harold's eyes widened. "After all of your spouting about the nuns and the priests, you became a religious leader." He grinned and shook his head.

The man behind the counter placed two steaming cups of coffee on saucers in front of them, then handed Harold a little jar of cream. As Harold sweetened and diluted his coffee like a woman, Will forced himself to smile. "James and George do some construction work. They just finished up a job over on the bridge over in City Park." He took a sip of his black coffee, ready to play his next card in the plan he'd devised. "We're hoping to find some other construction-type work, but with Thanksgiving in just a couple of weeks and it being so close to Christmas . . ."

Harold set his cup into his saucer with barely a clink. "We just started some construction work here at the hotel."

"Really?" Will widened his eyes and put on what he was sure was a surprised expression. He'd practiced it over and over for the past week just for this moment.

Harold nodded. "Yes. We're adding in a restaurant and a courtyard along the side of the hotel. I'm sure we could use more crew workers. Dad will be back soon. I'll introduce you. I know you'll like him. He's great. I bet we'll be able to hire you and the guys." Harold took another sip of coffee. "And you all must come for Thanksgiving. We always have quite the spread—turkey, stuffing, mashed potatoes, green beans, and so many pies that you can't eat a slice of each one at one sitting."

"That sounds swell." Will smiled against the fake friendliness. "Oh, and I go by Will now. Will Youngblood."

18

ADDY

"You look as pretty as a picture, Addybear." Vincent smiled.

Addy nodded at her father, even as she felt the blush. She'd debated for quite some time between a dress and the pantsuit, finally going with the pantsuit for more comfort. "You look rather dashing yourself, there." Addy studied him for any sign of tiredness. "Are you sure you feel up to going?"

"I'm not wild about wearing the monkey suit, but it'll be nice to mix and mingle with people for a bit. I'm a little tired of being stuck in this hotel room, nice as it is."

"Well, you make that tux look good, Daddy."

"Has Beau told you anything more about the case?"

"Nothing more than what you already know." She let out a little sigh as she touched up her lipstick in the parlor mirror, silently wishing, just a little, that Zoey had asked her to babysit little Sam. Since she hadn't gotten a call, she was stuck going to the art show as an adult, complete with heels. At least she'd get to see Tracey. She couldn't wait to see her best friend and Geoff together. She'd be able to get a read how serious they were as a couple once she saw them together.

"I've gone over my research in depth." He fidgeted with the bow tie.

She caught his reflection in the mirror and turned to fix the tie for him. "Oh?"

"Yeah. The common MO of all the attacks was the way the Axeman entered the houses—through a chiseled hole in a door, and the weapon he used—an axe."

Stepping back, she smoothed his tuxedo jacket. "Right."

"Well, isn't that a little odd? The way he got into the houses?"

"Everything about him is odd. What do you mean?" She grabbed the lint roller and ran it over his back.

Her father waved off her fussing. "Do you have any idea the amount of work that it takes to chisel a panel from a door? Not to mention how small those were, even back then? Many claimed that the openings were too small for a grown man to pass through."

She ran the lint roller over her black slacks. "Yeah, but in the current cases, the person mimicking the Axeman doesn't use a chisel or anything. At least, Beau hasn't told me any differently."

Vincent continued. "With the original Axeman, the motive for the attacks was never considered to be robbery since the Axeman never took anything from his victim's homes. I'm going to assume that's the same with the attacks recently."

Addy shook her head. "Beau hasn't said anything was taken."

"Since the majority of the original attacks were against Italian-Americans, back in the day some believed the attacks were racially motived. That doesn't apply to the copycat today. Also, many of the original victims were grocers, so some theorized that the attacks were Mafia hits conducted to pressure the businesses into paying *protection taxes*. But neither applies to the attacks of today."

"True. I'm not even sure if one of the people attacked is even in the grocery business."

Vincent grabbed a tin of Altoids from the desk and slipped them into his front right pants pocket. "Some researchers pointed out that most of the Axeman attacks seemed to target women and could have been sexually motivated, especially since the Axeman seemed to only attack the men when they blocked his attempts to murder the women. That, too, doesn't seem to apply to the current attacks."

Addy had just about had enough of the Axeman. If only her father realized that when he was attacked, most likely an axe had been what caused the gash on his head.

But Vincent continued. "The Axeman's ability to quickly flee the scene—as if he had wings, as one witness stated—and the fact that the door holes he used to get into the houses were so small led the townspeople to wonder if the Axeman truly was, as his infamous letter stated, some sort of ungodly demon."

She was done with the conversation, the Axeman, and demons. *Done.* Addy checked the time on her cell. Man, she'd forgotten to charge her phone. It was already down to twenty-five percent. She should charge it before the event. Maybe she could charge it in Dimitri's office. "Are you ready? I need to check with Dimitri and everything before this event actually begins." She tucked her cell phone into the pocket of her slacks, another benefit of choosing the pantsuit over the dress—pockets.

"Sure, honey. Let's go." Her father held out his arm to escort her.

They made their way down the hall. She smiled at Richard, the elevator attendant as they stepped into the car.

"Good evening, Mr. and Ms. Fountaine." He nodded at Addy. "You look especially lovely, ma'am."

"Thank you." The door slid shut and music filled the space. It startled her. "Richard, when did we start having, literally, elevator music?"

He shrugged. "I just noticed it this evening. It

wasn't playing when I came on right after lunch. It's kind of catchy. Jazzy. I like it."

Addy went very still as she listened. Her heart began to race as she recognized the tune. She stared at her father. "We didn't upgrade to any elevator music. I don't even know how it's playing in here. I think it's the same tune that the music box I got yesterday plays."

"What music box?" Vincent's stare penetrated through her.

"One was delivered to me yesterday morning. Wrapped in a box. A gift with a bow. I'm pretty certain it plays this tune. My phone app can't really identify the song. It gives me a different one every time I check."

"Where's this music box?"

"In my office."

The elevator door opened. "Show me." Her father's tone left no room for argument. Not that she had an argument.

"Is there something I should do?" the elevator attendant asked.

"No. I'll have someone check into it. Thank you."

She quickly led her father across the lobby and down the hall to her office. She flipped on the lights and steered her father toward the settee table with the music box. "There."

He lifted the lid and the upbeat tune filled the office. "What was inside?"

"Nothing." Her stomach twisted into knots. She didn't know what was going on, but that someone had the ability to get music into one of her elevator cars without her knowledge unnerved her more than a gift of a music box.

"Did you tell Beau about the box?"

"No." She caught the disapproving line of her father's face. "To be perfectly honest, I thought it might have been a gift from Dimitri."

"Since you have both those boys on a string, you didn't want to tell Beau." Again, the disapproval.

"Not anymore."

"What?"

She let out a slow breath. "Not that it's really any of your business, Dad, but I told Dimitri that there wasn't a future for us." She should've felt sadder at saying that aloud, but she didn't, which just confirmed—again, that she'd made the right decision.

Her father struggled to refrain from smiling, but it was so obvious. She narrowed her eyes at him. "Daddy."

"He's a nice-enough guy, honey, but just not for you." He gave her a quick hug. "But I'm sorry you had to have a hard conversation."

"It was, surprisingly, easier than I would've thought. Dimitri's a gentleman and was extremely gracious and kind. I don't think it'll be too awkward to transition back to our friendship."

"That's good." Vincent lifted the music box and inspected it, much like Addy had done. "So, um, what did Beau say when you told him?"

She should teach her father a lesson and tell him she called everything off with Beau, too, but she wasn't that cruel. "I haven't said anything to him yet."

He waved the music box before setting it down. "But Dimitri didn't send you this?"

"I forgot to ask him. We had a harder conversation to have."

He nodded. "Hang on a minute." He pulled out his new smartphone. He wound the music box and listened for a minute, then shut the lid. He tapped on his phone, then the same tune as the box spilled out from his phone.

"You got it to recognize the song? Man, I guess I'm really going to have to upgrade my phone now."

"No, it's not a song recognition app."

"What is it?"

"It's the midi version of the 'Axman's Jazz (Don't Scare Me Papa)' by Joseph John Davilla, written in 1919."

Her heart free-fell to her gut. "It's the same song that was playing in the elevator, too, isn't it?"

Her father nodded. "Somebody's sending you a message, Addybear, and I don't like it. Not one little bit."

"Me either." Thoughts pummeled her mind like a raging hurricane. "Okay, I need to get with our security team and tech team and find out how the music's getting into the elevator and get it stopped."

"They should be able to backtrack it and find the origin."

"You wait here. I'm going to security." She reached for her door handle.

"No, I'm going with you. Beau made it clear that someone could be out for either of us. We should stay together."

She nodded, but led the way to the security office. Her heels tapped on the smooth tile floor. She made a point to pay attention to any music, but heard nothing. She opened the security door and stepped inside with her father. She nodded at the two men in security uniforms sitting in the office. One was Sully Clements, and the other was Hixson Albertson.

She let out a little breath. "I'm glad to see you're on duty tonight, Hixson."

"Yes, ma'am?" His brow furrowed.

Hixson was a twenty-four-year-old brilliant technician that knew a lot about computers and hacking. He'd been a lifesaver last month when they'd been hacked.

"There is music in the elevators."

He glanced at her, quizzically. "Um, yes, ma'am?"

"We don't have music in the elevators."

"Oh." Without another word, he turned to his bank of screens and keyboards and began pounding away. "Which elevator, in particular, did you hear the music in?"

"I was in car one. It might be in the other two as well."

"Let me see." He typed and clicked the mouse. Three monitors flashed to the elevator cars' interiors. "Hang on, I'm getting the reading of the location. Give me a minute."

More clicking. Typing. Flashing of monitors.

"Hmm . . . Well, it's not in the hotel's system."

"Then how did I hear the music in the elevator?" She looked at her father. He'd heard it, too, so she wasn't imagining things.

"Hang on, Ms. Fountaine." Hixson kept clicking and tapping and the screens flashed from different views to different areas.

If nothing else, she could thank Claude Pampalon for installing the best and most elaborate security system that he could. Of course, he did so to protect his criminal and nefarious actions, but she was grateful for it today.

"There." Hixson pointed at the largest monitor where he'd split the screen into three different views.

"What am I looking at?" It looked dark and like something in the broiler room or some such place. Visions of old horror movies raced through her head.

Hixson ran his finger along the cable in the pictures. "These are live feeds of the top of each of the three elevator cars." He pointed to a small, black square. "See this?"

She nodded.

"It doesn't belong there, but it's on top of each of the cars." He clicked a button and a fourth image filled another monitor. "That's the inside of car one."

He tapped the screen in the top corner of the elevator car. "You can't really see it very well, but there's a black dot. I think it's a small hole there. I can't get a close-up of it, but I'm betting those squares on each of the cars is a remote MP4 player and those little holes are how the speaker is filling the car with the music."

"How did someone get up there to set that up?" That someone could get in the elevator shaft of all three elevator cars and no one know it . . . well, that was a problem she would have to correct immediately. Especially since they'd worked very hard to lock down all the hidden passageways from the original construction of the Darkwater Inn.

"It's actually not as hard as you would think. You'd assume you'd have to get into the shaft to put something on top of the car, right?" Hixson asked.

She nodded.

He shook his head. "You don't. The ceilings of the elevators are easily accessible to assist firemen and other officials in getting out stuck people. Anyway, because of that, you could use a little pole to push up one of the panels, use something like a selfie stick or something like it to slide the MP4 player to the roof, then just pull the little wire into the corner for the speaker. If you practiced it, you could probably do it in less than a minute or two."

"But we have elevator attendants." How hadn't they seen someone doing this?

"That, I don't know." Hixson shrugged.

"How does the music play?"

"I'm sure it's remote activated or programmed."

"Programmed?"

Hixson smiled. "Like people can automate parts of their house by phone? They have programs to turn lights off and on, open or close a garage door, lock or unlock doors . . . all kinds of stuff like that. You just have to have the electronic device set up to the app and have the app on your smartphone. Easy peasy."

Addy couldn't help but wonder if technology, while making lives easier, wasn't going to be the world's downfall. For the moment, however, she had something more pressing to deal with. "How do we get it down?"

Hixson shrugged. "I can go pull them out

for you. Won't take me but like ten or fifteen minutes."

"Then do it."

Her father grabbed her arm. "Maybe you should call Beau first, honey. Someone tampering with the elevator cars in the hotel, on top of you receiving an anonymous music box, and considering the tune . . ."

She nodded. "Hold off on removing them, Hixson, until I can contact the police, but is there any way you can stop the music without actually touching it and contaminating evidence?" She pulled out her cell and quickly called Beau.

"Let me see." Hixson did his thing on the computer.

The call went straight to Beau's voice mail, very unlike him. He must be making a call. "Beau, it's me. Call me when you get this message, please. We've had someone place music players in the elevators here at the Darkwater Inn."

"It's off now, Ms. Fountaine," Hixson whispered.

She smiled and nodded. "And I received an anonymous music box yesterday. Both the music box and the elevators are playing the same song—the 'Axman's Jazz (Don't Scare Me Papa)' from 1919."

DECEMBER 25, 1938

"We need to hurry, Will. My family will be expecting me to open presents once Henri wakes up." Harold followed his friend down the hallway.

Will glanced over his shoulder. "It won't take but a minute. It's your present from me." He opened the door to the construction area and waved Harold into the dimly lit room. The candles flickered, there not only for light, but there to purify the space.

"Surprise!" James and George gestured to the big box with the bright, red bow on top that sat between them.

It was fitting to do this today, the celebration of the birth of Jesus.

Harold grinned and took a moment to shoulder clap each of them. "Guys, you are the best. This is great." He moved to the box and tore off the bow and opened it. Tissue paper spilled onto the concrete floor as he pushed it aside, digging into the box.

Will slipped into the black robe, as did George and James. Will lifted his arms and began to speak. "Dear Lord, whose nature is ever merciful and forgiving, accept our prayer that this servant of yours, bound by the fetters of sin, may be pardoned by your loving kindness."

Harold stood and turned, his face a mask of confusion. "What's going on?"

Ignoring him, Will continued, praying the specific prayers he'd researched through old texts at the library to learn over the last couple of weeks. "Holy God, Almighty Father, Everlasting Lord and Father of our Savior Jesus Christ, who once and for all consigned that fallen and apostate tyrant to the flames of hell, who sent your only Son into the world to snatch from ruination and from the clutches of the noonday devil this human being made in your image and likeness. Strike terror, dear God, into the beast now lurking, through a direct bloodline, into this mere mortal. Let your mighty hand cast him out of your servant, Harold, so he may no longer hold captive this person whom it pleased you to make in your image, and to redeem through your Son; who lives and reigns with you, in the unity of the Holy Spirit, God, forever and ever."

Harold's face twisted. "I don't know what kind of sick game you're playing, but I'm leaving. I'd suggest you all leave as well."

He made a move to bolt, but James and George grabbed him and held him.

"Let me go!" He twisted and jerked, but the young men had been well instructed by Will, who'd explained the demon would make Harold flee in order to stay within him.

Will walked to Harold and made the sign of the cross in front of him.

"Stop this, Will. Your prank has gone on long enough."

"Prank?" Will stepped back and stared at Harold. "This is no prank. There's a demon in you, passed down from your father."

"My father? What are you talking about?" He thrashed about, but James and George held tight.

"Your biological earthly father, Robert Holmes."

"What about him?"

"He was weak and allowed a demon to take possession of him. Through this, he acted as the Axeman, who attacked many people. My mother was one of them."

Harold jerked and twisted. "You're crazy."

"No, it's true. We've done the research." George held tight as he spoke.

"James, you can't believe this nonsense," Harold pled with the other man.

Hesitating for just a moment, James then shook his head. "I do. I did most of the research myself. Your father was the Axeman."

"But he's dead." Harold leaned against their arms as he raised his voice to Will. "If he was, and if he killed your mother, I'm sorry. That has nothing to do with me."

Will smiled. "Poor soul. Tobit 3:5 clearly tells

us, *'And now thy many judgments are true in exacting penalty from me for my sins and those of my fathers, because we did not keep thy commandments. For we did not walk in truth before thee.'* "

"You're insane." Harold jerked and even tried to run, but George and James held fast.

"When your father left this earthly place, the demon could only depart the body through a direct bloodline. To you." Will made the sign of the cross in front of him again. "The demon is dormant within you for the moment, waiting for the perfect time to rise up and begin his evil crusade once again."

Fear settled over Harold's face as he wiggled and kicked, bucking his legs, but George and James supported him by his arms.

Will began praying in Latin. He was pretty sure he was pronouncing everything correctly. If not, God knew. God had set him on this path from birth. Will just knew it.

"George, James . . . you guys. You know me. You know I'm not evil. Haven't I been nothing but a friend to you ever?"

"Silence, demon!" Will broke his prayer as he saw the uncertainty pass over James. "You are banished from here. From this servant. You are not allowed to use his tongue."

"Listen to yourself, Will. I'm me, Harold. The kid who told you stories at St. Vincent's when you couldn't sleep. Your friend who helped you with your lessons at St. Mary's so the Mother Superior wouldn't get her ruler after your knuckles." Harold sagged against James and George's hold.

"You do not fool me, demon!" Will continued his praying in Latin, but all the time, he knew what he would end up having to do. Had known it before they'd even come. That's why he'd brought the axe he'd hidden under the box.

"Guys, I don't have any demon in me. My father may have been the Axeman, but I have no idea about that. He died from the flu. He and my mother both."

Will took a step closer. "I command you, unclean spirit, minion from Lucifer, by the ascension of our Lord Jesus Christ, by the descent of the Holy Spirit, and by the coming of our God for judgment, that you depart! I command you to obey me as I am a follower of God despite my unworthiness."

"Even if my father was the Axeman, his evil died with him."

"Demons can't just die, Harold. That's the evil within you telling you lies."

"He didn't have a demon in him."

Will smiled. "You were a child. How would you have known? All the nuns said that the Axeman was a mortal who allowed a demon to possess him so that he could kill. You remember that, don't you, demon?"

Harold shot up to his feet and began to scream. "Dad! Help! Somebody, help!"

Both Harold and James looked to Will.

It was time. He'd wanted to wait and say a couple more prayers, but he couldn't. He grabbed the axe and lifted it. "Depart, you serpent, full of lies and cunning. For He has already stripped you of your powers and laid waste your kingdom, bound you prisoner and plundered your weapons. He has cast you forth into the outer darkness, where everlasting ruin awaits you and your demons. You are guilty before almighty God, whose laws you have transgressed. You are guilty before His Son, our Lord Jesus Christ. You are guilty before the whole human race. You are sent back to the bowels of hell." He brought the axe down with all his strength, right on top of Harold's head.

19

BEAU

"Detective Savoie." He didn't recognize the number on his cell's display, but answered anyway.

"This is Mother Mary Bernadette from the Archdiocese of New Orleans's office."

"Yes, ma'am." Beau lifted his pen and opened his notebook.

"Were you the officer who asked about records from St. Mary's Asylum for Boys?"

"Yes, ma'am, I am."

"I was able to speak to some of the older nuns who were trained under the staff of St. Mary's. Some of the teachers there during that time kept prayer journals regarding the wards in their care."

Beau jotted it down.

"While there are no records of the boy you specifically asked about, a boy named William Lowe is mentioned in several of these prayer journals. He apparently had been left at St. Vincent's as an infant because his mother died following a vicious attack of a serial killer who terrorized our city. The injuries she sustained eventually killed her."

So he really was the son of Harriet Lowe, victim of the Axeman.

"Several journals mention him as well as three other boys—George Rouzier, James Isnard, and Harold Holmes. According to what has been written, the four boys were good friends and considered inseparable."

Harold!

Beau wrote the names quickly, checking the spelling. "What about George, James, and Harold . . . are they in the records after St. Mary's moved and became Madonna Manor?" He knew about one, but wanted another layer of verification.

"I thought you might ask, Detective, so I checked. Neither George nor James were listed as had been checked into Madonna Manor, just like William wasn't."

"What about Harold?"

"He was adopted in 1931 by Louis and Eva Pampalon."

Yes! It *was* all connected! "Thank you, ma'am."

"Good luck, Detective."

He disconnected the call and quickly gave the information to Marcel. "So Harold was big buddies with the other three guys. I know we have nothing on William, but maybe we can find something on George or James."

Marcel was already typing on his keyboard. "I'm checking on James. You run George."

Beau nodded and began his search.

Before Beau's results were returned, Marcel let out a slow whistle. "Bingo. I'm looking at his record."

Beau reached for his pen and notebook.

"James Isnard, date of birth is November 13, 1918. Orphaned during the flu epidemic, he was sent to St. Vincent's, then to St. Mary's. He married Etta Thibodeaux in 1936. Etta died in 1993 and James in 1994. They are survived by their three children: Rachel, Leigh, and Esau." Marcel typed on the keyboard. "Let me see where his kids are."

Beau glanced at his monitor. "Here's what we have on George Rouzier. Born January 10, 1917. Orphaned after an auto accident killed his parents, he went to St. Vincent's, then St. Mary's. He married a Marie Boudreaux in 1940. George died in 1990 and Marie in 1999. They had no children." He clicked to go to the next screen.

"James's daughter Rachel is married and lives in Las Vegas with her husband. Leigh is divorced with two little girls and lives in Colorado. His son, Esau, died from an overdose in 1992 before Etta and James died."

Beau looked back to his monitor again. "Looks like George didn't have much listed." He scrolled. "Wait! Here it is." Tingles tickled up and down his spine. "George was a founding member of the *Cretum Deus* religious group of New Orleans until the time of his death."

"Same with James!"

Grinning, Beau updated his notebook. "We need to talk with anyone in this *Cretum Deus* group who might have known James or George, and maybe William. Someone has to know something because there's a connection in some way. I'll see if the department has any open files on them." He opened the search option and typed in the name of the cult.

This was it . . . he could feel it. Everything was connected. He played it over in his mind.

Harold got adopted. The other three boys ran away a year later. Maybe it was planned for them all to connect later or whatever. Either way, they had to have connected while Harold was living with the Pampalons. Something somewhere went sideways for whatever reason, and Harold was murdered and walled into the Darkwater Inn. William, James, or George should have known something. There had to be a lead somewhere.

The computer beeped. Beau read the file the department had on the cult. "The *Cretum Deus* might call themselves a religious group, but some who have left are very adamant about it being a cult. They were demanded to give over all their money to the group. Women were and are considered second-class citizens, and the only way any man in the group can marry is with the permission of the leader, a Will Youngblood. Several of the women reported that their marriage could not be consummated with their husband until they gave this Will Youngblood a son." Beau's stomach coiled.

"Yeah, sounds like a cult to me." Marcel typed on his keyboard. "But looks like every complaint was buried. No action ever taken."

Beau scrolled through statements, feeling sicker with each report. "Will Youngblood kept everyone in one house. The men could have sex with any women they wanted to—sounds like they were treated as sex slaves. But I hope that doesn't mean . . . young girls. And incest."

"Probably does. You know how cults are," Marcel said. "But it looks like the ones who got out and made complaints were ignored. No action was ever taken."

Beau looked up. "Nothing?"

Marcel scratched his head. "No. And—get this. According to our database, Will Youngblood doesn't exist."

"What?"

Marcel shook his head. "No birth certificate, no driver's license . . . no house or vehicle deed of any kind. Nothing. Nada. Nil. He doesn't exist."

Beau read back over the reports. "Every single account lists the name of the leader of *Cretum Deus* as one Will Youngblood. Yet, not a single charge—or even a full investigation—has ever been made."

Marcel cocked his head. "Maybe we should try for a warrant."

"On what grounds? Right now, we know everything connects, but at the moment, there's nothing concrete linking the cult to any crime."

"Well, then, just another thing we need to ask Mr. Youngblood when we meet him, wouldn't you say? I've got the address. We can always pay a visit. Who knows? We might get lucky and have them talk to us."

Beau unlocked his drawer with his gun. "Why don't you go update the Captain right quick and I'll meet you at the car?"

Marcel sprinted toward Captain Istre's office. Beau holstered his gun and grabbed his keys. He slipped his notebook in his pocket and grabbed his cell. He noticed he had a voice mail, and a missed call from Addy. He quickly played the message as he headed to the car. The uncertainty and controlled fear of Addy's voice nearly stopped him cold.

He got behind the wheel and dialed Addy's number.

"Hey, Beau."

"Are you okay?" His heart pounded, feeling as if it would rattle his ribcage.

"I'm fine. Daddy's with me and we're okay. A member of our security was able to get the music turned off remotely without having to touch it. We thought you might need it for evidence or something, so we didn't want to touch anything."

"No, don't touch it."

"Also, we have a location on the remote . . . wait—" Rustling sounded over the phone before Addy came back clear. "Let me have you talk to our guy. His name is Hixson Albertson."

Before Beau could say anything, a guy's voice came over the phone. "Sir, I don't know if you're up on cyber matters or not—"

"I'm not."

"Okay. Well, I was able to trace the location of where the remote signal is coming from. I have the address where the person who turned the music on is."

Marcel opened the passenger's door and slipped inside.

"So, it's not there at the hotel?"

"No, sir. The physical address is in the warehouse district."

Well then, Addy was safe. "Okay. Put Ms. Fountaine back on the phone, please. And thank you."

"Yes, sir."

Only a moment passed before Addy's voice soothed his frazzled nerves. "Beau?"

"Look, it doesn't sound like you're in any physical danger at the moment, but stay with your dad, okay? Marcel and I have a lead we need to follow, then we'll go by and check out the remote location Hixson came up with and look around. I should be at the hotel in an hour at the latest. Just stay with your dad to keep you both safe."

"Okay."

"Text the address that Hixson has. I'll call you if I'm going to be later than an hour. Again, stay with your dad."

"I will. Be careful, Beau."

"You, too, Addy."

He ended the call and filled Marcel in as he started the cruiser's engine. "We'll run by there after we finish talking to the cult."

Marcel rattled off the address for the cult, and Beau steered the car in that direction. "It's about time we get some answers. I hope somebody there remembers the boys."

Nodding, Marcel clicked his seatbelt. "Well, since James and George have only been dead for twenty or so years, there should be at least somebody who remembers them. And you know how the cults usually are—telling the stories down the generations. Hopefully we'll have some answers."

Beau made another turn. "Yeah. Like if anybody there is William's descendant and maybe doing all these copycat killings." His cell phone sounded the message tone. "Check the address and see how far it is from where we'll be. I don't think it'll be too far out of our way, since I'm guessing whomever is doing this is linked to the hotel."

Marcel made a snorting sound as he opened the message. "No, it won't be out of our way at all."

"Good."

"It's the cult's address."

Beau slammed on the brakes. "Now you can call and see about that warrant."

DIMITRI

"I don't know where Solomon is." Zoey paced the restaurant around the workers setting everything up.

Dimitri gently rocked the infant carrier Sam slept in with his foot before turning to Zoey. "Tell me again what happened." He gently eased her onto one of the bar's stools.

"When I left here earlier, I called Solomon and told him he could stay with you. He was grateful and said he would pack his clothes and toiletries and never go back to his family's home." She stood, gripping the edge of the bar. "He was supposed to pick me up promptly at four, and we were going to drop Sam off at the sitter's, then come here. When he didn't show at four, I tried calling him, but it went to voice mail. I left a message." Tears filled her eyes.

Dimitri rested his hands on hers. "Take it easy. Just tell me."

She let out a breath. "Four thirty came and he still hadn't shown or returned my call. I thought maybe our wires got crossed, so I headed to the babysitter's, only she wasn't there. I banged on the door, but no answer. I didn't have Addy's number and knew I needed to get here, so I brought Sam."

"It's okay. He's sleeping. When Addy gets here, I'm sure she'll be more than relieved to watch him."

Her bottom lip quivered and she nodded. "I hoped Solomon would be here, but clearly he isn't, and it's five forty-five and his show starts at seven."

"Plenty of time, Zoey. Over an hour. Maybe he stopped for something. Maybe he had car trouble and didn't have reception. Just calm down. He'll probably be here soon and you'll feel silly for being so worried over nothing."

She nodded. "I do need to make sure all the pieces are marked correctly, description and price."

"Then go do that. Sam's sleeping fine. I'll have one of the waitresses keep an eye on him while I finish up in the kitchen. Addy will probably be here early anyway, so it'll all be okay."

She squeezed his hand, then turned and moved toward one of the bigger paintings.

Dimitri watched her for a moment, staring at the painting that had already creeped him out. It wasn't the actual image painted, but the feeling it evoked. A crooked cross tilted on a hill in the distance against a raging thunderstorm. It made him feel lonely. Destitute. Hopeless. He couldn't imagine anyone buying such a painting, but what did he know? Some of the ugliest paintings he'd ever seen were famous and worth millions.

He waved Holly over. The young waitress worked in his church's nursery and loved kids. He nodded at the sleeping toddler. "Have you met Sam?"

She grinned. "I have. He's a sweetheart."

"Would you mind keeping an eye on him while you fold the napkins? I need to finish up in the kitchen and his mommy is checking on the paintings placement. Her babysitter flaked and Addy had volunteered to watch him, so we're hoping she can and will."

"If you don't need me to walk trays of food around, I'm happy to watch Sam."

Dimitri smiled. "We might take you up on that."

"Sure. Let me grab the napkins for now."

"Thanks." Dimitri headed to the kitchen, his mind wandering as the enticing spices filled his senses. He checked the Cajun crawfish bread on the front tray that one of the kitchen workers was cutting and stabbing with the *fleur de lis* topped toothpicks, even as his thoughts tumbled over one another.

What was Solomon thinking? Had Zoey pushing him to leave his family cult been too much for him? Had he changed his mind about leaving and was too scared to tell her?

He turned to watch Yvette make patties for the creole scallop cakes that were always a crowd pleaser. She would gently fry them so they'd be nice and warm to serve to the first round of guests at straight up seven, just as scheduled. Dimitri didn't worry too much as long as his sous chef was on the job.

Poor Zoey. She had come so far to have her heart broken by someone who couldn't escape the clutches of his family and wasn't enough of a man to tell her. Or maybe something happened to him on the way. They'd find out soon enough.

Dimitri nodded at the young worker smiling up at him over the prep counter for the crawfish beignets. The young man was working the dough just right. The bowl for the accompanying Cajun dipping sauce set off to the side. Yvette would oversee the mixing before it was put on trays to go out into the restaurant.

He made his way out of the kitchen, stopping at the bar to make sure there was plenty of sparkling grape juice ready to be poured in the glasses. Three bartenders were shining the champagne flutes with the Darkwater Inn logo etched into the glass.

The wait staff all looked sharp in their black tuxedos and white gloves. Dimitri checked his watch—six twenty. Everything on his end was ready. He looked over the space. Maybe Solomon had slipped in and was with Zoey.

He rounded the corner and literally ran into Zoey. She had an older man of about fifty with her. "Dimitri!" No mistaking the desperation in her voice. "This is Solomon's brother, Moses. He came to get me because Solomon's had an accident and we need to go." She made her way to where she'd left her son.

"What kind of accident?" Dimitri stared at Solomon's brother. He was medium-height, muscled, with squinty eyes. He didn't look intimidating, but Dimitri didn't trust anyone when it came to the cult.

The older man cleared his throat. "Solomon was preparing for his show tonight, anxious to get here. He was in an accident. He's unconscious."

"We have to go, Dimitri. Now." The worry lined every delicate feature of hers as she kept moving.

But Dimitri wasn't just going to follow blindly. "What hospital was he taken to?"

Moses frowned and shook his head. "I don't know." He shook his head again. "I can't think very clearly right now. I need to get to my brother."

"Where's Sam? I need to take him and go. Moses is going to give me a ride." She looked over to the counter where Sam still slept in his rocker. Holly sat in front of him, folding napkins. She startled as Zoey moved around her.

"I can watch Sam, Ms. Zoey." Holly stood, glancing back to Dimitri.

Moses spoke up. "It will be fine. We have people who can look after the child. He should be with his mother." However, he looked less like a concerned brother and more like a freakish cult member to Dimitri.

"Why don't I drive you to the hospital, Zoey? Sam can stay with Holly and once you see about Solomon, I can bring you back whenever you want."

But Zoey shook her head. "I need someone here to oversee the show. Explain why Solomon isn't here. Explain why I'm not here in case my boss from the gallery drops by." She leaned closer to Dimitri and whispered. "We need the sales now more than ever. You know why." She straightened and grabbed the handle of Sam's carrier. "Please, Dimitri. I'll call you as soon as I know how Solomon is."

"Let me keep Sam here at least. You need to focus on Solomon, not have to worry about Sam."

Moses took the handle of the carrier from Zoey's hand. "We will help her with her son." He put his other hand under her elbow. "Come along, we need to get to Solomon."

Zoey began to move with Solomon's brother.

"Wait. I'll go with you." Dimitri snapped for his restaurant manager, Betti, and quickly filled her in on the situation as they walked toward the door.

"All the pieces are priced. Just collect that amount and I'll send out receipts." Zoey let herself be hurried by Moses.

"Call me if you have any questions. Fill Adelaide in on everything as well." Dimitri would text her from the car so she could contact Beauregard and have the police check out Moses's claim of Solomon's accident.

Because everything about this felt very wrong.

20

ADDY

"Come on, Daddy." Addy's heels clicked on the marble floor as he headed into the restaurant through the back way. A nice crowd had formed outside the restaurant in the lobby, so at least they'd have a good turnout.

"You go ahead, honey. I'll catch up."

She stopped and spun, taking in the paleness of his face. "Are you okay?" She moved to take him by the arm.

"I'm fine. Just a little dizzy. The medication makes me a little loopy sometimes. And nauseated."

"You probably didn't eat dinner either, did you?"

He slowly shook his head.

She wanted to snap at him, but the look on his face told her that he regretted taking pain medication on an empty stomach. "Once we get into the restaurant, you are to eat as many of the hors d'oeuvres as you can."

"Yes, mother hen." He flashed her a weak smile.

"I'm serious, Dad. I can't have you collapsing because you didn't eat."

He nodded. "I will. You go ahead and do your

job. I'll be right behind you. I just need a little fresh air."

Beau's warning to stay together reverberated in her mind. "Why don't I walk you outside for a minute? I could use a breath of fresh air myself."

"Addybear, stop. This is your job, and I know you have things to do. I just need a little nip of the cooler fresh air to clear my head and ease my nausea. I won't be more than five minutes, then I'll come right into the restaurant."

It was her job, but this was her father. The only family she had. "Don't be silly. Dimitri will have everything under control. I could use a little fresh air, too." She linked her arm through his and headed toward the side exit of the hotel.

As they stepped into the cool March night, Addy felt her father pull in a long breath before he moved from her to lean against the building.

"Daddy?"

He held up a hand. "Just queasy, honey. Give me a second."

She turned away to give him a little privacy in case the nausea wouldn't be denied. The courtyard was on the other side of the hotel and she could hear the familiar strands of Zydeco music. Not the jazz tune, for which she was grateful.

She glanced along the alley and noticed a car's headlights. No one was supposed to park in the alley. She started to take a step in that direction when she saw Zoey and Dimitri slip into the back seat, followed by a man holding Sam in his carrier who got behind the wheel. The back door stayed open for a moment, then she caught a glimpse of Dimitri's head as he reached for the door and pulled it shut. The car sped away before Addy could move.

What in the world?

"Addy." Her father sounded weaker.

She turned and rushed back to his side.

"I just can't shake this upset stomach and dizziness, honey. I think I need to go back to my room and lie down."

"Of course." All the action of the last few days must have taken more of a toll on her father than she'd thought. On top of that, taking strong pain medication and not eating . . . well, no wonder he didn't feel well. "Let me take you back to your room." She helped him to the door.

"I can make it myself. I'm just sorry I've delayed you this long. Your party should be starting."

"It's okay. You're more important. I'll get you to your room, then I'll go check on the event." She opened the door.

He shook her off. "I'm fine. You go. If I get to feeling better, I'll come down. I'll just eat some of that fruit you keep having sent up."

"Eat the bananas. The potassium is good for you, and it'll stick to your stomach. If you feel

318

better, come down. I know Dimitri made some awesome food for tonight."

He leaned over and kissed her temple. "I will, honey. And I'm sorry."

"Don't be." She put her hand on his cheek. "You just go take care of you."

She watched him make it to the elevator before she turned and headed to the restaurant. Now to find out what had happened with Dimitri and Zoey leaving so mysteriously.

Less than three minutes after entering the restaurant, the manager, Betti, rushed up to Addy. "Ms. Fountaine, I'm so glad you're here. We're about to open the doors, but Mr. Pampalon and Ms. Naure had to leave."

"I saw that. What's going on?"

"The artist, Mr. Youngblood, was in an auto accident and is unconscious at the hospital. Ms. Naure and Mr. Pampalon left with Mr. Youngblood's brother to go to the hospital."

"Which hospital?"

"I don't know, ma'am."

Holly, one of the regular waitresses came up to them. "It's really weird, Ms. Fountaine." She shook her head.

"What?" A very unsettling feeling grew in her stomach.

"Little Sam was sleeping in his carrier. I know him from church since I work in the nursery. Mr. Pampalon asked me to keep an eye on Sam while

319

his mom checked on everything. I offered to watch Sam tonight if you weren't able to."

She nodded, trying to keep up. Zoey's baby-sitter probably backed out at the last minute again. Of course she would watch that sweet boy.

"When the artist's brother—I heard him say his name was Moses—said they should take Sam, Zoey agreed. Moses couldn't even tell them what hospital his brother was in. Mr. Pampalon tried to get her to leave Sam here with him and me and you, but Moses was really pushing her to take him. Eventually, she agreed and they started to leave."

Betti picked up the story again. "Mr. Pampalon didn't want her and Sam going off with that man alone, so he said he was going with them. He told me to tell you what was going on."

One of the waitresses rushed to the group. "Betti, it's two after seven and this is supposed to start at seven. Can we open the doors?"

Betti looked at Addy. They needed to go forth as if nothing was wrong. She gave a little nod. "Open the doors and run the event. I'm going to see if I can get in touch with Dimitri and get an update so we can tell the guests." And find out what hospital they were at and send Dimitri's car over there so he wouldn't be stuck.

"Yes, ma'am. All the pieces are priced and the descriptions are correct. Yvette said the trays of food are ready to be loaded. I can handle the guests and inform them of the artist's accident. Who knows, it might help some of the pieces get sold. Some people are weird like that." Betti went to the front door of the restaurant and began greeting guests.

Addy retreated to Dimitri's office in the kitchen, grabbing her cell phone from her pocket. Her cell was at twenty-one percent, so she would have to charge it soon. But right now, she needed to call Dimitri.

It went straight to voice mail.

Dimitri never turned his phone off. Ever. Maybe he was dialing out. She'd call back in a minute. To save power on her phone, she brought up Dimitri's computer and ran a search for the area hospitals. Using the landline from the phone on the desk, she called the first one—University Medical. No record of a Solomon Youngblood in the ER or having been admitted.

She tried Dimitri again. Straight to voice mail.

Addy dialed the number for the next local hospital, New Orleans East. Again, no record of Solomon. She tried the next hospital—Tulane Medical. They, too, had no record of Solomon.

That little nagging suddenly became louder and stronger as she tried Dimitri's cell again. It went straight to voice mail.

Something was wrong. Very wrong.

She called Beau. It rang only once. "Addy, what's wrong?"

"Nothing. Well, I don't know." She quickly told him what had happened. "But no hospital has any record of an accident involving Solomon Youngblood. I'm worried about Zoey and Dimitri and little Sam. Beau, what's going on?"

"I don't know, but we just got to the address where Solomon and his family live, which is also the address Hixson gave us as being the source of your music. I'm going to get some answers. I'll update you when I can. Stay with your dad." He clicked off before she could explain about her father being in his suite.

Still, it didn't seem like there was a threat here, but she was more than worried about everyone else, especially little Sam. Everything in her screamed that things were bad.

She bent her head and sent up a silent prayer for their protection.

Her cell phone rang.

She jumped, startled, but yanked it up. It wasn't Dimitri as she'd hoped, but it was the hotel. "Hello."

"Ms. Fountaine, this is Hixson. I found something else you might want to come see."

She stood. "I'm on my way." What now?

BEAU

"I'm Detective Savoie with the New Orleans Police Department and this is Detective Taton.

322

We only need to speak to whomever is in charge. It won't take but a moment." Beau held his shield out where the young man could see it.

"Hang on." The door shut in their face.

Beau looked at Marcel. "Did he really just go there?"

Marcel shook his head. "I still can't believe we were denied a warrant. Religious freedom? Seriously?" He jammed his cell phone in his back pocket. "No cell reception here either."

"Someone pretty high up must be a member of the cult." They'd gotten warrants on much, *much* less. Not today though. No, it was probably one of the kids of an official who belonged to the cult—that was the latest fad, right? To belong to some off-the-wall group. Even law enforcement would protect their kids over enforcing justice. Didn't matter, Beau supposed, since they'd still do their job. Beau checked his cell display—no bars either. He shook his head as he took a step back and looked around the house.

The house was one of the older ones in the warehouse district of the city. Many of the homes in the area were run-down. Some had even been condemned. This particular one wasn't in as bad of shape, but it wouldn't be gracing any *Southern Living* issues anytime soon. The steps were sturdy up to the front door, but the need for a fresh coat of paint and a good pressure washing was definitely evident.

The door opened again and an older man had replaced the younger one in the doorway. "Detectives, my apologies." He stepped onto the narrow porch with them. He stood hunched, his advanced years obvious in the curve of his stance and the wrinkles on his face. "I'm Levi Youngblood, how may I help you?"

"Are you the one in charge here? The leader of *Cretum Deus*?"

A flash moved in his eyes for a moment before the guard fell carefully back into place. "No, that would be my younger brother, David. At the moment, he's unavailable. What may I help you with?"

"We're looking for information on the founders of *Cretum Deus*. Who could help us with that?" Marcel had clearly had enough of playing nicely.

Beau understood. Standing out on a porch, getting what was clearly a runaround, didn't bode well for the cult. Especially not in light of learning someone here was the source of the Axman's Jazz at the Darkwater Inn. Warrant or no, he was going to get some answers.

Levi narrowed his eyes, deepening the crow's feet in the corners. "What type of information do you require?"

Why not just get it out there? "We're looking for information regarding Harold, William, James, and George." At least to begin with. They'd get to the jazz and Addy and the hotel once they had someone who could tell them something.

Levi hesitated. "Just a moment. Let me see who I can find for you to speak with." He retreated into the house so quickly that Beau couldn't even catch a glimpse inside.

"I can't believe we couldn't get a warrant," Marcel mumbled.

Beau wondered if he should have asked about Solomon as his lead-in to get more of a response, but something told him to hold off on that. Call it cop's hunch or gut instinct, he didn't know, but he'd kept silent about how he knew about the accident as well as the jazz tune in the hotel's elevators and the music box sent to Addy.

"These people are weird with a capital W, buddy." Marcel paced the small confines of the porch. "That Levi guy looks like an undertaker in a graphic novel."

"Comic book, you mean?" Beau smiled at his partner, who had a love of gore-filled graphic novels, resenting people who referred to them as big comic books.

The door opened and Levi stood there again. "My father has deigned to speak with you. I hope you understand what an honor it is for my father to take such time." He led them just inside the door, then to a small room to the immediate right.

The little room had a draft, but also was lit only by candles. Their flickering on the old wallpaper depicting a French countryside scene went beyond eerie. Two ratty-looking high back chairs sat facing a couch that had seen its better days decades ago. The room smelled stuffy like mothballs.

"Father will be with you momentarily." Levi left the little room, shutting the door behind him.

"Uh, I'm not sitting on that rat-infested thing." Marcel nodded toward the couch, wiping off the seat of one of the chairs before he sat.

Beau took the other seat. At least they were facing the two floor-to-ceiling windows. Gauzy-looking curtains with holes in them hung from old rods. The overall feel of the room was cold. Impersonal. Definitely lacking a welcoming touch. Even the old Oriental rug looked as if it deserved a proper burial.

The door opened with a creepy creak and Levi led an old—really old—man inside. The old man's face, lit by the candles, looked like very worn leather. His eyes had a bugged-out quality to them as Levi assisted him to the couch. Once he sat, he nodded at Levi, who promptly left, closing the door.

"Gentlemen . . . detectives." The old man's voice cracked, but was much stronger than Beau expected from the whip of a man in front of him.

"Thank you for seeing us, Mr. Youngblood. We hate to intrude, especially in the evening." Beau watched the old man's eyes flash with a wildness he hadn't anticipated.

"Not a problem. Happy to help the police in any way. What is this regarding, if I might ask?" The old man leaned against the back of the couch, releasing a pouf of particles to dance in the air visible with the flickers of the flames.

Beau glanced at Marcel, who shrugged and addressed the old man. "I don't know if you've heard the news about some attacks that have been happening in our city lately."

"Ah, yes. Reminds me of the tales of the Axeman attacks." He ran a hand over the top baldness of his head.

"Yes." Beau pulled out his notebook and pen. "We're following up on the possibility that it might be someone mimicking those attacks from 1918 and 1919."

Mr. Youngblood smoothed the frazzled bits of hair on either side of his head, just over his ears. "I remember hearing about them. Horrible. Had to be some sort of evil doing such things to people."

"We were hoping that perhaps you might have some information regarding the four founders of *Cretum Deus*: Harold, William, George, and James."

The man's eyes narrowed and his voice thundered in the silence of the room. "Harold was never part of *Cretum Deus*."

"Are you sure?" Marcel asked. "Some of our research shows that he likely was."

"I'm positive Harold was never part of our group."

Beau looked up from his notes. "How can you be so positive?"

"Because, young man, I *am* the founder of *Cretum Deus*."

"Wait." Beau gripped the pen so tight it was a wonder it didn't break. The hairs on the back of his neck were standing at full attention. "You're William Lowe?" *This* man was Harriet's son? The lost William? The man whose mother was murdered by the Axeman?

The old man shrugged. "I haven't gone by that name since I was a teenager. I'm Will Youngblood, and under God's guidance, I formed *Cretum Deus* and invited my friends, James Inard and George Rouzier to join me, which they did." He straightened. "So, what specific questions may I answer for you that could help you with your investigation? I apologize for being blunt, but I have plans later this evening."

21

DIMITRI

"Both of your cell phones—in the basket." The man holding the gun on them in the back seat of the car wore a no-nonsense glare.

"Don't try anything funny, or your son will pay." Moses looked at Zoey in the rearview mirror.

She tossed her cell phone into the basket. Dimitri did the same. The man waved the gun toward Dimitri. "Shut the door."

Dimitri reached for the door handle, quickly assessing where they were parked. He glanced up to the camera mounted over the side door of the Darkwater Inn. He took a split second to look straight up at the camera and mouth the words *HELP CULT* before he shut the car door.

Moses gunned the engine and then sped out of the alley.

"Who are you? What do you want?" Dimitri figured if he could get the man talking, maybe he could figure some way out of this mess. He *knew* he should've listened to his gut instinct. Too bad he hadn't.

"Not that you're owed any explanation, but I'm Jacob Youngblood."

329

"You're Solomon's brother?" Zoey kept trying to position herself so she could see her son in the front seat. "Is he okay?"

"Stupid woman. Solomon wasn't in a wreck. He's currently at our home, going through a program to rid himself of all the evil and wanton things you did to him to turn him against God and his family." The anger in the man's voice rattled his words.

"I didn't do any such thing." Zoey spoke through clenched teeth.

"Yes, you did. Harlot." Jacob kept the gun trained on Dimitri, even though he spoke at Zoey.

Dimitri discreetly took Zoey's hand and squeezed. "So, where are you taking us?"

Jacob cut his eyes off of Zoey. "Home, of course. We have big things planned for tonight. To rid the world of this demon again."

They were crazier than Dimitri had thought, but at least he was talking and had lowered the gun. "The demon? What demon?"

Jacob narrowed his eyes. "Don't try to distract me. You're the one who released the demon our father had contained years ago. You and that woman you let run your hotel."

This wasn't making any sense. "I didn't release anything, much less a demon. I'm a God-fearing man."

Jacob snorted. "God-fearing? You don't even

know what that means. You let women rule over you like that Fountaine woman. You hang out with harlots like this one." He waved the gun at Zoey, then back at Dimitri. "You turned on your own family . . . your father. Flesh and blood. You can't be cleansed. You must be held accountable for your sins, and you will."

Dimitri knew Scripture. "I am responsible for my own actions, my choices, and my decisions, but I'm also forgiven by the blood of Jesus Christ."

"Don't you try to mess with my mind. My father is in constant communication with God, and while he's allowed his sons to oversee our group, he has been instructed by God himself to come out and rid the world of the demon once again. Tonight."

There was no reasoning with them . . . they were that crazy. But maybe if he kept Jacob talking, it would build a rapport that would eventually allow Zoey and Sam an opportunity to get away. "I'll accept whatever the Lord has in store for me, but I'm confused about the demon. You said I released it. How?"

Jacob sighed. "As if you don't know."

"I don't. I'm sorry. Please explain."

The man hesitated for only a moment. "My grandmother was murdered by the Axeman in 1918. She was an original sinner." He turned to Zoey. "Much like you. A trollop who entices

331

married men to sleep with her. Who bears children from another woman's husband."

Zoey shifted, but Dimitri squeezed her hand very tightly.

Jacob smiled as he looked back at Dimitri. "She was in such a compromising position when a demon-possessed man, called the Axeman by men but he confessed to being a slave to Satan in hell, attacked her. She died, as she should have for her wanton ways, but it left my father an orphan."

Dimitri swallowed against a dry mouth, not daring to speak and interrupt Jacob.

"He grew up in the care of nuns at orphanages. Did you know that they called them asylums back then? Now the definition is an institution offering shelter to people who are mentally ill. It just goes to show the mind games played with the poor children with no parents. But those nuns, they were good to inform my father of how much of a sinner his mother was and how God sent a demon-filled man to get rid of her."

Dimitri held tight to Zoey's hand. These people were past crazy and right into insane. Talk about someone needing an asylum . . .

"Even as a teen, Father began hearing from God. He got instructions. God told him when to leave and who to invite to leave with him. God led him to create our group, *Cretum Deus*, in order to fulfill God's work here. On earth. In this city. In our community. God provided everything as my father obeyed."

The car turned, sending Zoey almost into Dimitri's lap. A knock sounded in the front seat, then Sam began to whine. Zoey leaned forward.

Jacob held the gun up, pointed right at her.

"I'm just going to hold my son." She ignored Jacob and his gun and reached over the seat to unsnap Sam from the seat and pull him into her lap, sitting back beside Dimitri with a thud. She held him tight and rocked him, humming.

"His father was another woman's husband." Jacob glared at Zoey.

"How do you know?" She kept her tone light as she rocked Sam, but lasers shot from her eyes. Sam snuggled against his mother and his eyes closed again.

"Weren't you listening? I told you, my father hears from God."

Zoey rolled her eyes and kissed the top of her son's head.

Jacob's stare hardened. "You doubt my father?"

"Doubt your father? I don't even know him. Or you. I don't care what you believe. I think you're crazy—and your father, too. Solomon told me all about your *family*. You're a cult."

Moses spoke from the front seat. "You need to shut up. We are not a cult. People call us that who don't understand our high calling from God. Miserable sinners can't grasp a family and group

333

who follow the leading of God as He instructs. You aren't even worthy to speak about my father, my family."

The car lurched forward as Moses continued in a shaking voice. "That you touched my brother literally makes me sick. You, who gave yourself to man after man after man . . . putting yourself on my brother. Using temptation to try and estrange Solomon from the calling upon his life as the youngest son of Will Youngblood, as he is the last direct descendant of the founder of *Cretum Deus*. You even had poor Solomon send that woman at the hotel a warning. One of our very old music boxes. Our father was very unpleased with his actions. You are an evil woman, and I'm glad the world will be rid of you soon."

Dimitri needed to act fast, or this was about to go sideways. "So your father left and started *Cretum Deus*. How does that connect to the demon?"

"The Axeman was killed, struck down by illness sent straight from God, but my father discovered he'd had a son, and we all know that bloodlines are strong—much is passed through a blood connection."

Dimitri still didn't see the connection of the son of the Axeman to him. "How did I let the demon out?"

Jacob jutted out his chin. "You opened the walls where the demon had been contained."

Walls? Mere walls could contain a demon from hell? These people didn't even have logic on their side.

"Our father had killed the son of the man with the demon. Our father is pure of heart, as were the two disciples with him, so the demon was trapped. They put the body that held the demon against a wall, and bricked over him. The demon had nowhere to go, and no way to get out without a human he could possess. He was trapped." Jacob sighed. "Until you knocked down the wall and released the demon."

The skeleton. Of course. It all started with that.

The car turned again. Dimitri glanced out the window into the darkness. They'd gone far into the warehouse district. Near the run-down area, and were on the back end. They had to be getting close to the cult's headquarters . . . their home.

He sat up straight. "So hold me accountable for releasing the demon. I accept responsibility for that. But let Zoey and Sam go. They're innocent in my actions."

Jacob snorted again. "She's not innocent, and neither is her child. His father was another woman's husband." He flashed her a look of utter disgust.

Zoey spoke up. "You don't know who his father is. For all you know, he could have been a single man I loved who died before we could get married."

335

Dimitri cocked his head. He'd never asked Zoey who Sam's father was, assuming it was none of his business, which it wasn't.

But Jacob smiled. "That's a lie, you fornicator. His father is Matthew Scordamaglia, who was married to another woman at the time of your bastard's conception."

Zoey's face went ghost white, and Dimitri knew Jacob was right. The fact that the cult knew such private details frightened him.

"Ahh, you realize I speak the truth. I've not lied to you at all. It's not in me to lie. My father would not tolerate it because God does not."

The car came to a stop. Moses killed the engine and got out.

"We're here. You'll soon allow Matthew to meet his offspring." Jacob lifted the gun pointed at Dimitri.

Moses opened Zoey's door and grabbed Sam out of her arms. The child stirred, but stayed asleep. Zoey reached to snatch him back, but Jacob put the end of the gun's barrel against her chest. "No."

Moses shut the door. Zoey reached for the handle.

"You go out the other door." Jacob dug the gun harder into her chest. "Or you'll leave this earth without ever seeing your son again."

She sagged against Dimitri, who reached for the other door handle and spoke firmly. "Let them go. She has nothing to do with me releasing the demon." He was careful not to use the word *innocent* again.

Jacob shook his head. "We cannot let her and her son go because they're important parts of the ritual tonight. The one that will finally rid the world of the demon once and for all." He pulled the gun from Zoey and pointed it at Dimitri. "Open the door and get out. Slowly."

ADDY

"What is it?" Addy stepped into the security office to a tight fit. Geoff and Tracey were crammed in there with Sully and Hixson. "Well, hi, everyone."

"Hope you don't mind. I stopped by to check on things on the way to the party and Hixson brought me up to speed." Geoff gave her a half-smile.

"He's the one who told me to check all the side entrance video recordings to see if we could see someone coming in who wasn't supposed to come in one of the employee or private entrances. That's when we found it."

"What?"

Tracey reached out and took hold of Addy's hand. The warmth of her bestie's touch reassured her, but also made her realize how cold she felt.

Geoff nodded at Hixson. "Replay it."

Hixson tapped the big monitor, whose screen displayed a still screen of an alley. A second passed, then movement filled the side entrance alley. The car that she'd seen Dimitri and Zoey climb into filled the screen. Two men got out of the car.

One climbed into the back seat, but faced the back seat. The car was like a limo, but not. It had one reverse seat in the back that faced the actual back seat. That's where the man sat. There was a flash of a glint before the other man shut the door and headed toward the door to the Darkwater Inn.

"Was that a gun he had?" Addy's heart pounded. It had flashed so quickly, she couldn't be sure, but it sure looked like the shiny metal of a handgun.

"We think so, but can't be sure." Geoff nodded to Hixson. "Fast forward it to the next frame with people."

The monitor filled with static, then slowed as Dimitri, Zoey, and the driver who now carried Sam in his carrier filled the screen.

"I saw this."

"Pause." Geoff gripped Hixson's shoulder and looked at Addy. "What?"

"Daddy needed some fresh air, so we stepped outside. We were at the corner, near the front of the hotel so we could be under the lights. I saw them from the corner of my eye get into the car.

I thought it was weird, but they drove off so fast, then my dad needed to go back to his room."

"Just watch." Geoff let go of Hixson.

On the screen, Zoey slid in, then Dimitri. While they weren't clearly in focus, an image of the man in the back moved. Again, a flash of metal in his hand.

It had to be a gun.

It looked like Zoey sat in the middle of the seat, turning her knees toward the open door like she didn't want to be near the guy in the back seat. Very un-Zoey-like. She was usually comfortable with all men, and Addy didn't mean that in a rude way. Zoey just had an overdose of self-confidence and always seemed very sure of herself.

Dimitri reached into his pocket and tossed something at the man, it looked like.

Geoff tapped the monitor. "We think that's his cell phone."

Which would explain why he hadn't answered any of her calls.

Dimitri's hand came out of the car, reaching for the door bar. He turned his face slowly toward the camera and mouthed two words. Then he withdrew into the back seat, shut the door, and the car sped away.

"What did he say?" He'd deliberately looked at the camera, knowing it was recording, and mouthed something. It had to be important.

"We don't know." Geoff took her other hand in his. "I called a friend of a friend who has a deaf son, and he's agreed to look at the video. I need your permission to send it to him."

"Yes, yes. Of course. Send it."

Geoff nodded to Hixson, who clicked a button. "It's sent."

"How long will it take?" This was so unbelievable. How could this even be happening? Addy couldn't even think straight.

"Just a few minutes. Long enough for it to download and for him to watch it. He said he'd call as soon as he did."

She pressed her hand against her forehead and closed her eyes. *Oh, Lord, please.* She didn't even know what to pray for.

"Have you checked on your dad?" Tracey smoothed Addy's hair behind her ear.

"No. I really haven't had time. I need to." The tears threatened to spill out.

"Call him now. While we're waiting. Just a quick check-in." As usual, Tracey was right.

She pulled out her cell phone—blast it, she'd forgotten to charge it! At least she still had eight percent. Addy called Vincent's number.

"Hey, honey." He answered on the first ring. Thank goodness somebody was answering her calls.

"How're you feeling, Daddy?"

"A little better. I got sick as soon as I got to the

room, but I ate some of that fruit—yes, a banana, and then some of the peanut butter crackers you gave me. I'm feeling better now. About to clean up and head back downstairs. How's the party?"

Geoff's cell rang and he answered.

"I've got to go, Daddy. I'll see you soon. Love you." She ended the call and pocketed her phone, then listened to Geoff.

"Got it. Are you sure?"

A pause. Tracey wove her fingers through Addy's.

"Yep. Thanks, man. I appreciate it." Geoff looked at Addy.

"Was he able to read his lips? Did he know what Dimitri said?"

Geoff nodded. "We need to call the police, Addy."

Her heart was going to beat out of her chest. "Why? What did he say?"

"Dimitri mouthed the words *help* and *cult*."

22

BEAU

Beau flipped through his notebook, a little shaken. He hadn't expected to find the William Lowe he'd read so much about. To be honest, he'd thought the man had to be dead. He did the quick math. The man was one hundred and one years old. He cleared his throat. "So, um, Harold was never part of the—of *Cretum Deus*?"

Will raised his head, sitting up straight on the old couch, and looking down his beakish nose at him. "No. Harold was adopted before we left St. Mary's. He was never part of *Cretum Deus*."

"Oh. I thought you guys were inseparable. That's what we were told."

"We were, up until he left St. Mary's. He was adopted. I'm sure there are records regarding that."

Something about the way the man spoke down to them. All of Beau's training in the art of microexpression and deception detection seemed to scream at him. "Do you know who adopted him?"

A car's light shined in the window, only for a moment, as it turned down the side alley that ran alongside the building.

Will waved away the question like he was swatting at pesky mosquitos. "I was a teenager at the time. Why would anyone have given me such information?"

Marcel inched to the edge of his chair. "Harold didn't tell you? Maybe when he said goodbye?"

Will shook his head and smiled, as if they were silly, stupid children. "In an orphanage, most aren't given the option to say goodbye. They are just there one day, gone the next. That's how it was with Harold. We woke up one day and he was gone. One of the sisters told us to celebrate as he had been adopted."

The man was very good at redirection and evasion. Not very productive for the investigation. Beau flipped the page in his notebook, but before he could speak, Will shoved to his feet.

The old man stood straight, as if to defy his own age. "If you have no more questions, I really need to see to some items as I do have plans for the evening." He stared directly into Beau's eyes, like he could make them submit to *his* power.

Marcel bounced to his feet and took a step toward Youngblood, almost invading his personal space. "How is your son Solomon? We heard he was in an accident and was in the hospital."

A brief flash of annoyance lit in his eyes before a smirk tugged at his lips. "He's resting now. He will be fine soon, with the care and prayers of his family. Thank you for your concern." He waved toward the door. "Now, if there's nothing else, I really must—"

Beau stood and popped his notebook against his hand. "I do have one more question for you, Mr. Youngblood." He struggled to keep the respect in his voice. Every time he looked at the man, the statements of so many women raced through his mind and turned Beau's stomach. "Some music devices were placed in the elevator shafts at the Darkwater Inn hotel. Would you know anything about that?"

He slapped away the question. "What does an old man like myself care about music devices?"

But Beau recognized the deflection as Youngblood didn't answer the question. Beau pressed on, refusing to accept the non-reply. "One of the electronics specialists on the hotel's security team was able to trace the origin of remote back to this address."

Youngblood stared at him, almost through him. "There are many people here at our home of refuge."

Cult or no, if this guy was a religious freak, he would tell the truth, or at least not out-and-out lie. Beau hoped not anyway. "I'm asking what do *you* know about those music players?"

Will Youngblood's brows drew together until they almost formed a perfect V over his bent and oversized nose. He held his mouth slightly open, his lips forming a square and revealing his teeth. Or rather, a good pair of dentures. His lower jaw thrust forward. "I don't care for your tone, Officer."

"It's Detective, and I simply asked what you knew about the music players placed illegally at the Darkwater Inn that are remotely controlled by someone at this address." Beau held his pen over his notebook and raised a brow at the old man.

"Illegally, huh?"

A second passed. Two. Three.

Youngblood lifted his chin. "I'm afraid our conversation must end now, *Detective*." He opened the door and in seconds, Levi Youngblood was at his father's side. "These policemen are leaving now. They won't be back without a warrant."

The old man gave a final glare to Beau and Marcel. "Gentlemen, I bid you good evening." He turned and disappeared down the hall.

Marcel took a step to follow, but Levi stepped in his way. "This way." He blocked the hallway and gestured toward the front door.

Not having another choice, Beau and Marcel headed out the front door.

"If you come back, officers, please do have that warrant my father mentioned. Good night." He shut the door.

Beau led the way down the stairs to the cruiser.

"I want to know who is killing any investigation into these people." He pulled out his cell. Still no service.

"Has to be somebody high up in order to stop us at every turn." Marcel slipped into the passenger's seat. "To have our request for a warrant so quickly dismissed and denied . . . well, you know it's got to be somebody with power. Someone who has some serious sway over the legal system."

Beau shoved the keys into the ignition and turned over the engine. "All the complaints that had been filed against the cult and Youngblood himself . . . all buried or disregarded. Somebody's controlling the police department, too." Without more to go on, they couldn't go back and ask for a warrant.

Backing out of the driveway, Beau steered just a few feet past the building, then slammed the car into park on the street, just out of view of the cult's place. "We need a warrant."

That didn't seem very likely. Not if someone high on the food chain was set on protecting them. The whole thing made Beau angry. Not only were countless women over the decades subjected to sick perversions, but people had to have been brainwashed out of their wages and savings.

But if the cult was being protected, they'd never get a warrant.

"Nah, man, we need to figure out a way to get around the warrant." It was as if Marcel was reading Beau's mind. He pulled out his cell. "Still no service."

Beau thought out loud. "We don't have time to send someone in undercover." To get in and get into a position where the undercover could access useful information could take months . . . years even.

Marcel nodded. "Well, if someone's life was in danger . . ."

"That's the problem—none of these people think they're in danger. They think everything's hunky dory. Like Youngblood in there is *saving* them." Beau shook his head. "These people need to go to a real church and hear the real gospel, not some man's twisted version of the truth, bent to support whatever craziness is filtering through his mind."

"What about the kid, Solomon? According to what Addy said, Zoey was told he was in a serious accident and taken to a hospital, which he wasn't. Youngblood said he was okay. Maybe we could go in to check on him?"

Beau shook his head. "Youngblood was very careful in how he answered my questions about Solomon. He never said he was here, only we know he probably is. We don't know if the son is involved in whatever is happening over at the Darkwater. That's not enough for us to move without a warrant." He snorted. "At least not if someone is protecting the cult."

"Well, we need to think of something."

Beau nodded. What, though? He didn't want to leave. His gut screamed at him not to leave, that he needed to be close. Something was going to happen. Even the ominous way Youngblood said he had plans tonight sent shivers—

"What the—?" Marcel jumped out of the car.

Levi loomed down toward the car. "You officers having car trouble?"

"No." Marcel's hand rested on the butt of his service handgun.

Levi held up his hands. "I'm just being a Good Samaritan and checking on you. Because if my father thought you were surveilling our home, well, that might be considered harassment, and we wouldn't want that, now would we?"

The threat was barely veiled.

Beau sighed. "Come on, Marcel. It's not worth it," he said in a low voice so Levi couldn't hear.

Marcel gave a jerk of his head. "You have a nice night, Mr. Youngblood." He got into the passenger's seat and slammed the door.

Beau put the car in drive and eased away from the curb. He glanced in his rearview mirror. Levi stood on the street, staring at the car.

"We could've stayed, man. Public street. He has no right to imply we can't be there." Marcel clicked his seatbelt into place.

348

"Yeah, but we don't need a hassle. If they do have someone that powerful in their pocket who says we're harassing them, it'll roll onto Captain's shoulders and then you know we'll get a chewing." He came to the stop sign and put on his blinker. Through the flashing light, he could make out Levi's silhouette easing back from the curb. He still had that feeling that he shouldn't leave. "We'll just make a block or two, then circle back. Unless you have a better idea?"

"I'm good with staying. Anything that'll bring these guys down."

"Yeah, me, too." Beau went down another block before making another right turn. If only he could get in that commune. They were hiding something.

Beau just knew.

ADDY

"Yes, call the police immediately and tell them. Send the video if needed," Addy instructed Geoff. She looked at Hixson. "Can you send that video to my phone?" She pulled it out of her pocket and handed it to him.

"Your battery is almost dead, but, yes, ma'am." Hixson plugged it into one of the computers and began working.

Addy turned to Tracey. "Can I use your cell for a minute?"

Tracey bit her bottom lip. "Ads, I'm sorry. I made a rule for myself that I'd stop carrying my cell on dates where I know the person well. So I'm not tempted to send a gazillion selfies or not pay my date due attention."

Of all the times for her best friend to lessen technology's grip on her! Addy sighed.

"Here you go, Ms. Fountaine." Hixson handed her back her phone. "You need to charge that soon or it's going to die."

"Thanks. Please send a copy of the video to this number." She rattled off Beau's cell phone number, then turned back to Tracey. "I'll call Beau on my way."

"On your way? Where do you think you're going?"

"To the address we have for the cult." She still had a hard time believing such things as cults had a place in the world. Then again, with everything else familiar to New Orleans, why should a cult be so shocking? Many people in the gritty undersurface of the city thought themselves a witch or vampire or voodoo priest.

"How do you have that address?" Tracey asked. "And why do you have it?"

"Because it's Solomon's address, and I had to have it for the records for tonight's events." She waggled her phone. "And, it's the same address of where Hixson was able to trace the remote access of the music."

"You can't go there." Tracey shook her head.

"I have to." No way was she *not* going to go.

Tracey cocked out her hip. "And do what, pray tell? Knock on the door and nicely ask if Dimitri can come out and play?" She straightened and shook her head again. "Look, I know you and Dimitri have some romantic ties and you care about him, I get that. Trust me, I understand. But, you can't play with these people, Ads."

"I care about Dimitri, yes, but we aren't dating any more. He's my friend and I love him in that capacity."

"Wait, y'all aren't dating?" Tracey held up her hand.

"Long story, but no." Addy knew she'd have to do a full confession soon, or Tracey would drive her crazy. "It doesn't matter, I have to go."

"You can't, Ads."

"Dimitri came for me last month when I was abducted."

"He went after you with Beau. He was with a cop. You know, someone who can carry a gun, arrest people, and uphold the law?"

"I said that I'll call Beau and have him meet us there. I just *need* to be there."

"Then I'm driving you." Geoff set down his cell on the counter and dug his car keys from the pocket of his slacks. "The police dispatcher said she'd have someone look into it. It was odd.

She seemed very interested until I gave her the address, then she said she'd have someone look into it."

"I can't ask you to go, Geoff. Stay here and watch over everything." Addy put her phone in her pocket. She'd have to run up to her apartment and grab her car keys.

"Good thing you aren't asking then." Geoff glanced at Tracey. "I'm sorry to run off on you."

"Oh, I'm going with y'all."

"No." Both Addy and Geoff spoke in unison.

Geoff took her hand. "Look, I don't know what we're going to walk into over there, but whatever it is, I want to know that you're here, safe. We'll be back as soon as we can. I'm sure the police will send us away almost as soon as we get there."

She shook her head. "I'm not letting either of you go without me."

"Trace, will you please get with Dad? He was cleaning up to come back down to the show. Considering everything, I don't want him alone."

Tracey's eyes narrowed. "Adelaide Fountaine, don't you dare try to give me busy stuff so I won't demand to go with y'all."

"I'm not. There's a very good chance that Dad's head injury was caused by an axe, and both Beau and I think the cult may have been his attack. Please." Tears burned her eyes. "You know how ornery Dad can be. I need someone I can trust to make sure he doesn't go off half-cocked or something."

Tracey hesitated a moment, chewing her bottom lip. She then leaned over and gave Addy a quick hug. "You take care of you, Ads, but also of Geoff, cuz I really do like him," she whispered in Addy's ear.

Addy nodded as she stepped back. "Thanks."

"Let's go." Geoff bent and gave Tracey a very quick, but very intense-looking kiss before he opened the door to the Darkwater Inn's security office.

"You come back soon. And safe." Tracey flashed him a look that everyone knew meant she wasn't playing around.

He nodded and started across the lobby with Addy. "I parked by the courtyard today." He led the way to his car.

"Thank you for driving me. For going with me." Truth be told, Addy didn't know if she'd have been able to drive. Her hands were shaking as she latched her seatbelt. Fear of not knowing what was going to happen or fear for Dimitri and Sam and Zoey, she didn't know which. All she knew was that her trembling hands were nothing compared to the double-time pounding of her heart.

"Of course. I owe you and Dimitri my freedom. You two believed in me, were there for me during one of the darkest times of my life. I won't ever forget that." He started the car and revved the engine.

She pulled her cell out of her pocket and showed Geoff the address she had for Solomon. The cult. That Dimitri, Zoey, and sweet little Sam were probably there by now to face . . . heaven only knew what. She swallowed and sent up yet another silent prayer as she called Beau.

"Addy?" He answered on the second ring.

"Listen, my battery is almost dead. Hixson is sending you a video. Watch it because it shows Dimitri was taken at gunpoint. Well, we think at gunpoint. Just watch the video and see. And Zoey and her little baby are with him."

"Addy, slow down. What are you talking about? What video?"

"I asked Hixson to send it to you. Didn't you get it?"

"Not yet, I guess not."

"Let me send it. Hang on." She tried to send the video Hixson had loaded on her phone, but she disconnected the call.

Addy glanced at the battery icon. Two percent. She quickly sent the video. "Can I use your cell to call Beau back? Sending this will drain mine, if it's even enough to send."

"Sure." Geoff reached to his back pocket. "Uh, Addy, I left my phone in the office."

The little chirp sounded that the file had been

sent. "It's okay. I have one percent." She dialed Beau's number.

"Hey."

"Did you get it? It's the video from the hotel's security—" The phone shut down.

Addy groaned, then tossed the phone onto Geoff's console. "It's dead."

"But the video went through?" Geoff asked.

"I think so. It showed that it did."

"Then Beau will figure it out and meet us there. He's smart."

She nodded. Beau was smart. He would figure it out, surely. As long as the video went through.

Lord, please. Be with little Sam, Dimitri, and Zoey. Let Beau have gotten the video and know what it means. Protect us all, God, I pray.

23

DIMITRI

"Dimitri, do you have any idea where we are? Where they have Sam?" Zoey's voice, while only a whisper, cracked.

He tightened his grip on her hand. "I don't know," he whispered back. "I think we're at the cult's home base. Don't worry, we'll find Sam."

"I want my son. What do you think they mean by ritual? I'm scared, Dimitri."

"I know. I know." He squeezed her hand again. He was scared, too. He'd been praying ever since Jacob had led them across an alley into the back door of a run-down building. Men of varying ages had greeted Jacob like a prodigal son, this time returning with his own fatted calves. Dimitri had a strong feeling that they were like lambs being led to slaughter as they climbed creaking old stairs in a dimly lit, enclosed staircase.

Jacob's gun pressed into Dimitri's back. "Stop."

Dimitri and Zoey did as instructed. Jacob opened a door off the hallway and pushed Zoey inside. Dimitri followed. Jacob didn't enter, but shut the door behind them.

The click of the lock echoed.

"Who are yo—" A tall blond man about Dimitri's age rushed toward Zoey. "Zo! What are you doing here?"

Her face was as white as the moon lighting the night. "Matt?"

"What are you doing here?"

"I was brought here at gunpoint with . . . with my friend." She turned and beckoned Dimitri over. "This is Dimitri Pampalon. Dimitri, this is Matthew Scordamaglia."

"What's this all about?" Matt looked from Zoey to Dimitri, then back. "They told me I had a child, that a DNA test proved it, and wanted me to meet him. A son." He shook his head. "But when I got to the house, they stuck me with a needle or something and when I woke up, I was in here. That was just a few minutes ago, that I woke up, I mean."

Zoey looked stricken as she stared at Dimitri.

Dimitri knew she wanted answers. Wanted him to tell her what to do. But he couldn't. He wouldn't condone misleading this man, but he couldn't make that decision for Zoey. All he could do was give her the most understanding smile he could muster.

She tightened her lips into a thin line, and gave a quick nod of her head, then turned to face the other man. "Matt, there's something I need to tell you. They didn't lie to you in order to get you here. You do have a son."

"How do you know?"

"Because . . ." she licked her lips. "Because I'm his mother."

"You?" Matt shook his head. "But you are—I mean, you were a professional back when we, uh, hooked up. I mean, pregnancy isn't supposed to be a concern with . . . well, with your type. I meant, what you did. Before." He shook his head again. "Look, I'm not trying to be a jerk, but no matter how I say anything, it comes out all wrong."

Dimitri pressed his lips together to not say anything. He used the moments to inspect the room holding them. Wasn't much. No windows. No closets. Just a room with a locked door.

Zoey leaned against the wall and slid down to floor. "Yeah, well, sometimes, things just don't go as planned, you know."

"How do you know the boy's mine?"

Despite wanting to punch the guy in his face, Dimitri knew it was a fair question.

Zoey sighed. "I ran a DNA test. I don't know how the cult got those private results and found you, but they apparently did."

"But how did you get my DNA?"

Zoey glanced up and stared at him. Not saying a word.

A moment passed.

"I knew I was pregnant the last time you hired me. I got a DNA sample then to run the test later."

"Oh." Matthew sat on the floor opposite her. "Why didn't you tell me?"

She gave a sad smile and shook her head. "What would've been the point? I mean, like you said, I was a professional. You came to me because you still loved your wife and didn't want to leave her. Having a child on the way would've only complicated your life."

"I didn't love her. Not really, but I get what you're saying. No offense, but I should have never hired you." Matt was quiet for a moment. "I still deserved to know."

"You did. You do. I'm sorry."

He stared at her. "Had it not been for this situation we're in right now, would you have told me?"

"No, probably not."

"Would you have ever told me?"

She stared at him, then shook her head.

They were both quiet.

Dimitri felt like an intruder, but he had no choice. The bare bones of the situation had been revealed, so now they needed to move on. He cleared his throat to get their attention, but also remind them both that he was in the room with them. "We were told that all of us were part of a ritual tonight. Do you have any idea what they mean?"

Matt shook his head. "Like I said, I was knocked out. But I heard a voice say that it was God's provision that my last name was Scordamaglia, which is so close to Cortimiglia." He looked up at Dimitri. "I haven't ever heard of the name Cortimiglia, and it certainly doesn't sounds like mine. I don't know why they said that."

"Me either." Zoey looked at Dimitri.

"I have no idea, and certainly not why that's important." Dimitri crossed his arms over his chest. "What else can you tell me? Anything else you've overheard, even if it seems like nothing." He suddenly caught himself channeling his inner Beauregard. Had he not been terrified of what was happening to little Sam, he might find the humor in that.

"I've heard a lot of footsteps. Men's voices, always kinda muffled sounding, but that could be a side effect from whatever they dosed me with."

Dimitri squatted down in front of the man. "Close your eyes and try to remember any of those conversations."

Matt nodded slowly, then closed his eyes. He rested his head against the wall. "Something about jamming cell signals, just in case one slipped by." He looked at Dimitri. "When I woke up, my cell phone was missing."

"Yeah, they took mine and Zoey's as well. Anything else you remember?"

Closing his eyes again, Matt went silent.

Dimitri could hear his own heartbeat, deafening in his ears. Zoey rubbed her hands together in her lap.

Matt opened his eyes again. "Something about Moses called and has the owner, too." He shrugged. "That's all I can remember."

So, it hadn't been their intention to bring him along. Dimitri didn't know if that meant they hadn't expected him, so would delay whatever ritual they were planning, or if that bode even worse for him because of his being there.

A key rattled in the lock. All three of them shot to their feet.

Jacob, gun still in hand, entered the room. "I take it you've all had a chance to become reacquainted."

"Where is my son?" Zoey took a step toward him.

Jacob leveled the gun at her head, effectively stopping her in her tracks. "Yours and Matthew's offspring is being prepared."

"Being prepared? What does that mean?"

"It means you'll see him soon enough. Don't worry, all three of you are required for tonight's ritual." He pointed the gun at Matt. "Come on, it's time for you to be prepared."

Matt took a defiant stance—feet planted about a foot apart, shoulders squared, and hands curled into fists. "I'm not going anywhere with you until we get some answers."

Jacob made a *tsking* noise as he slowly shook his head. "Make no mistake about it, you are going to die tonight. You all are. The choice is how painful that will be. If I shoot you now, it will hurt, and you will be in pain for the hours it will take to conclude the ritual." He shrugged. "But the choice is yours. It makes no difference to me. I just need to know if I should call someone to drag your bleeding and sobbing body to be prepared or if you're going to walk."

"Kill me? I haven't done anything!"

Jacob lifted the gun to point in Matt's face. "You're an adulterer."

A second or two passed as the two men stared off.

"Fine." Matt moved out the door, Jacob following. The door closed behind them, then the rattle of the key echoed.

Zoey burst into tears and rushed to Dimitri. "I'm sorry I got you into this."

He hugged her, feeling her trembling. "No, you did nothing wrong. You can't be responsible for the actions of these crazy zealots."

"I don't want to die," she took a step back, letting the tears still fall, "but if I do, and you have a chance to get Sam out, Dimitri, I beg you to save my son."

He knew he would die before he'd allow her to be harmed, but he also knew she needed reassurance at this moment. "I promise you, Zoey, I'll do everything in my power to save Sam." He just didn't add he'd do the same to save her. He gave her another hug. Her heart beat against his chest. He sent up a prayer of protection over them and Sam.

"Thank you." She turned and began to pace. "What do you think they mean by preparing for the ritual?"

A million images of cult rituals danced across his mind, none of which he was inclined to share with a terrified mother. "I don't know."

"I wonder where Solomon is." She kept pacing. "They've probably got him drugged somewhere around here."

Unless Solomon was in on all this. Dimitri didn't want to believe Zoey had been deceived, but he wasn't going to discount anything at the moment. Not when their lives were clearly at stake. Especially little Sam's. An innocent child. Dimitri clenched and unclenched his fists.

"You don't think they'd hurt Solomon, do you? I mean, he's their flesh and blood, right?"

"I don't know." Dimitri shook his head. He didn't, but he was more concerned about what type of ritual they were planning.

A child's wail split the silence of the house.

Zoey and Dimitri both turned toward the door. "Sam!"

BEAU

"Our call disconnected again." Beau shook his head. "But whatever she sent is still down-loading." He pulled closer to the cult's location, staying out of view.

"The cell service here is awful." Marcel checked his own phone. "I barely have a bar. Let me try to call Addy while your phone is downloading."

Beau stared hard at the status circle on the download. Not even fifty percent yet.

"Went straight to voice mail. Do you have any idea what she's talking about?"

Beau shook his head. "No. She said she was sending a video and then the call dropped." Yet everything in him said this was very important. To not only his case, but to saving lives. Whose lives, he didn't know yet. It might just be a feeling, but he'd been saved by *feelings* many times before.

"A video, huh?" Marcel waggled his eyebrows.

Shaking his head, Beau rolled his eyes. "You're too much, man."

Marcel chuckled. "Just giving you grief. How is that romance going?"

"I wish I could tell you it was going well, but right now, it's in slow motion." He hadn't had time to wine and dine her all that much since last month. Then this case hit . . . as soon as he could, though, he'd ask her out. They'd been on such a good path, but now Addy and Vincent were pulled into the vortex of danger.

He knew he had her father's blessing—Vincent had told him that much. That the two men spent so much time together and were bonded . . . well, he wasn't sure if that was reassuring or annoying to Addy, but it couldn't be helped. Vincent had stepped in as a surrogate father when Beau's father had died in the line of duty, and he couldn't help that he loved the man. The dynamics of their relationship were certain to change once him and Addy . . .

Wow, he'd automatically begun to think of him and Addy as a single unit. A pair. A couple.

"I'm just bustin' your chops. I know this thing with you and her and Dimitri is . . . well, complicated."

Wasn't that the understatement of the season? Of his life?

"That video isn't downloaded yet?"

Beau checked the status. "Fifty-two percent."

"I can download movies faster than that." Marcel pulled out his cell. "You know, my reception is low here." He glanced at the warehouses. "Think we're getting interference from something?"

Beau glanced up at the cult's building a few hundred yards away, remembering that someone in there possessed enough technical savvy to remotely access music players at the Darkwater Inn. "Or some*one*." He put the cruiser in gear. "Let's test that theory, shall we?"

He'd barely driven over a block and his cell phone beeped.

Marcel grabbed it. "Download is complete. Pull over."

Beau inched the car to the curb and took his cell. Holding it so his partner could see the screen as well, he tapped the file to open it.

A black and white video began. A dark sedan with a longer-than-usual body pulled into what looked like an alley. Beside the Darkwater Inn, maybe? Two men got out of the front seat of the car. The sedan's headlights were off, but the engine was most likely still running since the dashboard lights were reflected in the video.

The two men spoke for a moment, then one climbed into the back seat, in a smaller seat facing backward. There was a flash of something metallic before the other man shut the door and headed out of the camera's view.

The video went all staticky, then slowed as Dimitri Pampalon, an attractive woman, and the other man returned to the screen. The man carried a child carrier with a sleeping child in it.

"What the . . . hey, is that woman Zoey Naure? You know, the uh . . ." Marcel cleared his throat.

"Yes. I think it is."

On the screen, Zoey slid into the back seat,

then Dimitri. While they weren't clearly in focus, an image of the man in the back moved. Again, a flash of metal in his hand.

"That looks like a gun to me." Marcel leaned closer to Beau's cell phone.

"Me, too."

On the video, it looked like Zoey sat in the middle of the seat, sitting almost sideways facing the open door. Dimitri slid in beside her, then reached into his pocket and tossed something toward the man.

Dimitri grabbed the car door, but turned his face to the camera and mouthed two words. Then he withdrew into the back seat and shut the door. The car's headlights came on, then it sped away.

"What did he say?" Marcel asked.

"I don't know, but Dimitri knew that camera was there, knew it would be recording, and used it to get a message out. We need a lip reader."

"Already on it. Calling one now." Marcel had his own cell phone in his hand.

Beau tried Addy's cell, but it went straight to voice mail. This was it . . . he could feel it. The case was going to break wide open, one way or another.

He just hated that in some way, once again, Addy was involved and in danger.

24

DIMITRI

Two men entered into the room where Dimitri and Zoey were being held. One was Moses, the driver who'd brought them here, and the other man, younger, was someone he'd never seen before. Dimitri moved to stand almost in front of Zoey.

But she was having none of that. She stepped around Dimitri, looking like a wild woman, ready to claw their eyes out. "Isaiah, where is my son? I want to see my son right now."

Dimitri held her firmly so she wouldn't do anything to provoke these men.

The man Zoey had nearly accosted spoke. "Your son is with his father at the moment. Getting to know one another."

Dimitri sized up Isaiah as he pushed Zoey behind him, placing himself between Zoey and the men. Isaiah was late thirties to early forties, but very slight of build. Moses stood off to the side, wearing an expression of indifference and anger. It was a strange mix on a person, but it seemed everything about this night was strange.

"Why are you doing this? Where's Solomon?

What have you done with him?" Her voice cracked.

"Zoey, please. I must take you to prepare you for tonight's ritual." Isaiah looked tired. Or maybe he was just run-down. Dimitri didn't know, but it wasn't boding well for any of them at the moment.

"Where are Sam and Matt?"

"You will be with them soon enough. After I prepare you, I promise you, I'll take you to them both."

Dimitri faced her. "I think you have to go with him. To see about Sam." He hated to encourage their separation from each other, but he remembered he wasn't part of the original plan or ritual. Whatever they had planned, she would at least get to see Sam again. He glanced back at the two brothers. He would do whatever he could to get away from Moses and save her and Sam. He lowered his voice. "I'll do my best to find you and get you out of here."

She lifted onto her tiptoes and planted a kiss on his cheek. "Thank you. For everything." Tears shimmered in her eyes.

"Come along." Isaiah waited at the door.

Zoey gave Dimitri a final weak smile, then left with the younger man.

Dimitri crossed his arms over his chest and leaned against the wall, propping a foot up, hoping he looked casual and nonthreatening. "So, Moses, it's just you and me. Are you going to prepare me for the ritual?"

The older man smirked. "I am."

"How, exactly, is this going to work?"

"As you've been told, you're partially responsible for releasing the demon." He jerked his head toward the door. "Those three will represent the Cortimiglia family murdered by the originally possessed man back before God struck him down."

Dimitri tilted his head. "You know, I've been thinking about that since you and Jacob told me. There's a fatal flaw in your thinking."

Moses raised his bushy brows. "Really? I can't wait to hear this."

"Yeah. See, if a demon had possessed a man and God struck the man down with the illness that killed him, as Jacob told me, then that would be the end of the demon. No going through a bloodline to any son. God's power of striking down that man would have killed the demon as well." Dimitri straightened. "The Bible is full of accountings of where Jesus himself drove demons out of men."

"That's a lie." Moses's upper lip curled.

"No, it's not." Of this Dimitri spoke with quiet confidence and assuredness. "The whole fifth chapter of Mark is about Jesus restoring a man who was once demon possessed. Matthew, chapter eight, verse sixteen tells of many who were brought to Jesus who drove out demons with a word and healed the sick. There are many instances of this." He ran a hand over his chin. "If you are a godly man, how do you not know Scripture?"

Moses's face turned red. "My father removed every reference to any demon from our Bibles. We would not allow evil an entry into our lives by even reading about demonic possession. We were taught well."

"Apparently not." Who tore out pages of a Bible they didn't agree with?

Moses pulled a gun from his pocket. "Enough. My father was instructed on what was important and what he was to do by God himself. You need to stop trying to corrupt my thoughts. I will not sway from my orders."

Dimitri held up his hands. Not a good idea to anger the crazy man holding a gun. "So your father's been having the original Axeman murders copied?"

Moses shook his head. "No, my brother Jacob did that. To prove to our father that the demon had been released and action was needed." He sneered. "Our brother David is the current leader of *Cretum Deus*, and is somewhat of a pansy. No backbone." He shook his head. "But Jacob is in line to take over next year."

Talk about dysfunctional. And Dimitri thought

his family connections between himself, Claude, and Lissette were bad.

Moses lifted the gun. "Enough trying to distract me from what I need to do now."

Again, not to anger the crazy with a handgun. "Okay. So, back to the ritual. Zoey, Sam, and Matt will represent the Cortimiglia family. I guess I'm supposed to represent someone?"

Moses nodded. "Steve Boca. It's not ideal that your name isn't similar, but our father said that was okay as we'll be driving the demon totally out tonight."

"So, Steve Boca was a victim of the Axeman's?"

"Yes. You will fill in. Then that just leaves Sarah Laumann and Mike Pepitone." Moses smiled.

That expression more than the gun alarmed Dimitri. "Who will represent those two?"

Moses's smile widened. "Why none other than that woman who helped you release the demon. And her father."

Dimitri's gut turned inside out. Adelaide and Vincent!

ADDY

"That's the car that took Dimitri and Zoey and Sam." Addy nodded at the sedan parked almost behind a big house. Well, it was one of the many buildings that had been converted into houses many years ago. "We were right to come in the back alleyway."

"We need to wait for the police, Addy." Geoff's whisper came out almost like a hiss. "Addy, stop." He grabbed her hand.

Addy shook off his hold. "Shh. I'm just going to have a quick look-see. Maybe I'll be able to see Dimitri or Zoey and that they're okay." She kicked off her heels and crept up the back stairs barefoot. Her heart pounded so loudly, she was certain Geoff could hear it as he crept up behind her.

She inched to the edge of the stairs and looked inside. The interior was dark, only flickers of light bouncing off the walls. Shadows stretched into darkness.

She turned the knob of the back door. It opened with ease. She held her breath. No alarms went off. No lights flashed. Only the slightest creak as she pushed the door open.

"No, Addy," Geoff hissed.

She ignored him as she crossed the threshold of a cavernous room. She couldn't make out any movement, but she could hear voices off in the distance. Each step was on tiptoe, but even so, a board would creak every third or fourth step.

Geoff continued behind her. She could feel his disapproval as tangible and real as the coolness of the floor under her feet.

Voices got louder and footfalls sounded.

Addy flattened herself against a wall. Geoff did the same.

Two men carrying a candle and a rifle passed by. They were both wearing black hooded robes.

She nearly cried out. These were the same people who had chased her and Beau outside the Square and who had thrown pig's blood at her feet. The cowards. But they'd attacked her father, too, and set his house on fire.

Now they'd abducted Dimitri, Zoey, and sweet little Sam.

The thought of these monsters with that baby . . . She pushed away the nausea. She couldn't just sit by and do nothing. Beau would be here soon and save the day, rushing in like the hero he really was.

Oh, mercy . . . her heart really had jumped right into Beau's arms.

Another group of men with robes and candles passed. The lump in the back of her throat blocked her breathing. She forced herself to breathe in . . . exhale. Breathe in. Out. Slowly inhale. Let it out.

She moved into the hall. All clear. She turned in the opposite direction the men had gone. Maybe if she could find where they were, she could open a door or something. She couldn't think clearly. All she knew was that this was all very wrong and she had to help.

"Did you hear that Will is going to lead the ritual himself?" Another set of hooded men approached. Their candles cast dancing shadows on the wall of the hallway.

"I can't believe it. We are so blessed we get to witness him driving a demon back to hell for the second time in his life."

"It is a miracle. Jacob said he'd prepared everything for Will. God must be so very pleased."

"We should have blessings raining down on us all as soon as the demon is vanquished. The angels and saints will celebrate. All of *Cretum Deus* will be rewarded. Moses said so."

The men passed Addy and Geoff who hid in the shadows.

Geoff's lips were almost touching Addy's ear. "That's it. We're getting out of here and waiting for Beau. These people are certifiable."

Addy couldn't disagree. While she needed to help, maybe the best thing to do was to go find a phone and call Beau and make sure he was on his way to rescue them. She slowly nodded.

Geoff led the way back down the corridor and into the room they'd come into. He eased the back door leading to the alley open, pausing as a creak sounded. He grabbed Addy's hand and stepped onto the stairs.

Addy followed, tiptoeing. She didn't want to think about all the filth and germs and heaven-only-knew-what-else was all over the bottoms of her feet. She let go of Geoff's hand. "I'll just shut the door."

He nodded and sprinted across to his car, pulling his keys from his pants pocket as he did. They would make a getaway, then call Beau and get him here ASAP.

She reached for the door, and just as her fingertips touched the cold metal, a baby cried out.

Sam!

Addy looked over her shoulder at Geoff, already unlocking the car. No time.

She opened the door and went back into the house, heading in the direction of where she heard Sam crying. The direction the men had been going.

Oh, Lord, help us all.

25

BEAU

"How much longer?" Beau didn't know how much longer he could wait. He literally felt like jumping out of his skin to get inside the cult's place and figure out what was going on.

His cell rang. He jerked it up and glanced at the display before he answered it. "Tracey?"

"Hey, listen, are you with Addy and Geoff yet?"

His stomach turned inside out. "No, why?"

"Didn't you talk to her?"

"We talked for a just a minute, then we got disconnected. I've tried to call her back, but every call has gone straight to voice mail. What's going on?" He gripped the steering wheel with his left hand.

"Her cell phone must have died. Long story short, Dimitri, Zoey, and her son were taken from the Darkwater Inn, we think at gunpoint."

"The video."

"You saw it, then?"

"We have a lip reader making out what Dimitri mouthed right now."

"We already did that. He says *help* and *cult*."

Beau tightened his grip on the steering wheel

until his knuckles popped. "Are you sure?" If that was correct, no warrant would be required.

"Positive."

They could go in!

"Beau, Addy refused to stay here. She and Geoff headed over to the address for the cult. Geoff left his phone here at the Darkwater Inn, and her phone was dying, so I have no way to check on them."

"What?" Of all the harebrained things she'd done, this was one of the worst.

"I know. Geoff called the police before they left, but he said he felt like they brushed him off as soon as he gave them the address."

Someone was definitely covering for the cult. He'd had enough. "I'll get them. Thanks." He ended the call and pocketed his cell. "We're going in." He started the car but left the headlights off, and raced up the drive, stopping right in front of the building.

"We still don't have confirmation of what Pampalon said." Marcel opened the passenger door and stepped out, putting on his bulletproof vest.

"I do. He mouthed *help* and *cult*." Beau grabbed his vest and slipped it on, pulling his gun out of its holster and checking the safety. "Call for backup. Now." He clipped his shield onto the vest.

Marcel grabbed the radio and sent the message,

pulled out his service handgun, then pulled his shield out from under the vest.

They crept up the stairs they'd vacated not long ago. The house looked darker, more ominous than before. Or maybe that was Beau's fear playing with his mind. "Addy and Geoff Aubois might be inside," he whispered to his partner.

"What?"

Beau quickly and quietly told Marcel what Tracey had said. "So, be extra cautious." He crouched behind the hedges by the front stairs. "What's taking backup so long?"

"Only been a few minutes, man. They'll be here soon."

Protocol demanded that they wait for backup, but Beau itched to get inside. He listened for the sound of a vehicle. Instead he heard voices . . . singing? No, chanting. Beau held his breath to make out what they were saying.

Oh, Archangel, St. Michael, leader of the heavenly army, hear our prayer. Defend us, the saints on earth, in the battle against principalities and powers.

Beau's gut knotted. These chanting cult members gave him the creeps. He met his partner's wide-eyed gaze. Marcel shook his head slowly as if in disbelief. Where was their backup?

Oh, Archangel, St. Michael, leader of the heavenly army, hear our prayer. Defend us, the saints on earth, in the battle against principalities and powers.

They either were speaking louder and clearer, or more voices joined the chanting. Beau repositioned his gun in his hand, letting his hand mold to the grip in the familiar, comfortable manner.

A door slammed inside the house. Another. A faint sound of a woman crying.

Oh, Archangel, St. Michael, leader of the heavenly army, hear our prayer. Defend us, the saints on earth, in the battle against principalities and powers. Oh, Archangel, St. Michael, leader of the heavenly army, hear our prayer. Defend us, the saints on earth, in the battle against principalities and powers.

The chants were almost deafening as the words were spoken faster and faster, almost whirling in the air like the wind.

"Please, stop." Definitely a woman's voice.

A baby cried out.

No more time to wait for backup. They had to act now.

Beau crouched up the stairs, his partner right behind him. Marcel nodded as Beau reached the door. His partner fell in line behind him, watching his back. Beau checked the windows— no lights or movement detected. He performed a quick self-check, as he always did just before going into an unknown situation.

Vest—check. Gun—check. Extra magazine loaded—check. Several tactical zip tie hand-cuffs—check.

Beau knocked on the door, gun in hand, Marcel at his six. They wouldn't be dismissed and turned away this time.

A younger man wearing a black robe eased the door open. Before he could speak, Beau leveled his gun at him. "New Orleans Police. Get down."

The man started to run. Beau pushed him down and pulled out one of the zip tie handcuffs. Marcel stood with gun drawn at the ready while Beau slipped the cuffs over the man's hands behind his back and cinched them.

The sound of sirens wailed.

The man on the ground screamed, "Cops!"

Pandemonium erupted as robed, hooded men rushed into the room. Shots were fired. Yelling. Screaming.

Lights from police cruisers filled the front of the house and spilled through the open door.

A child's scream echoed over the chaos.

Beau ran in the direction of the scream.

Bam!

He slammed against the wall. White, hot fire shot through his left shoulder. His eyes filled, blurring the darkness.

Beau glanced down. Moisture darkened his shirt sleeve.

Great. He'd been shot.

ADDY

The robe she'd lifted off the rack was way too long for her, but it served its purpose. With the hood covering her head, no one suspected she wasn't one of the other hooded robed people milling about. All she could hear was talk about a ritual and it was time for them all to go to the altar room. She'd been moving slower to stay out of the crowd. All the others were men, so if anyone suspected she was a woman . . . she'd be busted.

Pop! Pop! Pop!

Gunshots! Yelling! She had to act now.

Addy lifted the robe up a couple of inches and ran full speed toward the room where she'd seen them carry Sam into. Addy ignored the pandemonium and jerked open the door. She saw Sam in a portable playpen, crying. He was all alone in a room with nothing but a lantern to provide light.

She reached out and picked him up. "Hi, Sam. Remember me?" She spoke in soothing tones, desperate to keep him calm. Now all she had to do was get him out of there. By the sound of the sirens and guns, the police were here. Beau would save her. Save them. She just had to get them out of this room before someone from the cult came to get Sam.

Lord, please help me!

With Sam in her arms, Addy secured the hood to the robe and crept out the door. The main hall was filled with men in hooded robes, running. Some had guns, some didn't. Addy ducked down and took the only other way, away from the men. It would take her deeper into the house, but maybe she could find a way out.

Her bare feet made no sound as she rushed down the empty corridor. There was less light this way, but she didn't care. All she cared about was keeping Sam safe and getting him away from this awful place and these awful people.

She rounded a corner and nearly dropped Sam.

One of the men in a black hooded robe stood before her, but this one was wearing a unicorn mask. He froze.

She froze.

Sam whimpered.

The unicorn man held out his arms. "Give me the child." His voice sounded a little weak. Or maybe that was just her wishful thinking.

Addy twisted, putting her left shoulder toward the man while clinging to Sam on her right hip.

"Give. Me. That. Child." His voice had strengthened. "God has ordained me to rid the world of the demons."

Footsteps sounded louder. Closer.

She looked over her shoulder, back to the way she'd come. Shadows crept on the walls. They were coming closer.

Unicorn man had taken a few steps closer. She could see into his eyes through the mask. What she saw sent tendrils of fear throughout her body. Hatred. Anger. Rage. Darkness.

Evil.

Sam pulled at her, tugging the hood down.

Unicorn man gasped, and his eyes under the mask went blank. "You imposter! Give me that child!" He raised his voice and called out, "*Cretum Deus* members, come to me. A woman has stolen the child. The demon is escaping!"

Yells and footsteps increased as they came rushing to his protection.

Addy took a deep breath and barreled right into him as hard and as fast as she could. She didn't think of anything else, just to run.

She hit the man and he fell to the ground. A thud sounded, followed by a groan.

Addy kept running hard. The roughness of the floor dug into her feet, but she kept running as fast as she could. She almost tripped on the long robe, but she kept running.

Her mind screamed with every step: Get out! Get out!

She bolted down yet another corridor, no clue where she was heading. Addy had gotten all turned around inside the house as she tried to escape. Little Sam clung to her, his whimpers pushing her faster.

Bam!

She'd hit a muscled chest and fell back against a wall as Marcel reached out to steady her. "Addy? Is that you?"

"Marcel?" She'd never been so happy to see Beau's partner before. She slumped against him as exhaustion pulled on her limbs.

"You're okay." He took Sam from her arms. The child started crying.

"Sam? Sam?" Zoey raced to them, taking her son into her arms, crying and kissing his face.

"He's okay. They hadn't hurt him." Addy left off the word *yet*.

Zoey reached out and hugged Addy, leaving her almost breathless. "Thank you, Addy. Thank you."

A uniformed officer led Zoey away.

Addy stood on her own. "Dimitri?" she asked Marcel.

"He's fine."

"Where's Beau?" She couldn't wait to see him. To hold him. To tell him that she'd made her decision and she'd chosen him.

Marcel frowned.

"Marcel?" She suddenly felt like she was going to be sick. "Where's Beau?"

"Addy . . . he's on the way to the hospital. He was shot."

26

BEAU

"Thanks, Doc." He stared down at the nurse sewing stitches in his shoulder.

"Just keep it clean and go to your regular doctor next week to make sure you're healing well and to set up an appointment to remove the stitches. I'll send a copy of your records to his office. It's really nothing more than a flesh wound. You were lucky you were wearing your vest." The doctor left the triage room.

Beau glanced at the slugs still embedded in his Kevlar vest. While his chest may be bruised for a while where he'd been hit, the slug over where his heart was would forever be a reminder just how precious life is, and how blessed he was that he was still alive.

He closed his eyes as the nurse's actions tugged on his skin. They'd gotten in before the cult could start their ritual. Marcel told him there had been a makeshift altar with candles ready beside a tray with several axes. It was downright creepy just to imagine.

Where was Marcel? He'd wanted to come to the hospital with Beau, but Beau had refused to go to the hospital unless Marcel promised to stay and find Addy. The ambulance had gotten him to the emergency room fast, and since he was a police officer, he'd been seen to immediately, but still, Marcel should have called or been here by now.

His heart tugged harder than the stitches pulling at his skin as he worried about Addy. Had he known this was such a slight injury, he would've never left. Even though Captain Istre had ordered him into the ambulance with the threat of firing him from the police force.

If anything had happened to Addy . . .

A uniformed officer slipped through the curtains of the triage room. "Detective Savoie?"

"Yes?"

"Detective Taton said to tell you he's on his way here with Ms. Fountaine."

Beau released a long breath. "Thank you."

"Yes, sir." He turned to go.

"Officer?"

"Yes, sir?"

"Do you have an update on the status of the cult's raid?"

"Yes, sir. No civilian casualties or serious injuries. Two cult members were shot and died at the scene. Five more are on their way to the hospital for treatment. Eighteen arrests. Oh, and the leader of the cult, Will Youngblood?"

William Lowe. "Yes?"

"He's dead."

"Shot?"

"No, sir. Best that those on the scene can figure is he was knocked down and hit his head on one of the brass candleholders. He was wearing a unicorn mask, sir."

Fitting, actually. "Thank you."

The officer nodded, then left.

Beau glanced down at his shoulder. The nurse applied a gauze over the four stitches. "Keep it dry for twenty-four hours. You can remove the bandage then, but still keep it as dry as possible to reduce the chance of infection."

Beau nodded.

"They're okay in the shower after twenty-four hours. Just pat them dry with a towel. If you see any redness or they ooze, call your doctor for a follow-up, otherwise, go to your doctor as instructed for care."

"Yes, ma'am."

She stood and pulled off her gloves, putting them in the trash before she grabbed the electronic tablet. "You can put on your shirt. I'll start your discharge papers and be back in a few minutes." She disappeared before he could thank her again.

He eased his shirt over his head. They'd cut the sleeve in the ambulance to get access to the bullet wound. Blood stained the area of his shirt. This one would go in the trash tonight. Well . . . maybe not. Maybe he'd hang on to it, just to remind him of how blessed he really was.

The curtain split again, this time Marcel stepped into the space. "He's decent."

Addy rushed in and hugged him, careful to not get near his injury. "I'm so glad you're okay. I can't believe you were shot."

He hugged her back, inhaling, pulling in every scent that was fresh and all Addy. "You scared me. I about died a thousand deaths when Tracey told me you and Geoff had gone to the cult house." He gave her a hard stare. "You know better, Addy."

"I just couldn't sit by, not once I knew that Dimitri, Zoey, and Sam were abducted. I know what that feels like."

Marcel nodded at Beau, then discreetly stepped out of the triage room, pulling the curtain closed behind him.

Beau didn't know what hurt more—his arm or knowing that Addy had risked her life to go after Dimitri. Sure, it was her nature to take up for others, but this . . . this was taking it a step too far. He knew she had feelings for Pampalon, of course, but he hadn't thought they'd run this deep.

He wasn't sure how to feel about that. Jealousy had worked its way through him last month and he thought he'd gotten over those feelings. But now? Now that he realized just how precious his own life was, he didn't want to waste a minute of his life without Addy.

The dilemma was how to tell her how he felt. He didn't want to rush her or push her into a decision. He'd told himself he wouldn't ever issue her an ultimatum. On the other hand, he couldn't keep these feelings to himself. Even if she rejected him, even if she chose Pampalon, Beau knew he had to tell her the depth of his love for her.

Yes, it was love. He'd been toying around the word for some time now, but it was love. He knew it. He *felt* it. It was time to call it as it was. Only one thing made him hesitate . . .

The thought that she might refuse that love scared him in a way the cult or being shot never could.

ADDY

She just wanted to hold him forever. The fear she'd had on the drive over, even though Marcel had sped like a demon chased them, had almost caused her to have a breakdown before she got into the emergency room. She'd gone between lamenting her fears to Marcel and praying silently that he was really and truly okay.

But he was okay. He was sitting here, smiling at her, holding her hand. He was really and truly okay.

"I was so scared when Marcel told me you'd been shot."

"Just like I was scared when Tracey told me you'd gone there."

"Like I said, I had to go. You and Dimitri had come for me last month when I was abducted. And sweet little Sam. I was terrified for him." To see him safe in his mother's arms, Zoey crying tears of relief and happiness, made Addy realize that she wanted a family of her own. Not immediately, but definitely in her future. For so long after Kevin Muller had hurt her so badly, she had shied away from any man. Then, after Geoff had killed him and she'd told her father and Beau and Dimitri what she'd been through, she'd accepted that she'd survived and deserved to be happy.

She hadn't really considered having a family until she'd held little Sam. Now . . . well, now she knew she wanted that for herself.

Addy just hoped Beau did as well.

"I'm glad Sam and Zoey are safe. And Dimitri." Beau's hand twitched in hers.

It was now or never. "Me, too." She took a deep breath. "Beau, about Dimitri . . ."

The curtain ripped open, and a nurse with a wheelchair stood there. "You're all set." She handed him the tablet. "Just use the stylus or your finger to sign, and I'll wheel you out."

Addy swallowed the frustration. Maybe this was God's way of telling her to wait.

She only prayed it wasn't His way of telling

391

her it wasn't meant to be between her and Beau. She didn't know if she was prepared to accept that.

Beau handed the device back to the nurse. "I can walk."

"No, sir. Hospital policy. You have to go out in the wheelchair."

"That's ridiculous. The doctor said it was basically a scratch. I'm fine." He jumped down from the bed—and wobbled.

Addy and the nurse eased him into the chair.

"Fine, but a little shaky on your feet. That's normal, which is why it's hospital policy to go out in a wheelchair. We can't have you falling out on the floor, now can we?" The nurse situated him and put the tablet on the counter as she pushed him toward the exit. She looked at Addy. "Why don't you bring the car around, honey?"

"Um . . ."

Marcel joined them. "I'll bring it around." He winked at Addy, then jogged toward the exit.

"I can wheel him out for you." Addy reached for the handles of the wheelchair.

The nurse smiled. "Okay, honey. One of the boys out there will bring the wheelchair back." She patted Beau's right shoulder. "You take care, Detective."

Addy wheeled him outside.

The full moon and array of stars filled the night

sky. Peaceful. Calming. A masterpiece of God's handiwork.

Addy rolled him beside the benches just outside the door. She sat down beside him and took his hand again. She couldn't wait any longer. "Beau, about Dimitri."

"Look, I said I wouldn't pressure you or rush you. I'm not going to do that."

She smiled.

He kept talking. "I mean, you're a grown woman and you're entitled to make sure of your heart and what you want despite—"

Addy leaned over and kissed him. Full on the mouth. Full of all her emotions. Full of the fear she'd had earlier of losing him. Full of fear of not being able to have a family with him. Full of her chosen.

She pulled back, breathless. "I choose you, Beau. If you'll have me."

He let out a rush of air. He reached out and grimaced as he moved, but held her face with both hands. "Oh, Addy. I love you. I love you. I love you." He leaned, closer, pulling her against him, and kissed her as ferociously as she'd kissed him. But *more* because now she could feel the love in their embrace.

She melted against him. Her heart sang as she prayed a silent prayer of thanks. This was what she wanted in her life, this warm love and peacefulness. This was a dream come true, she had her heart's desire. Only God could have brought her life full circle and given her what she wanted—and needed most.

Peace, love, and a lifetime of happiness with Beau.

Dear Reader:

Thank you, once again, for returning to New Orleans with me and the crew of the Darkwater Inn. I loved sharing the dynamics of Addy-Beau-Dimitri with you readers, and hope that you are satisfied with the outcome. These characters have been living with me for the past year, and saying goodbye is hard. Look for Darkwater Inn novellas to be released in the future.

As I've said before, Louisiana is in my blood, and Cajun country has a large piece of my heart. If you get the opportunity to visit the area, I encourage you to do so. The laid-back, generous, and hospitable attitudes of most of the people who live in south Louisiana will steal part of your heart too.

The research for this novel was intense, but as soon as I read the history of the Axeman, I knew I wanted to blur the lines between past and present. I hope I did the plot justice. It is a fact that the identity of the Axeman was never discovered.

There are many cults throughout the United States, and sadly, many are settled in or near the New Orleans area. New Orleans is home to not only a smelting pot of cultures, but also beliefs. I tried to portray the reality of such, as per my experience.

Additionally, I took liberties in twisting the

truth to make my plot work. I would love to hear from you. Please visit me on social media and on my website: www.robincaroll.com. I love talking books with readers.

Blessings,

Robin

ACKNOWLEDGMENTS

I have been so blessed to work with some amazing people on this book. Thank you to Lora Doncea for your in-depth editing on this manuscript. Your comments and insights were so incredibly helpful.

Thanks to my agent, Steve Laube, who not only respects my business decisions, but is always looking out for me. Thank you so much for all that you do, especially when I'm on a tangent!

This book was so much fun to write. I enjoyed delving into the research of New Orleans and bringing the past, no matter how unattractive, to the present.

Once again, a big thanks to fellow author Pam Hillman, who was the best sport on our research trip to New Orleans. She let me drag her through cemeteries, the French Quarter, and on tour buses. I'm so glad I didn't have to go alone!

Thank you to my mom, Joyce Bridges, and dear friend Rosemary Troquille who helped fill in some of the research holes with tracing the facts of the real Axeman and the homes for the children. Thank you, Carrie Stuart Parks for stepping in with research answers when I wrote myself into a corner.

Thanks to Brian Sparks, who sent me the Death Investigator Handbook to help with my research.

Thank you to FACES in Baton Rouge, Louisiana, who provides a wealth of information on their website alone. Thank you to Dr. Sharon Kay Moses, who answered my questions regarding forensic anthropology.

I'm forever grateful to my amazing prayer partners, beta readers, and encouragers: Pam Hillman, Heather Tipton, Tracey Justice, Ronie Kendig, Dineen Miller, Cynthia Ruchti, and Cara Putman. You ladies don't let me get away with anything or take any shortcuts, and I appreciate each of you for that!

To my immediate family, who help me brainstorm, plot, and cause havoc in my poor characters' lives: Casey, Remy and Bella—*thank you* for taking the active part in my stories. I can't tell you how much it means to me for y'all to rock the fiction process with me.

Lots of love for my extended family's encouragement. I so appreciate your continuous support: Mom, my grandsons—Benton and Zayden, Bubba and Lisa, Wade (because you are more family than not).

Special thanks to my hubby, Casey, who keeps me going when I want to quit, makes me laugh out loud, and understands the craziness that is me. I love you!

Finally, all glory to my Lord and Savior, Jesus Christ. I can do all things through Christ who strengthens me.

ABOUT THE AUTHOR

Best-selling author of more than thirty novels, ROBIN CAROLL writes Southern stories of mystery and suspense, with a hint of romance to entertain readers. Her books have been recognized in several awards, including the Carol Award, HOLT Medallion, Daphne du Maurier, RT Reviewer's Choice Award, and more. Robin serves the writing community as Executive/ Conference Director for ACFW.

For More Information
www.robincaroll.com

Books are produced in the United States using U.S.-based materials

Books are printed using a revolutionary new process called THINKtech™ that lowers energy usage by 70% and increases overall quality

Books are durable and flexible because of Smyth-sewing

Paper is sourced using environmentally responsible foresting methods and the paper is acid-free

Center Point Large Print
600 Brooks Road / PO Box 1
Thorndike, ME 04986-0001 USA

(207) 568-3717

US & Canada:
1 800 929-9108
www.centerpointlargeprint.com